GANSETT EPISODES
VOLUME 1

EPISODES 1 & 2

MARIE FORCE

Gansett Island Episodes
Volume 1
Episodes 1 & 2
By: Marie Force

Published by HTJB, Inc.

Cover Design: Diane Luger
Print Layout by E-book Formatting Fairies
ISBN: 978-1946136350

View the McCarthy Family Tree*marieforce.com/gansett/familytree/*

View the list of Who's Who on Gansett Island here *marieforce.com/whoswhogansett/*

View a map of Gansett Island *marieforce.com/mapofgansett/*

The Gansett Island Series

Book 1: Maid for Love *(Mac & Maddie)*
Book 2: Fool for Love *(Joe & Janey)*
Book 3: Ready for Love *(Luke & Sydney)*
Book 4: Falling for Love *(Grant & Stephanie)*
Book 5: Hoping for Love *(Evan & Grace)*
Book 6: Season for Love *(Owen & Laura)*
Book 7: Longing for Love *(Blaine & Tiffany)*
Book 8: Waiting for Love *(Adam & Abby)*
Book 9: Time for Love *(David & Daisy)*
Book 10: Meant for Love *(Jenny & Alex)*
Book 10.5: Chance for Love, *A Gansett Island Novella (Jared & Lizzie)*
Book 11: Gansett After Dark *(Owen & Laura)*
Book 12: Kisses After Dark *(Shane & Katie)*
Book 13: Love After Dark *(Paul & Hope)*
Book 14: Celebration After Dark *(Big Mac & Linda)*
Book 15: Desire After Dark *(Slim & Erin)*
Book 16: Light After Dark *(Mallory & Quinn)*
Book 17: Victoria & Shannon (Episode 1)
Book 18: Kevin & Chelsea (Episode 2)
A Gansett Island Christmas Novella
Book 19: Mine After Dark *(Riley & Nikki)*
Book 20: Yours After Dark *(Finn McCarthy)*
Book 21: Trouble After Dark *(Deacon & Julia)*
Book 22: Rescue After Dark (*Mason & Jordan*)
Book 23: Blackout After Dark

More new books are always in the works. For the most up-to-date list of what's available from the Gansett Island Series as well as series extras, go to *marieforce.com/gansett*

Enjoy Victoria Shannon!

Marie Joyce

CHAPTER 1

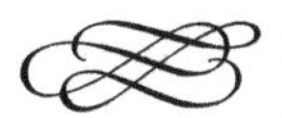

Desperate times called for desperate measures, or that was what Victoria Stevens told herself as she took an early lunch break for an errand she'd put off long enough. She had tried everything she could think of to get her boyfriend, Shannon, to open up to her without success, and there was only one person on this island who could help her figure out what to do next.

On paper, Victoria was one half of a perfect relationship. Together nearly a year, she and Shannon O'Grady enjoyed a lot of the same activities, TV shows and friends. They'd lived together for almost a year, laughed often, hardly fought and had the hottest sex she'd ever had with anyone almost every day. Though she told herself it couldn't be better, that was a big, fat lie. It could be better. It could be a *lot* better.

What they had, she'd finally been forced to acknowledge, was a lovely, wonderful surface relationship that lacked the kind of true intimacy she craved. She saw what she wanted for herself every day in the couples she worked with as a Certified Nurse Midwife, and refused to settle for less in her own life. So even if her relationship with Shannon seemed perfect on the surface, the foundation was shaky.

For one thing, they never talked about anything important beyond their work schedules, what was for dinner or whether they should go to a party they'd been invited to. In some ways, she felt like she didn't know him any better now than she had the day she met him, and that was a problem she couldn't continue to ignore as much as she might want to.

Five years ago, she would've ignored it. She would've told herself to stop being melodramatic and enjoy what she had. The future would take care of itself. But staring down her twenty-ninth birthday had her taking stock of where she'd expected to be by thirty—and it was *not* in a go-nowhere relationship with the hottest guy she'd ever met, let alone dated.

She'd waited until Shannon, a deckhand for the Gansett Island Ferry Company, departed on the eleven o'clock boat to the mainland. As she walked into town from the clinic where she worked, she saw the boat he was on way off in the distance. That meant the coast was clear for her trip to the ferry landing, which bustled with activity on a Friday in late June.

This was the right thing to do, or so she told herself. If she allowed in any other thought, such as the propriety of asking Shannon's cousin questions she probably ought to ask Shannon himself, she might chicken out, and that was not an option. Outside the door to the ferry company's main office, she took a deep breath and knocked on Seamus O'Grady's open door.

He was on the phone and waved her in.

Victoria went into his office and took one of the chairs that sat in front of his desk.

"I understand," he said in the lyrical Irish accent that was so familiar to her after a year with his cousin. "I appreciate the call. I'll have a talk with him tonight and get back to you tomorrow. Very good. Thank you." Sighing, he ended the call and placed his cell phone on the desk. "Sorry about that."

"Everything okay?"

"Jackson is having a few challenges at summer camp," Seamus said of one of the two brothers he and his wife, Carolina, had taken in after their mother died of lung cancer. "Getting into some scrapes with the other kids and 'acting out,' or so the director says. I'll admit to being out of my league with things like this."

"You're doing great, and you'll figure out what to do."

"I hope you're right, but you didn't come by to talk about my woes, did you?"

"No," she said with a smile, "I came to talk about *my* woes."

His brows knitted with concern. "What's wrong?"

"Shannon."

"What about him? I thought things were going great for the two of you."

"Things *are* great." Victoria paused and shook her head. "No, that's not true. It *could* be great, but it's like there's this gigantic brick wall standing between us, and I can't get around it or over it or through it no matter how hard I try."

"Ahhh," Seamus said, nodding. "I see."

"I hope you know... I'd never bother you with this if I wasn't feeling sort of desperate about what to do."

"First of all, love, you're never a bother. We're friends, aren't we?"

"I'd like to think so." She and Shannon spent a lot of time with Seamus and Carolina and now their boys, too. They regularly went out to dinner, played cards and spent holidays together.

He stood. "Take a walk with me. This isn't a short conversation."

Victoria got up to go with him, eager to hear what he had to say even if part of her was afraid, too.

They walked to the pier where the fishing boats came and went, bringing in fresh catch-of-the-day that was sold to island residents and restaurants. In the middle of the day, the pier was mostly deserted, with many of the boats out on the water.

"Has he told you about Fiona?" Seamus asked after a long silence.

"Who?" Victoria immediately thought of the woman who worked with Grace McCarthy at the pharmacy, but clearly Seamus meant someone else.

"I didn't think so."

"Who is she?"

"She was his first love back in Ireland." He rested his arms on one of the pilings and stared out at the ocean. "It's still hard to talk about her even after all these years."

Suddenly, Victoria was sorry she'd sought him out and particularly sorry she'd asked questions she had no business asking. "I, um, maybe it would be better if I didn't know."

"Would it?"

He was giving her an out, and Victoria wanted to take it because she sensed that whatever he was about to tell her would change everything. Was that what she wanted? To change everything? "I... I don't know."

"You want to understand him, right?"

She nodded.

"Then you need to know about Fiona."

Resigned to hearing the story, Victoria leaned against the next piling, needing the support it provided.

"I can't remember a time when they weren't together. They met in school and were inseparable from then on. After they finished school, they moved to Dublin so she could pursue a career as a model. Shannon got a job as a bartender to help make ends meet so she could focus on her career, which was really taking off. She had a top agent and a couple of photographers who loved to work with her."

Victoria wanted to run away from whatever was coming next. "Wh-What happened?"

"I'm only going to tell you this much, love. She was murdered."

Victoria felt like she'd been punched. "Oh God," she whispered.

"I'll leave it to him to share the details, if he chooses to. I've already said more than I should have. He's intensely private on this topic. He doesn't talk about her at all."

Her heart ached for Shannon. Tears flooded her eyes, spilling down her cheeks.

"As you can imagine, he's never been the same since she died. For a long time afterward, we worried he'd take his own life rather than have to live without her. So we made sure someone was always with him the first year. We watched him around the clock. The second year, he started drinking and spent most of that year and the next drunk. By the time he finally snapped out of that stage, we were about to send him to rehab. But one day, he got up, took a shower, got dressed and went back to work at the bar, as if nothing had happened. That's what he did for years—got up, went to work, did what he had to do to survive. Then, eight years after he lost Fiona, he came here and met you, and he's been different."

"How so?" she asked, her voice scratchy. "How has he been different?"

"He smiles again. He laughs. He participates. You have no idea what a huge improvement those things are from the way he was for so long."

Using her sleeve, she tried to mop up the tears. "I've wondered," she said haltingly, "why it seemed he was willing to go only so far with me. Now I know it's because he isn't capable of more."

"A year ago, I would've agreed with you. Now, I'm not so sure that's true."

"Why do you say that?"

"I've spent a lot of time with the two of you. I've seen the way he looks at you and watches you when you're in the room, looks for you when you're not. He's as invested in you as he's able to be, even if he doesn't say so."

"I'm not sure what to do with this information, Seamus." She'd gotten way more than she'd bargained for from Shannon's cousin.

"What do you want to do with it?" he asked.

"I want to find him and hold him and tell him I love him and I always will even if he's not capable of loving me back."

"He's capable. He just doesn't know it yet. You'll have to lead him to it if you're interested in a future with him. Is that what you want, Vic? A future with him?"

"I think so," she said softly. "But I can't compete with her. I feel awful even saying that."

"I understand, and you shouldn't feel awful. For what it's worth, I see the way he is with you, and I think he cares for you more than either of you realize."

"Do I tell him what I know?"

"That's up to you, love. I can't tell you how to play this. I wish I could."

"Will he mind that you told me?"

"If he does, that's between the two of us. Don't you worry about me. I can fight my own battles. I told you what I did because I like you for him. I like you two together, and I wanted to help. My intentions were pure, and that's what I'll tell him if it comes to that."

"I really appreciate this, Seamus."

He held out his arms to her, and she walked willingly into his embrace. "He's lucky to have you in his life, and he knows it. Have some faith in that."

"I'll try," she said, smiling up at him. "Your wife is lucky to have you, too."

"Aye, I tell her so every day."

Victoria laughed at the predictable comment. "I'll see you later." She walked back to the clinic lost in thought and grief-stricken over what Shannon had been through losing his first love in such a horrific way. So many things made sense to her now that she knew what'd happened to him.

Most of the time, he came off as a happy-go-lucky sort of guy. However, every so often, the darkness would swoop in, and he'd punch out of their relationship for a day or two, even if he never physically left the home they shared. Victoria had learned to give him space during the dark moods, even as she wondered what caused them. Now she knew, and understood, for the most part anyway. If only she could figure out how best to use the information Seamus had given her to improve their relationship.

In her heart of hearts, she believed they had what it took to make this the kind of love story that lasted a lifetime. But that could happen only if they both wanted it. She couldn't do it on her own. She was still pondering her predicament when she walked through the main doors to the clinic. Dr. David Lawrence stood at the registration desk, speaking with Katie Lawry, their nurse practitioner, and Anna, the receptionist.

"Oh, there you are," David said. "I was about to call you."

"Why? What's up?"

"Tiffany Taylor is in labor in Exam Three." He took a closer look at her. "Have you been crying?"

She shook her head. "No."

"Vic... What's wrong?"

"Let's talk about it later." As her colleagues looked at her with concern, Victoria took Tiffany's chart from David and went through the double doors to the exam rooms, knocking on the door to number three. "Hi there," she said to Tiffany, owner of the Naughty & Nice boutique, and her husband, Blaine, the island's police chief. "What's this I hear about labor?"

"We were in bed, and she woke up in a puddle," Blaine said, seeming incredibly stressed.

"Any contractions?"

"Over the last day or two, I've had like a rolling ache that comes and goes pretty regularly, but since it didn't feel like the labor pains I had with Ashleigh, I thought they were Braxton-Hicks contractions. Not the real thing."

"Let's take a look." Victoria washed her hands and put on gloves before helping Tiffany into position. As this was Tiff's second child, she knew the drill.

Victoria performed an internal exam and discovered Tiffany was fully dilated and effaced. "You work fast, Mrs. Taylor. You're about to have this baby."

"Right now?" Blaine asked, sounding panicked. "She's not due for another week. This was supposed to happen on the mainland."

"Well, it's happening right here and now."

"What if something goes wrong or she needs a C-section?"

"We have everything we need if that should happen." After David had delivered his ex-fiancée Janey Cantrell's baby by emergency C-section last year, they'd taken steps to bring in the proper equipment to perform emergency surgery, if necessary. They never again wanted to be unprepared for an emergency of that magnitude. "The best thing you both can do is relax and breathe. Tiffany had an easy labor with

Ashleigh, and there's no reason to believe this one won't be routine, too."

As she said the words, Tiffany's face tightened with obvious pain. "I'm feeling the need to push." She clung to Blaine's hand. "Can I push?"

"Not quite yet. Let me get everything ready, and then we'll get that baby out." She left the exam room to round up help.

"What's going on?" Katie asked.

"She's ready to deliver now, and I think it's going to be quick. Can you give me a hand?"

"I'm all yours in five minutes. I've got to move a few things around."

"Ask Anna to clear my afternoon, will you?" In Victoria's world, nothing took precedence over a mom in labor.

"You got it." Katie went to speak to the receptionist.

"You're sure you're all right?" David asked when they met up in the hallway.

"Can we talk after work? I've got a baby to deliver."

"Of course."

"Thanks." David was one of her closest friends, and there was no one else she'd rather talk to about what she should do with the information Seamus had given her.

Victoria put her long dark hair up in a bun, donned a gown and thoroughly washed her hands. Right now she needed to focus on the new life that Tiffany was about to bring into the world. She'd have plenty of time later to figure out what she was going to do about her own life.

CHAPTER 2

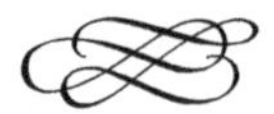

Victoria used the sleeve of her gown to wipe sweat from her brow. "Come on, Tiffany. One more big push."

"I can't," Tiffany said, weeping.

"Yes, you can, babe," Blaine said, cheering her on as he had for two hours now.

It was taking longer than Victoria had thought it would to get the baby out. She was keeping a close eye on the baby's heart rate and Tiffany's vital signs. So far they were both hanging in there, but she was anxious to see the baby safely delivered.

"Why's it taking so long?" Tiffany asked. "I had Ash in thirty minutes. Aren't second babies supposed to come faster?"

"They're all different," Victoria said, eyeing the monitor. "Here comes another contraction."

Tiffany pushed as hard as she could, but the baby was obstinate.

"We're almost there." Victoria tried to stay cheerful and upbeat during deliveries, hoping the moms would take strength from her positive attitude. "Rest for a minute, and then we'll do it again."

Blaine sat behind Tiffany on the delivery table, his arms around her, and spoke softly to her between contractions as he wiped her tears with a tissue and her face with the cool cloths that Katie handed him after every contraction.

A knock on the door sent Katie to find out what was up. She came back with an odd expression on her face. "Jenny Martinez is here. She might also be in labor."

"You've got to be kidding me," Victoria said.

"Wish I was. David is with her for now."

Didn't it figure that all hell would break loose on a day when she wanted nothing more than to go home and be with Shannon?

Tiffany's sister, Maddie McCarthy, came to the door, looking frantic and overheated, which wasn't recommended due to her own pregnancy. "I came as soon as we got back from the mainland," Maddie said.

"Come in," Tiffany said, holding out a hand to her sister, who rushed to Tiffany's bedside to hug her.

"How're you doing?" Maddie asked.

"Terrible. The baby won't come out."

"She's doing great," Victoria said. "Her little one has a mind of his or her own."

"Just like his or her mom," Blaine said, drawing a small smile from his wife.

Victoria eyed the monitor and noted the start of another contraction. "Let's do it again, Tiffany."

"Come on, sweetheart," Blaine said, his arms around her as he supported her from behind. "You got this. I can't wait to meet our baby."

With Maddie holding her hand and offering added encouragement, Tiffany pushed harder than she had in a while.

Victoria watched as the baby crowned. "That's it. Don't stop now, Tiff. You're almost there."

Tiffany screamed from the effort it took to keep pushing.

Victoria delivered the baby's head and then the shoulders. "One more good push." And with that, the baby slid into Victoria's waiting hands. Holding the squalling infant, she stood to show her off to her exhausted parents. "You have a little girl. Congratulations! Dad, do you want to cut the cord?"

"I'll let you take care of that," Blaine said, wiping tears from his own face as well as Tiffany's.

Victoria took care of the cord and handed the baby to Katie to be cleaned up before she got to officially meet her parents. Victoria delivered the placenta and determined that Tiffany needed a few stitches to deal with some tearing. She worked through the post-delivery steps one after the other with single-minded focus on her patient.

David evaluated the baby and declared her perfectly healthy. He wrapped her in a receiving blanket and brought her to meet her overjoyed parents.

"Oh my goodness," Blaine said on a long exhale. "Will you *look* at that face?"

"Another girl who looks just like her mother," Maddie said.

"Three of them will be the death of me," Blaine replied as he contended with a new flood of tears.

"Hi, baby," Tiffany said, running her finger over her daughter's cheek.

"What's her name?" Victoria asked.

"Adeline Francine Taylor," Tiffany said. "Adeline is Blaine's grandmother's name, and Francine for my mom."

"That's beautiful," Maddie said. "I love it, and Mom will be thrilled. Do you want me to call her?"

"Yes, please. Everything happened so fast that I never got around to calling anyone. How did you hear?"

"Katie told Shane." Katie's fiancé, Shane, and Maddie's husband, Mac, were cousins. "He called Mac. We got back on the first ferry that had room for the car."

"I feel bad that your trip got cut short."

On Victoria's recommendation, Maddie and Mac had gone to the mainland to consult with the specialist at Women & Infants in Providence. After her last pregnancy ended in miscarriage, they were leaving nothing to chance.

"Only by a day that we were going to spend at the beach," Maddie said. "Nothing to worry about."

"And everything is okay?" Tiffany asked.

"So far so good. It's the waiting that's the hard part."

"You're already past the point you were when you lost Connor."

"I know." Maddie smiled at her sister. "No talk of sad things today. This is baby Adeline's day. Let me call Mom to get her, Ned and Ashleigh over here to meet their new granddaughter and sister."

"Thanks, Maddie."

"I'm going to check on another patient," Victoria said. "I'll be back to look in on you guys shortly."

"Thanks for everything, Vic," Tiffany said. "I never could've gotten through this pregnancy and delivery without your support."

"I'm so happy for you all." Victoria left them with a smile, removed her gown and tossed it into a hamper. Then she went into her office to send a quick text to Shannon. *Outbreak of babies around here today. I'll be late.*

He responded right away. *No bother, love. I'll keep dinner warm for you.*

Don't worry about dinner for me. Will grab something here.

Okay, see you when you get home.

Every time she helped bring a new life into the world, she wondered if she'd ever get to share that experience with a man she loved above all others. Seeing Blaine and Tiffany with their newborn baby made Victoria yearn for a child of her own with the man she loved. Interestingly enough, she'd never had such yearnings until she met Shannon O'Grady.

She took a deep cleansing breath, the kind she encouraged her laboring moms to take, and left her office to see to Jenny Martinez, a first-time mom at age thirty-eight. Victoria had kept a close eye on Jenny, especially during the last few weeks. Like Tiffany, Jenny had planned to deliver on the mainland, but her baby apparently had other plans.

Victoria couldn't wait to see what these strong-willed babies would be like as two-year-olds.

"Hi there," she said to Jenny and her husband, Alex, when she entered the room where Jenny was hooked to monitors. Alex stood next to the bed holding her hand, looking as stressed as Blaine had earlier. "How're you doing?"

"Not so great," Jenny said. "The pain is pretty bad. Worse than advertised."

"I wish I had a dollar for every time I've heard that from a first-time mom in labor," Victoria said. "Let's take a look." During the internal exam, Victoria determined that Jenny was fully effaced but only seven centimeters dilated. "You've got a little ways to go before you'll be ready to deliver."

Jenny groaned at that news. "How little of a ways?"

"Three more centimeters, but you're doing great."

"We hadn't planned to have the baby on the island," Alex said, looking a little wild around the eyes. "Are you sure it'll be safe?"

"We'll do everything we can to make sure it's perfectly safe," Victoria assured him. "As we've talked about over the last few weeks, there's always a possibility of complications. I don't expect any problems, but if we encounter something we can't handle, we can have a chopper here within minutes and get you to Providence. Okay?"

Alex nodded in agreement, but she could tell he was only partially pacified by her answer.

She didn't blame him for being concerned. Island deliveries were never recommended, but they happened. Not usually two in one day, but Victoria delivered, on average, about six babies a year in the clinic. She'd delivered Laura Lawry's twins in March when they arrived early. In her line of work, best-laid plans often went awry.

"What're you thinking about pain meds?" Victoria asked Jenny.

She glanced at Alex and then said, "I'm going to try to go without."

"Are you sure? If we wait much longer, it'll be too late."

"I think I'm sure."

"Babe, if you need it, do it," Alex said. "Victoria wouldn't give you anything that would hurt the baby."

"I know, but I really want to be drug-free."

"Then that's what we'll do," Victoria said, patting Jenny's knee. "I'll be back to check on you in a little while."

"Thanks, Vic."

David met her in the hallway. "You need food."

"I'm okay."

"Could be a long night. I'll order from Mario's. You want your usual?"

She wasn't sure she could eat, but she nodded anyway. "Sure, that'd be great."

"Coming right up. Go take five while you can. I'll find you when the food gets here, and I'll keep an eye on everyone in the meantime."

"Thanks, David."

"No problem."

Victoria went into her office, took her hair down from the bun and stretched out on the sofa she'd bought at a yard sale for occasions such as this when she was required to stay at the clinic after hours. Rarely did she have to spend an entire night, but it happened once in a while. In a way, she was thankful for the outbreak of babies, because it bought her some time to figure out her next move with Shannon.

Looking up at the ceiling, she thought about the night she'd met him at the Beachcomber, the same day he'd arrived from Ireland with his aunt Nora, Seamus's mother. He'd planned to stay for two weeks and go home with Nora. Victoria wasn't particularly proud of the fact that she'd invited him back to her place the first night they met. That wasn't something she'd ever done before him. But it had been a while, years really, since she'd connected with a man the way she had with him. And, let's face it. The man was smoking hot.

She smiled thinking about how bowled over she'd been by his charm, the accent and a face that defied description. He was male beauty personified, with longish brown hair infused with red highlights that went blond in the summer, hazel eyes, a body built for sin and lips made for kissing. To this day, when he spoke to her in that lyrical Irish accent, she went stupid in the head. He could be talking about taking out the trash, and it had the same impact as when he whispered sweet words when they made love.

Closing her eyes, she thought about that first time, when he'd silently helped her out of her clothes and then let her do the same for him. She'd been slightly appalled at how easily she'd capitulated to his overwhelming charm, but once they were in her bed, she hadn't had the mental capacity for regrets *or* recriminations.

She'd had the best sex of her entire life that night—and just about every night since then. It was safe to say she was completely addicted to sex with him. Just thinking about it made her want him. Closing her eyes, she allowed herself to indulge in thoughts about the part of their relationship that worked effortlessly. All he had to do was look at her, and she was ready. It had never been like that for her before with any guy, even Stuart, the man she'd dated for two years after college.

Marrying him would've been a huge mistake. What if she'd been married to him or someone else when she met Shannon? How would she have resisted the instant temptation he presented? She'd wanted him from the minute he sat next to her at the Beachcomber bar and asked for a beer. He had her at "I'll have a Guinness, please, love."

Even Chelsea, the bartender, had reacted the way any normal red-blooded American woman would in the face of so much Irish hotness. The "holy cow" look she'd given Victoria had been priceless. But Shannon... He'd had eyes only for her, something that still had the power to amaze her so many months later.

They'd had an intense two weeks, fueled by the time limit on his visit. She'd actually taken vacation days so they could spend more time together before he had to leave. Okay, truthfully, they'd spent all those vacation days in her bed, getting up only to shower and eat before going back for more. Then, when the time had come for Nora to depart, he'd asked Victoria if she'd like him to stay.

She'd cried from the relief of knowing she got to keep him—for now anyway. He'd moved into her place that day and had been there ever since, paying his half of the rent and other expenses by working as a mate on the ferries that were managed by his cousin. Seamus had secured a work visa for Shannon that allowed him to stay in the country. Since then, they'd fallen into a satisfying routine that consisted of spending every free minute together. She still couldn't get enough of him or the way she felt when she was with him.

But the longer they'd been together, the more she'd begun to wonder about what he *wasn't* telling her. The dark moods, his refusal to say much of anything about his life in Ireland and his seeming intention to keep things light rather than serious between them had driven her to seek some answers. She'd gone to Seamus wanting to know why Shannon seemed only capable of a satisfying domestic and sexual relationship but nothing more than that.

Now she knew, and after hearing what he'd endured, she wished she'd left well enough alone.

A knock on the door snapped her out of the introspection. She sat up and ran her hands through her hair. "Come in."

David poked his head in. "Food's here. Katie said for us to eat first, and then she will. Is it okay if we eat in here?"

"Sure."

He came in with the bag from Mario's and set up their dinner on the coffee table she'd bought at the island's weekly flea market.

She opened the fragrant container of pasta primavera and poured Italian dressing on the tossed salad. As usual, David had gotten chicken parmesan for himself. "I hope Jenny likes the aroma of garlic in her delivery room," Victoria said.

"She'll be too busy having a baby to notice. I just looked in on her, and she's doing okay. Tiffany is taking a nap while Blaine is with the baby. All is well."

"Thank you. What a crazy day."

"Good thing this doesn't happen very often."

"No kidding. Let's hope Sydney Harris behaves herself and doesn't go early, too."

"Don't even say it."

They ate in companionable silence for a few minutes. Then he glanced over at her. "Are you going tell me why you were crying when you came back from lunch?"

CHAPTER 3

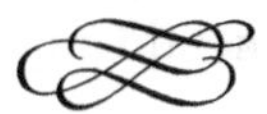

Victoria wiped her mouth with one of the paper napkins Mario's had sent with their order and took a sip from the bottle of water David had gotten her. "I went to see Seamus."

"Okay..."

"I asked him about Shannon. I... I wanted to know why our relationship seems to be stuck in first gear. Not that first gear is bad. It's actually really nice, but..."

"You want it to be more."

"I was hoping it could be more. Eventually. Now..." Victoria shrugged. "It's probably not going to happen."

"Why do you say that? What did Seamus tell you?"

She sighed deeply. "He told me about Shannon's first love, Fiona, the woman he was with from childhood who was murdered."

"Oh my God. How?"

"Seamus said I'd have to let Shannon tell me the details, if he chooses to. He didn't want to go too far in filling in the blanks for me."

"And Shannon has never told you anything about her?"

Victoria shook her head. "I'd never heard her name before today."

"Oh wow."

"I don't know what to do with this info, David. Do I tell him I know about her or respect his obvious desire to never speak of her? Do I settle for the perfectly good thing we have now, or do I rock the boat and hope we can make it something even better?"

"That's a tough one, for sure. Would he be angry with Seamus for telling you?"

"Seamus says probably not, and if he is, they'll work that out between them."

After a long moment of quiet during which Victoria picked at her food while David wolfed his down with his usual enthusiasm for all things edible, he looked over at her. "It comes down to what *you* want. Mentioning this to him would be a risk. He might not appreciate questions about her from you. That could put a wedge between you, but it could also bring you closer. Maybe he's been trying to find the right time to tell you about her. There's really no way to predict which way it'll go. Are you prepared for the possibility that you knowing about her could make him angry?"

"No, I'm not prepared for that, and I'd never want to do anything to resurrect painful memories for him, but I feel like the ghost of his dead love is standing squarely in the middle of our relationship. We'll never be able to move forward until we confront her."

"And you're sure that's what you want? To move forward with him?"

"Yes. I want everything with him. I'm crazy about him. I have been from the very beginning."

"I know," he said with a smirk. "I was there and had to hear the gory details."

"There was nothing gory about those details."

"Depends on which side of the conversation you were on."

Victoria laughed. "I suppose that's true." She sighed again. "I'm so afraid of bringing this up with him. The last thing I want to do is hurt him."

"Maybe you could bring it up without mentioning her name. You could say, 'I understand that you have reasons for not wanting this to be more than it already is, but I was hoping we might talk about the future and where we might be heading.' That would give you a chance to tell him what you want and to hear what he thinks."

"Why does the thought of saying that make me feel sick?"

"Because you're scared of losing something that's come to mean a lot to you."

"I don't want to lose him," she said softly, blinking back tears that made her feel weak. Victoria Stevens, badass Certified Nurse Midwife and overall happy person, did not *cry* over men. At least she never had before, even when she broke up with Stuart before he could propose and force her to turn him down.

David put his arm around her, and Victoria rested her head on his shoulder.

"Thanks for letting me dump this on you."

"You can dump on me any time. That's what friends are for."

"I need to check on my patients."

"I've got Tiffany and the baby. You focus on Jenny."

"Thanks for sticking around to back me up."

"Happy to help."

Victoria left the office to stash her leftovers in the fridge. She went into the bathroom to wash up and brushed her teeth so she wouldn't knock poor Jenny out with her garlic breath. Then she put her hair back up and stared at her reflection in the mirror. "Where's the magic mirror when you need it?" she asked the familiar face looking back at her.

Even after airing it out with David, she was no closer to a plan than she'd been before. Although she did like his idea to infer that she knew about Fiona without specifically saying so. That would be better than directly confronting Shannon's painful loss. With nothing she could do about her own life at the moment, she went to see to Jenny and the new life she and Alex would welcome into the world tonight.

BLAINE COULDN'T STOP STARING AT HIS BABY DAUGHTER AS SHE SLEPT IN his arms. Everything about her fascinated him, from the quiver of her feathery eyebrows to the purse of her little bow lips to the squeeze of her tiny hand around his finger, he was completely besotted with her.

Adeline... His grandmother would be so pleased when she heard the baby's name. He had a daughter named *Adeline*. Tiffany said they'd call her Addie since Adeline was too much name for a little girl. That was fine with him. After what Tiffany had given him today—and every day since he'd had the good sense to marry her—she could have whatever she wanted.

Tiffany awoke with a groan that had him immediately on alert.

"What's wrong, babe?"

"Everything hurts." She shifted to a different position and winced. "Even my hair hurts. I'd forgotten how bad the aftermath was the first time around."

Still holding the baby, Blaine stood, moving carefully because God forbid he should drop his precious bundle. "Let me see if they can get you something for the pain."

"In a minute. I want to see her first."

He turned so she could see the baby's little face. "Isn't she pretty?"

"She sure is."

"Just like her mama and her sister," he said, leaning over the bed rail to kiss Tiffany. "I'll check with Vic and David about giving you something to make you more comfortable." Reluctantly, he handed the baby over to her, hoping she'd give her back when he returned. He was nowhere near finished holding her.

Blaine went to the desk in the hallway where David and Katie were working on computers.

"How's Tiffany feeling?" Katie asked.

"She's hurting. Is there anything you can give her for that?"

"Absolutely. I'll be in with something in a minute."

"Thank you."

Blaine was heading back to Tiffany's room when a shout from the other end of the long corridor got his attention. Ashleigh broke loose from her aunt Maddie and ran for him. He bent to scoop her up and loved the way she wrapped her arms around his neck and hugged him so hard, he nearly choked.

Laughing, he kissed his stepdaughter's cheek. "Is someone excited to meet her baby sister?"

"What do you think?" Maddie asked when she caught up to them.

"Can I see her?" Ashleigh asked, her green eyes big with excitement. She had her mother's shiny dark hair and exquisite face.

"You certainly can, but you have to be gentle with her and with Mommy, okay? She's tired after having the baby."

"Okay."

Blaine carried her into the room. "We have a very special visitor, Mommy."

"Hey, sweetheart," Tiffany said, lighting up at the sight of her firstborn.

Blaine settled Ash on the bed next to Tiffany and stood back to watch while Ashleigh met her baby sister.

Tiffany gently placed the baby in Ashleigh's arms. "This is Adeline, but we'll call her Addie."

"She's so little!"

"I know, and we have to be extra careful with her."

"I will. I'll take such good care of her."

Blinking back tears, Tiffany looked at Blaine, extending her hand to him.

He went to join his family, taking the hand of the woman who'd given him everything, his heart overflowing with love for all three of his girls.

"Let me get the first picture of the new family," Maddie said, holding her phone. "Get closer to Tiffany, Blaine."

"Nothing I'd rather do," he said with a grin for his wife.

"Put it on ice, buster. No extracurricular activities for six weeks."

"What does that word mean, Mommy?" Ashleigh asked. "Extracrricula."

Blaine cracked up laughing. "Yes, Mommy, what does that mean?"

"It means," Tiffany said with a pointed look for him, "that Blaine has to keep his hands to himself—literally—for six weeks."

He snorted out a laugh at her double meaning.

"They tell us that at camp," Ashleigh said. "You should know that, Blaine, cuz you're a policeman."

"I know, honey," he said with a long-suffering sigh and playful scowl for Tiff. "Don't worry."

"Everybody smile," Maddie said, framing the first picture of the four of them together.

Blaine, who hadn't stopped smiling all day, happily complied and then forwarded the picture Maddie sent him to his family, letting them know Tiffany and the baby would be home tomorrow if they wanted to visit. He had no doubt they'd have a line out the door. His parents had been so excited to see him become a father.

After an hour-long visit that got more exciting when Tiffany's mom and stepfather, Francine and Ned, showed up, Maddie took Ashleigh home with her for a sleepover with her cousins, Thomas and Hailey.

"She's some kind of excited, huh?" Blaine asked Tiffany after everyone had left.

"She's going to be the best big sister ever. Well, except for Maddie, of course."

"Of course. I'm glad Ashleigh has a sister. I know how much you love yours."

"I do love my sister. But you know what this means?"

"What's that?"

"We have to try again to get you a son."

"I don't care about having a son. I love my three girls."

"Still… I may have one more baby in me if you're game."

"You say that now that Katie gave you pain meds. When they wear off, you might not be so agreeable. And PS, I'm always game for making babies with you."

"I want to try for a boy."

"Not today," he said with a teasing grin.

She groaned. "Not any time soon."

"No extracurriculars, Mommy."

"Oh my God! I can't believe she asked me what that meant!"

"I can. She's a parrot. If you say it, she says it."

"I know. It's awful. I have to watch my mouth so closely these days. What if she goes to camp and tells them Mommy and Blaine were talking about extracrricula activities?"

"I'm the police chief, babe. They won't arrest you."

"Thank goodness for that."

Addie came to life with a little squeak that was among the most adorable sounds Blaine had ever heard. "Was Ashleigh like her as a baby? I hate that I missed that time with her."

"She looked just like Addie does, and she used to wake with an indignant squeak, too. I'd forgotten about that."

Addie's squeak quickly became a howl.

"Is someone hungry?" Tiffany asked her new daughter.

"How do you know that?" Blaine asked, fascinated.

"She's not wet, and she just woke up, so she's not tired. Process of elimination."

He watched, enraptured, as she opened the front of her hospital gown and guided the baby to her breast. "That is, without a doubt, the coolest—and *sexiest*—thing I've ever seen in my entire life."

She smiled at him and moved gingerly to one side of the bed. "Come up here with us."

Careful not to jar her, he got on the bed and wrapped his arms around her, letting her lean back against him as she fed the baby.

"Ahhh, that's better," she said with a contented sigh.

"This has been the greatest day of my entire life, Tiffany. Thank you so much for her—and for everything else. You and Ashleigh and now our little Addie… I love you all so much."

With her head resting against his chest, she smiled up at him. "We love you, too. You think I've given you so much, but you've done the same for me. You waited all that time for me to be free."

He ran his finger over her cheek. "Waiting for you—and our family —was the best and smartest thing I ever did."

CHAPTER 4

By the time Jenny was ready to push at one in the morning, Victoria suspected she regretted her decision to forgo pain meds. Jenny was having trouble focusing on her breathing, despite Alex's steady support and encouragement. Her friend Erin Barton had come in around ten and stood by the other side of Jenny's bed, wiping her face with cool cloths and feeding her ice chips to keep her hydrated.

Victoria prepared the bed and the room for delivery, again proceeding through the checklist. She had long ago memorized the steps involved in delivering a baby and went through each one with ruthless attention to detail. Ensuring the safety and comfort of her moms was her top priority along with delivering a healthy baby.

Although it wouldn't be her preference to deliver an older mom on the island, Victoria was determined to make sure the delivery was smooth, and David and Katie were nearby in case she needed them.

She eyed the monitor, watching for the next contraction. "All right, Jenny. Let's get this baby out. On the next contraction, I need a big push."

Jenny pushed for a long, difficult hour before her son emerged into the world, screaming with outrage at the bright lights, the noise and the general inconvenience of leaving the womb. He was absolutely perfect—and close to nine pounds.

"You have a son," Victoria said to Jenny and Alex, who were overcome with emotion. She wiped away a few tears of her own, knowing the long and difficult path Jenny had traveled from losing her fiancé in the World Trade Center on 9/11 to falling for Alex many years later to now becoming a mother.

Katie quickly cleaned up the baby and wrapped him in a receiving blanket before taking him to meet his elated parents and Aunt Erin, who was the twin sister of Jenny's late fiancé.

"Hello, little man," Jenny said softly to the baby, who stared up at her with big dark eyes. He had a smattering of dark hair and his father's olive-toned skin.

"What's his name?" Victoria asked as she tended to Jenny's post-delivery care.

"George Alexander Martinez the second," Jenny said. "After Alex's dad."

"I love that," Erin said. "He looks like a George."

"My dad would be so thrilled," Alex said, wiping away tears.

George let out a lusty cry.

"I think your little guy might be hungry," Victoria said. "Let's see how he takes to breastfeeding."

Two hours later, Victoria was dead on her feet but had two successful deliveries completed and two breastfeeding moms who were doing great. David had checked both babies again, declaring them healthy and strong.

It had been a great day for the clinic team—or was it two days now?

"Go on home," David said to Victoria and Katie. "I'll stay."

Victoria would've argued with him, but his policy was to remain on the premises any time they admitted a patient. Besides, she was so damned tired, she could barely function let alone argue.

"We'll clear your schedule until noon tomorrow," he said. "Sleep in."

"You're the best boss I ever had."

"I love how she says that, as if she's not the boss around here."

Katie laughed. "Seriously."

"Whatever," Victoria said, yawning. "I'm outta here."

"I want my bed and my man," Katie said as she walked with Victoria to the dark parking lot, which held many more cars than usual due to their patients.

"What you said." Victoria's stomach ached at the thought of having to talk to Shannon about what she'd learned about him. But that wasn't going to happen tonight. She'd wait and choose her timing carefully. "Sleep well, and thanks for staying."

"Of course, no problem."

The three of them made a good team, supporting each other through the various challenges they confronted on a daily basis as the island's only medical providers. That they were also great friends made their work environment much more fun and dynamic than it would've been otherwise.

After finishing the Certified Nurse Midwife postgraduate program five years ago, Victoria came to Gansett intending to spend a year gaining experience in midwifery before moving on to something bigger and better. But Gansett had worked its magic on her, and now it felt like home. She thrived on the challenge of providing top-level prenatal care to isolated island moms and liked feeling needed in her professional life.

Now she couldn't imagine living anywhere but on the remote island where she'd found such a satisfying life. That life had become a heck of a lot more satisfying a year ago when Shannon O'Grady arrived.

She drove home to the small house they shared near the Salt Pond, close enough to smell the sea air, which, along with the scenic water views, had become one of her favorite aspects of island life.

Shannon had left the outside light on for her, and she tiptoed inside, hoping she wouldn't wake him. He had an early morning on the ferry.

In the bathroom, she changed into an oversized T-shirt and brushed her teeth before creeping into the bedroom, where she plugged her phone into a bedside charger. She made sure she was always reachable by the expectant moms who depended on her.

When she crawled into bed, Shannon reached for her, the way he did every night when they went to bed together.

"Did I wake you?" she asked.

"Nah, I was dozing, waiting for you."

If she lived forever, she'd never get tired of listening to that lovely accent. She took a deep breath and let it out, aching all over again as she recalled the things Seamus had told her. Thinking about what Shannon had been through broke her heart.

"Long day, love?"

"Long but good with two healthy new babies. Tiffany Taylor had a girl named Adeline, and Jenny Martinez had baby George."

"That's great news."

"It's always a huge relief when island deliveries go well."

"They usually go well when you're involved."

"That's the goal." Yawning, she turned to face him. "How was your day?"

"Less eventful than yours."

Victoria kissed him. "I missed you today."

"Missed you, too. It's not the same around here when you're not home. It's far too quiet. I went over to Seamus's for a little while. It's definitely *not* quiet over there."

She wanted to ask about Jackson and his troubles at camp, but then she'd have to tell him she'd been to see Seamus. So she didn't ask. "That's actually good news. I love to hear the boys are acting like little boys again."

"They certainly are. We played football in the yard with them, and I've got a few new bruises."

"Aww, poor baby."

He slid his leg between hers and tugged her in closer to him. "You could make me feel better."

Victoria laughed at his shameless ploy. Suddenly, she wasn't quite as tired as she'd been a few minutes ago. Being close to him this way always had the same effect on her. If he was nearby, she wanted him. It was one of the simple facts of her life.

"But if you're too tired—"

She kissed him, pouring all the love she felt for him into that single kiss, wishing she could take away the pain he carried with him, even if he never spoke of it.

He rolled her under him, kissing her face and neck.

Victoria wondered if he remembered his lost love when he was with her this way. Did he close his eyes and imagine she was someone else? The thought of that possibility broke her heart and had tears pooling in her eyes that she hoped he wouldn't notice.

They'd come such a long way from the first night they met, or so she'd thought. As he helped her out of the T-shirt she'd worn to bed and left a trail of kisses down the front of her, she thought about the steps they'd taken in the beginning that had led her to believe they were starting a lasting relationship. They'd been tested so they could have sex without condoms and then officially moved in together after spending every night together that first month. Now they shared meals and bills and a bed and a life that had come to mean more to her than anything ever had before.

She'd never lived with a man or engaged in the kind of relationship she had with Shannon. But now she had reason to wonder if they'd been building a life or a house of cards that would collapse under the weight of his past. And why hadn't he told her about Fiona himself? In all the time they'd spent together, how could he have kept such a big part of himself from her?

"Where have you gone off to, love?" he asked, his cock hard against her center.

"I'm here," she said, reaching for him. "I'm right here."

He thrust into her, filling her so completely in every possible way. Her heart overflowed with love for him, with the desire to have everything with him. She wanted little Irish babies who looked just like him and yearned to watch them grow up with him by her side.

Victoria hadn't often entertained those thoughts, because she'd always suspected something was holding him back from fully committing to her. Now that she knew why, it was like the floodgates had opened and all the things she wanted so desperately surged to the surface, making her cling to him as he made love to her.

They'd been together long enough that he sensed something was wrong. "What is it, Vic? Why're you so tense?"

"I'm sorry," she said, unable to let go and relax after the emotionally charged day she'd had. Soon she would have no choice but to do something with the information Seamus had given her. But not now. Not tonight. She wrapped her legs around his waist and ran her fingers through the thick hair that curled at the ends.

"You're sure you're okay?"

"I'm fine. Don't stop."

He grasped her hips and picked up the pace.

Normally, she couldn't form a coherent thought when he was inside her, but tonight, pleasure was no match for the insecurities that filled her mind.

"Tell me you're close, love," he said, sounding tense.

"So close." She wasn't. She'd never faked it before with him. She hadn't had to.

"You feel so good."

Victoria held him tight, fighting the emotional firestorm that threatened to erupt at any second.

"Vic," he said, sounding desperate as he came with a gasp, surging into her.

She couldn't find the wherewithal to pretend she'd come, too. Instead, she caressed his back and continued to run her fingers through his silky hair.

"What's wrong?" he asked after a long silence. "If you were too tired, you could've said so."

"I know. I'm sorry."

"You're not going to tell me what's on your mind?"

"Not now, if that's okay."

He withdrew from her and moved to his back, bringing her with him and arranging her head on his chest, usually her favorite place to sleep. But now she had reason to wonder if the heart that beat so hard and fast belonged to her or if it would forever belong to the woman he'd loved and lost so tragically.

"Whatever it is," he said softly in the voice that touched her soul, "I hope you know you can talk to me."

"I know." Victoria closed her eyes tight against a new flood of tears that wanted out. She felt so raw and exposed, as if her heart were outside her body, unprotected. If she gave in to the tears, she feared they might never stop.

Exhaustion was her savior, dragging her into the oblivion only sleep could provide.

It was still dark when Victoria woke to her ringing cell phone. Groaning, she left the warmth of Shannon's embrace to grab the phone, taking it with her to the bathroom, where she closed the door so she wouldn't disturb him.

"This is Victoria."

"It's Luke Harris. I think Syd is in labor. It's come on fast and furious."

"Can you get her to the clinic?"

"I don't think so. She says she needs to push right now."

In the background, Victoria could hear Sydney's anguished cries. "I'll be there in ten minutes."

"Thank you so much."

Victoria ended the call and found David's number on her list of contacts.

"Dr. Lawrence," he muttered.

"David, wake up. Sydney Harris is in labor at home, and it's happening fast. Can you meet me at their place?" She pictured him sacked out on the sofa in his office.

"Yeah."

"Are you awake?"

"I am now."

"Hurry."

"On my way."

Victoria got dressed as fast as she could, took a second to brush her hair and teeth, and then grabbed the bag she kept at home, just in case. It contained some of what they'd need, but not everything. She left a note for Shannon and headed out. From the car, she called Katie.

"Sorry to wake you up, but Sydney Harris is in labor at home. I need a few things from the clinic. Can you help me out?"

"Of course," Katie said, sounding wide awake when she'd been fast asleep one minute ago.

Victoria gave her a list of the supplies she needed.

"Did you call David?"

"He's on his way. I didn't want to slow him down by asking for supplies."

"Understood. I'll be quick."

"Thanks, Katie."

Victoria yawned and glanced at the clock. Quarter to six. She'd gotten about two hours of sleep. Nowhere near enough. Three babies arriving in twenty-four hours was an island record. Fortunately, none of her other expecting moms was close to term, so she should get a break after the Harrises' baby arrived.

She felt a twinge of anxiety about how Sydney's much-anticipated child would enter the world at home and not in the clinic. Like Tiffany and Jenny, Syd had been due to deliver on the mainland in two weeks. But the baby apparently had other plans. Nothing could go wrong with this delivery. There was, Victoria thought, no room for error.

Sydney had lost her first husband and two children in a drunk-driving accident a few years ago. After she married her first love, Luke Harris, Sydney had undergone a procedure to reverse her tubal ligation and had soon conceived what she called her miracle baby. If anyone deserved a miracle, Sydney did, and Victoria was determined to make sure she got one.

Victoria pulled into the Harrises' driveway and parked next to Syd's Volvo. She'd been here a few times for one of the frequent girls' nights out that the island women were so fond of, especially since the guys always crashed. Grabbing her bag, she ran for the door, where Luke greeted her, looking tense and worried.

"Is it bad that the baby is coming so fast?"

"It's not uncommon when it's the mom's third child. Try not to worry."

"That's like telling me not to breathe."

Sydney let out a cry from a bedroom in the back of the house.

"Vic..."

"I know, Luke. We're going to do everything we can for her. David and Katie are on their way. We've got this, but she needs you, too. Get yourself together and come help her."

He nodded and gestured for her to head down the hallway to the bedroom on the left.

After being told that Sydney's first two children had arrived quickly, she'd tried to prepare Sydney—and Luke—for the possibility of that happening again.

"Vic," Syd said, sounding frantic, "the baby is coming."

She was propped up on pillows, towels under her, legs splayed.

On first glance, Victoria could see that the baby was crowning. "When you say fast, you mean it."

"I had a backache all day yesterday. Do you think that was labor?"

"I would say so. Let me wash up, and we'll get that baby out to meet her mom and dad."

"Please hurry. I can't stop it."

Victoria went into the adjoining bathroom to thoroughly wash her hands. Then she donned gloves and a gown before positioning herself between Syd's legs.

Luke came into the room, seeming noticeably calmer than he'd been when he greeted her. "Where do you want me?"

"Behind Syd so you can support her when she pushes."

He got on the bed and took his place behind his wife, gathering her long red hair and smoothing it back from her face.

"On the next contraction, I want you to push," Victoria said. "As hard as you can."

Sydney nodded, and though she looked determined, Victoria could also see a hint of panic.

"Everything's going to be fine, Sydney," Victoria said, praying that was true. "Focus on breathing. Deep breath in. Hold it. Now let it out." She walked her through several more deep breaths before Sydney tensed with the start of the next contraction. "Okay, let's do it."

She'd pushed twice by the time David and Katie arrived.

"We're almost there," Victoria told them. "One more big push, Syd."

With Luke's arms around her, Sydney screamed as she pushed her daughter into the world.

Victoria held her up for her parents to see.

"Oh, Syd," Luke said. "Look at her!"

The baby let out an indignant cry, her face turning red with the rage of being disturbed.

Victoria quickly cut the cord and turned the baby over to David so she could focus on Syd.

"Is she okay?" Luke asked.

"She's perfect," David said. "What's her name?"

"Lillian Alice Harris," Sydney said as tears ran down her face, "after Luke's mom and mine. We're going to call her Lily."

"What a beautiful name," Victoria said.

"My parents are going to be so bummed that they missed this," Syd said. "They're in Wisconsin until next week. So much for their plan to be back for my due date."

"They'll be thrilled to hear she's safely arrived and it all went well," Luke said.

"Yes, they will."

David brought the baby to her elated parents and put her in Sydney's arms.

These were the moments that made Victoria's professional life so very rewarding. She found herself wiping away tears right along with Sydney and Luke, which wasn't uncommon. After spending nearly a year tending to her moms—and their nervous partners—it was always an emotional moment to welcome a new baby, especially one like Lily, who truly was a miracle.

"She's so beautiful, Syd," Luke said. "Just like her mother."

"She looks like you," Syd said.

"No way. God wouldn't be that mean to her."

Everyone laughed.

"She should be so lucky to look like her gorgeous daddy," Syd said, gazing at the baby with amazement and joy that had been a very long time coming.

"Does Syd need to go to the clinic?" Luke asked.

"If you don't mind if I stick around for a couple of hours to keep an eye on both your ladies, they should be able to stay here," Victoria said.

"That's totally fine with us," Luke said.

"I need to get back to the clinic," David said. "We're having a regular baby boom around here."

"We heard Tiffany and Jenny had their babies, too," Luke said.

"I see a big first birthday party in our future a year from now," Katie said.

"I can't believe she's finally here," Sydney said, staring at her daughter.

Luke kept his arms around Syd as she relaxed against him.

Victoria left the room to give them a few minutes alone.

Katie had already left, but David lingered.

"Did you get a chance to talk to Shannon?"

Victoria shook her head. "It was so late when I got home. I didn't want to get into it then. Hopefully, we'll have time to talk later."

"We should be out of the baby delivery business for a while now."

"Let's hope so. Three in twenty-four hours is a new record."

"One I hope we don't beat any time soon." He squeezed her arm. "Call me if you need me—for anything."

"I will. You guys will take care of my appointments today?"

"We've got you covered."

Her absence would make for a busy day for David and Katie, but they could handle the extra appointments.

"Did Tiffany and Jenny have a good night?"

"The babies were up and down, but overall, everyone got some sleep. I'm going to send them all home today."

"Sounds good. Tell them I'll see them in six weeks or sooner if need be."

"Will do." He paused on his way out the door. "So this isn't the time or the place, but Daisy will kill me if I don't get this taken care of."

"Get what taken care of?" Victoria asked, looking up at him in confusion.

"I was supposed to ask you two weeks ago if you'd be in our wedding."

"For real?"

"Yes, for real," he said with exasperation and laughter. "You're one of my best friends and—"

Victoria hurled herself at him, taking him by surprise.

Luckily, he recovered and caught her before they landed on the floor. "Is that a yes?" he asked, laughing.

"Yes! I'd love to be in your wedding. You're one of my best friends, too. Am I a groomsman or a bridesmaid?"

"Bridesmaid," he said. "You'd look silly in a tux."

"No, I wouldn't. I could totally rock a tux."

"I'll let you work that out with Daisy," he said, cuffing her chin on the way out the door.

"David?"

"Yeah?"

"Thanks for asking me. Means a lot."

"Thanks for saying yes."

Victoria smiled and waved as he headed for the driveway. She was so happy for him and Daisy. After the guilt and recriminations he'd suffered through after his engagement to Janey had ended in dramatic fashion after she caught him in bed with another woman, David had worked hard to turn his life around. He'd been so happy since he'd fallen in love with Daisy, and Victoria couldn't wait to dance at their wedding.

While she was truly happy for her friends, she couldn't help but wonder if she'd ever get to dance at her own wedding.

CHAPTER 5

As the first boat off the island cleared the South Harbor breakwater and headed for the mainland, Shannon made his way to the bow, his favorite place to stand during the hour-long ride. He stood at the rail, letting the spray from below wash over him every time the big ferry crested a wave. With his cousin at the helm, Shannon relaxed and took in the scenery as they traveled along the island's rugged north coastline.

He loved this job and the island and the life he'd found there with Victoria, Seamus, Carolina and their vast circle of friends. After a year, Gansett felt like home in a way that Ireland hadn't for quite some time. When he'd accompanied his aunt Nora on her trip to visit Seamus, he certainly hadn't expected to stay when she left to go home.

But he also hadn't expected to meet Victoria his first night on the island. Two weeks later, he'd been nowhere near ready to leave her. He still wasn't, which counted as the biggest surprise of the last year.

Nine years after losing his beloved girlfriend in an act of senseless violence, he was a shell of the man he'd once been. But lately, since he met Vic, to be precise, things had been better. The dark moods didn't come on as often as they used to, and he had new reason to get up in the morning, to function, to put one foot in front of the other and carry on. She'd been perfect for him, a wonderful, sexy companion who didn't ask more of him than he was capable of giving. She would never know how much he appreciated that.

She was off delivering yet another baby. He hadn't heard the phone or her early morning departure. He greatly admired her professional competence and her devotion to her patients. The island's female population was lucky to have her, and they knew it. She was forever coming home with flowers or other gifts her grateful patients had given her.

"Gonna be another scorcher." Shannon immediately recognized the sound of home in his cousin's voice.

"What're you doing up here? You're supposed to be at the helm."

"One of the new captains was hitching a ride back and offered to relieve me. He needs the experience, so here I am."

"Does he know what he's doing?" Shannon asked, eyeing the bridge warily.

Seamus barked out a laugh. "I only hire the best. Not to worry."

"If you say so." His cousin was nothing if not meticulous when it came to running the company owned by Carolina and her son, Joe.

"Vic came to see me yesterday."

Shocked to hear that, Shannon stared at his cousin, almost afraid to ask. "How come?"

"She had some questions."

"About me?"

Seamus nodded.

Shannon's chest felt like it was being compressed by something heavy and unforgiving, the way it had in the days that followed Fiona's death. "What did you tell her?"

"What she needed to know."

"Seamus! *Are you fucking kidding me right now?*"

"Relax. I only gave her the big picture. None of the details."

His mind raced as he tried to absorb the implications. So that was why she'd been so tense last night. "You had no right."

"I had every right. She cares about you. She wants to understand you."

"It's not your place to fill in the blanks for her."

"Whose place is it, then? You're never going to do it."

"How do you know that?"

"It's been a year, Shannon, and she'd never heard Fiona's name."

White-hot rage ripped through him. "And now she has?"

"Now she has."

"It wasn't your place! I can't believe you'd interfere in my life this way! What gives you the right?"

"The woman who loves you asked me. That's what gave me the right."

"She doesn't love me. She enjoys fucking me. Big difference."

"You're a bloody fool if that's what you think. Open your goddamned eyes and look at what's right in front of you before she gets tired of competing with a ghost she didn't even know about and walks away."

Shannon didn't think before he reacted, punching his cousin in the face so hard that pain radiated from his hand up his arm.

Seamus went flying backward, falling hard against one of the benches and landing on the deck. For the longest time, he didn't move, and for a brief, terrifying second, Shannon feared he'd killed his cousin.

Filled with unreasonable terror, Shannon leaned over him. "Seamus, I'm sorry!" He shook his shoulder. "Seamus! Wake up!" They'd attracted a crowd of curious onlookers, including several of Shannon's fellow deckhands. "Please wake up."

"Quit yer bellowing," Seamus said without opening his eyes. The left side of his face was already swelling and turning purple.

"I'm sorry. I shouldn't have... I don't know why..."

Seamus held up his hand, opening the eye that still worked. "Stop talking and help me up."

Shannon took hold of his cousin's hand and hauled him to his feet, grasping his shoulder when Seamus wavered.

"Show's over, folks," Seamus said. "Move along."

"Go get some ice," Shannon said to one of the guys he worked with. "Hurry." He helped Seamus onto the bench. "I'm really sorry."

"I heard you the first time."

His colleague Mark returned with a bag of ice that he handed to Seamus, who applied it to his face. "Sit yer arse down," Seamus said to Shannon when they were alone again.

Shannon sat next to him on the bench.

"You've put me in an awkward situation here. Because half the crew saw you hit me, I have no choice but to suspend you for three days for disciplinary reasons. An official note will be placed in your employee file. In this company, it's two strikes and you're out—cousin or not."

Knowing he'd fucked up, Shannon took a deep breath and let it out. "Okay."

"I want to say something else, and I want you to *listen* to me." Seamus removed the ice from his bruised face. "For nine long years, we've stood by you and tried to support you as best we could through an unimaginable tragedy. In the last year, I've seen you come back to life, back to the man you were before you lost Fi. That's *because* of Victoria. You lost Fiona through no fault of your own. If you push Victoria away because she's gotten too close, that'll be your own tough shit."

Taking the ice bag with him, Seamus got up and walked away.

Filled with despair the likes of which he hadn't felt so deeply in years, Shannon watched him go.

"I'M SERIOUSLY IN AWE OF YOU," LUKE SAID TO SYD LATE THAT afternoon, after Victoria had declared both ladies to be in perfect health and left them alone to care for their new baby. Lily—he had a *daughter* named *Lily*—was asleep in her bassinette next to their bed.

"Is that right?" Syd said with a saucy smile. Before Victoria left, he'd helped Sydney take a shower and gotten her settled back in bed while Victoria watched the baby.

Though Sydney was exhausted, her eyes were alight with joy. "Mmm," he said, nuzzling her neck. "That's right. You amaze me. After months of planning and me stressing out about all the things that could go wrong, you go and give birth without even leaving our bed."

Sydney laughed. "Well, that wasn't exactly the plan."

"I'm still allowed to be amazed."

"I'm just glad she's here safely, and we didn't have to leave the island to have her."

"Do you think she'll always be so accommodating of her parents?"

"Doubtful. I expect her to be a strong-willed girl like her sister was."

"That'd be fine with me, as long as you promise to protect me during the teenage years, when my little princess turns into a demon child."

She patted his head. "I'll run interference. Don't worry."

"Sometimes I still can't believe..." His throat tightened and his eyes filled. He'd been an emotional disaster all day.

"What can't you believe?"

"That you came back. That you actually love me and agreed to marry me and have given me a daughter. I was so alone for such a long time... And now..." He caressed her face and gently kissed her. "Now, I have everything."

"I don't even like to think about what I'd be doing if I hadn't come to the island or if you hadn't come to find me."

"Don't you mean if I hadn't spied on you?" he asked with a chuckle.

"It doesn't count as spying if I knew you were there. The scrape of your boat landing on the beach was one of the most familiar sounds in my life back when we were first together. I used to listen for it every night."

"Best thing I ever did was row my boat to your beach, baby," he said with a lascivious grin.

Sydney laughed at the double meaning behind his words. "You're going to make sure I'm not a total freak show with her, right?"

"Of course I am."

"I don't want her to grow up to be afraid of everything the way I am now."

"You're not giving yourself enough credit, honey. Look at what you've already done to prove you're not afraid of what might happen."

"What do you mean?"

"You married me. You had the tubal ligation reversed. You allowed me to knock you up, which was a great pleasure, I might add. You've given birth to a new baby. To me, all those things indicate your tremendous courage, not debilitating fear."

"That's nice of you to say, but the fear is still there. Maybe I just hide it better than I used to."

"I'm not just spewing platitudes here, Syd. I mean it when I say you're not giving yourself enough credit. You aren't the same fearful person you were when we first got back together. You've come a long way from there. Maybe you can't see it, but I do."

"If that's true, it's because of you. Your love has given me the strength to go on, to be optimistic and hopeful and joyful and all the things I thought I'd never be again after I lost Seth and the kids."

Luke leaned in to kiss her. "Whatever I've given you is a fraction of what I've gotten back in return."

Her smile lit up her gorgeous blue eyes. "I was thinking..."

"About?"

"This one went pretty well. Easy conception, uneventful pregnancy and delivery..."

His heart stopped beating for a second. "What're you saying?"

"Maybe we ought to do it one more time so Lily doesn't grow up alone."

Luke stared at her, incredulous. They'd agreed that one child would be a miracle. The thought of another was almost more than he could process.

Sydney waved her hand in front of his face. "Earth to Luke. Have I totally shocked you?"

"No, sweetheart, you've totally thrilled me."

"So you'd be game for doing this again?"

"Anything you want. Anything at all."

"Hmm," she said, her expression mischievous, "that's a pretty big mandate you're giving me."

"It's a pretty big love I have for you."

Moving slowly and carefully, Sydney snuggled up to him, and Luke wrapped his arms around her, profoundly relieved to have the delivery behind them and a lifetime to look forward to with Sydney and Lily and whoever might come next.

AFTER LEAVING THE HARRISES', VICTORIA SPENT A FEW HOURS AT THE clinic, helping David prepare Tiffany and Jenny to take their babies home. Jenny was having some challenges with breastfeeding, so Victoria spent an hour trying to help. She was so tired that her brain was actually buzzing from the lack of sleep.

"Go home," David said at two. "Before you fall over and become a patient."

"I'm going." Victoria didn't have the energy to argue with him. "Back to business as usual tomorrow."

"Let's hope so."

Victoria drove home with the windows open, hoping the fresh air would keep her awake long enough to make it safely to her driveway. She couldn't recall the last time she'd been this tired. Well, maybe the week she met Shannon when they'd stayed up every night for days because they'd been having too much fun to sleep.

Thinking about those first days together made her smile. That had been the most exciting time, to have found someone who captivated her so completely. That was all she'd ever wanted for her personal life, a man who loved her as much as she loved him and to live happily ever after with him. Was that too much to ask?

This time yesterday, she would've said she and Shannon had laid the foundation for that kind of relationship. Now she wasn't sure of anything.

When she pulled into the driveway, she was surprised to see his motorcycle parked outside. He was supposed to be at work. What the hell? She got out of the car and went inside, where he was seated at the kitchen table, an ice pack on his hand.

"Hey," she said. "What's wrong?"

He looked up at her, his eyes bleak. "Got into a fight at work. They sent me home for three days."

Stunned, she said, "A fight about what?"

"If it's okay, I'd rather not talk about it."

"Oh," she said, stung by his dismissive tone. "Okay. I'm... ah... just going to get some sleep, then."

He nodded and returned his attention to his injured hand.

Victoria went into the bathroom and numbly went through the motions of changing into a T-shirt and brushing her teeth. In the bedroom, she closed the blinds and got into bed, staring up at the ceiling while trying to make sense of what he'd told her.

He'd gotten into a fight. Her Shannon, a pacifist down to his bones, had actually gotten into a *fight* at work and was sent home for *three days*. What the heck could've precipitated that? And why wouldn't he tell her what happened?

She, who had been thoroughly exhausted ten minutes ago, was now so wired she couldn't sleep. How was it possible that in just twenty-four hours, her entire world had been turned upside down? Why hadn't she left well enough alone and resisted the temptation to ask questions of Seamus? Now she had information she didn't know what to do with, and Shannon was getting into fights. Coincidence? Probably not.

Oh God. What if he'd fought with Seamus? The possibility had her sitting up in bed, reeling from the potential implications of Shannon fighting with a man who was not only his boss but also his cousin. Was that what'd happened? Victoria got out of bed and went to the kitchen to find the chair he'd recently occupied now empty.

Outside, the roar of his bike starting up had her running for the door, but she was too late. He was gone by the time she made it outside. Where was he going, and when would he be back?

Victoria went inside, but she was far too agitated to sleep. She needed answers, and she needed them now. Instead of going back to bed, she got dressed and shoved her feet into flip-flops, grabbing her purse and keys on the way out the door.

Mindful of her lack of sleep, Victoria made an effort to concentrate on her driving and not on the turmoil roiling inside her. She took a right turn into a driveway that had become familiar to her in the last year after many visits and parked next to Seamus's truck. In the yard, Kyle and Jackson were playing with their dog, laughing and running around the way little boys ought to.

Victoria waved to them on her way to the house, where she knocked on the back door.

Carolina came to the door and didn't seem surprised to see her. "Come in."

Her stomach aching with nerves, Victoria followed her into the kitchen, stopping short at the sight of Seamus's badly bruised and swollen face. For a long moment, she couldn't bring herself to move. She could only stare.

"Come in, Vic," Seamus said. "Looks worse than it is."

"It's all my fault," she said, her voice rough with emotion. "I never should've come to you. If I hadn't... He never would've... This..."

Seamus got up and came over to her. "It's *not* your fault."

"You two fought because you told me about Fiona. That's why, right?"

"We fought because he didn't like something I said to him."

"But it started because I went to you with questions I should've asked him." Blinded by tears, Victoria wiped her cheek with the back of her hand.

Carolina came to her, put her hands on Victoria's shoulders and guided her to a seat at the table. "You didn't throw the punch," she said.

"I started the fight, though," Victoria said.

"No, you didn't," Seamus said. "I pushed him too far."

Carolina raised the ice bag to his face and held it in place. "That doesn't give him the right to punch you."

"I've made such a mess of things," Victoria said. "I should've left well enough alone."

"If you'd done that, your relationship with him never would've been more than what it is right now," Seamus said. "I was under the impression you wanted it to be more."

"I did. I *do*. But not if it's going to cause this kind of trouble."

"You were trying to understand him better by going to Seamus," Carolina said. "You had no way to know the magnitude of what you were going to be told or how he'd react to hearing what Seamus told you. Your intentions were pure and came from a place of love. No one can fault you for that."

Carolina's softly spoken words broke something in Victoria, the core of strength that had been holding her together since learning of Shannon's tragic past. She dropped her head into her hands as her body shook with sobs, her heart broken for Shannon's loss as much as her worries about her own future with him.

A few minutes later, the unmistakable roar of Shannon's motorcycle outside had Victoria hurrying to dry her face and wipe her eyes with the tissue Carolina handed her.

Seamus put the ice bag on the table. "Let me handle this." He stalked to the door and went outside.

CHAPTER 6

The slam of the screen door closing startled Victoria out of the daze she'd fallen into. She got up to follow Seamus, who had Shannon by the arm in the yard.

"Wait," she cried. "*Stop.* Just stop!" She forced her way between the cousins and took hold of Shannon's arm. "Walk away. Right now." She marched him toward the path that led from the yard to the rugged coastline.

Jackson and Kyle stood off to the side, watching them go by with big eyes.

Victoria felt bad for bringing their drama to Seamus and Carolina's home.

"What're you doing here?" Shannon asked when they had left the yard behind.

"About two seconds after you left, I figured out who you fought with at work, and I came to check on him."

"You're awfully cozy with my cousin all of a sudden."

Victoria gave him a hard shove that he didn't see coming, making him stumble on the dirt path. "Shut up. I am not *cozy* with him. I am *friends* with him *through you,* as you well know."

When he turned to face her, she was taken aback by the stormy expression on his face. In all their time together, she'd never seen that particular look on him before. "I don't know who you think you are, poking your nose into stuff that's none of your business."

"*None of my business?* How do you figure it's none of my business when you're *living in my house and sleeping in my bed?*"

"Both of which can be easily rectified."

Stunned by the hostile rebuke, Victoria reeled from the meaning behind his words. "So that's how you're going to play this? You're going to run away because I wanted to know why we're stuck in the same place we were a year ago?"

"*That's* what you think? That we're in the same place we were a year ago?" He shook his head in disbelief.

"We're exactly where we were then. We haven't taken a single step forward from the day you moved in."

"That is not true," he said softly.

She couldn't miss the hint of sadness in his tone. "Shannon—"

He held up a hand to stop her. "I can't do this."

A shockingly painful bolt of fear jolted her. "What can't you do?"

"This. Any of it. I never should've… I can't." He brushed by her and started back up the path toward the yard.

"Shannon, wait! You can't just walk away from me after everything we've shared."

He whirled around. "According to you, we haven't shared anything."

"I never said that!"

"Didn't you?"

When he started walking again, she chased after him, grabbing his shirt and forcing him to stop.

"I never said that."

"What did you say, then, Vic? Explain it to me."

She swallowed the huge lump in her throat and tried to ignore the roar in her ears and the relentless beat of her heart so she could focus on him. "I said we are stuck in the same place we started. That's all."

"I don't know how you can say that." He raised his hands to his head and ran his fingers roughly through his hair, leaving it standing on end.

She had to resist the urge to straighten it the way she would have only yesterday, before she ruined everything by digging into his past.

"If you think that," he said, "you don't know me at all."

"I *want* to know you. Why do you think I went to Seamus in the first place? It's because I want that so badly."

"So badly that you couldn't ask me what you wanted to know?"

He had her there. "I was afraid to."

Seeming stunned, he stared at her. "You were *afraid* to talk to me? What the hell, Victoria?"

"I don't know why I felt that way. I guess I figured if you were ever going to tell me what was holding you back from fully committing to me, you would've by now."

"Fully committing," he said with a huff of incredulous laughter. "I live with you. I sleep with you. I have sex with you almost every day, sometimes twice a day. How do *you* define fully committed?"

Victoria had to fight the need to squirm under his intense green-eyed gaze. "Is that it? Is that going to be our life? Living together, sleeping together, having sex?"

"I thought you *liked* our life."

"I do!"

"Then what in the name of God is the problem, Victoria?"

"I..." She took a deep breath and forced herself to meet his gaze. "I want more."

Again she saw sadness and weary resignation in his expressive eyes. "I'm not capable of more."

"Yes, you are."

"No, Victoria, I'm really not. I like what we have. It works for me. If it's not working for you, all you have to do is say so."

"It does work for me, but—"

"No buts. It either works for you or it doesn't. Which is it?"

She once again swallowed a lump in her throat as a hundred scenarios flashed through her mind in the span of a second. One thing became crystal clear—if they weren't together, they'd never be able to move forward. Right here, right now, preserving the relationship they already had was her top priority.

"Vic? What's it going to be?"

"It works for me."

"No more poking around in my past, you got me?"

"Were you ever going to tell me about it?"

"No."

"Just no? That's it?"

"Just no. That's it." As he said those words, she saw more passion and fire in his eyes than she had ever seen before—and all of it for a woman who had died.

Something inside *her* died at realizing she couldn't compete with that woman. She couldn't—and wouldn't—compete with her. "I... I'm sorry. It turns out that this isn't going to work for me after all."

"What're you saying?"

Since she might not get another chance, Victoria decided it was time to lay it all on the line. "I love you, Shannon. I'm in love with you. I want a life with you. I want us to have so much more than a shared address, a shared bed and the best sex I've ever had. I want a family. I want kids and a husband and a commitment from a man who loves me and only me. I want the fairy tale."

"I'm not capable of fairy tales."

"Yes, you are!" She closed the distance between them, placing her hands on his chest and sliding them up to encircle his neck. "You're so capable. You're everything I want and need. All you have to do is be willing to accept what I want to give you and then give it back to me."

"I can't," he said, shaking his head. "I can't. I'm sorry. If I was going to have that with anyone, it would be you."

"Shannon, please. All I'm asking you to do is *try*."

"I have tried. I've tried my best for a year, and you're telling me that my best isn't enough for you."

"Talk to me about her. Tell me what happened. Let me share your burden."

He pulled free of her. "I don't talk about her. I hate that you even know about her."

"Why don't you want me to know? What do you think I'll do with that information besides love you more than I already do?"

Shaking his head, he said, "Don't love me, Vic. I'm not worth it."

"It's far, *far* too late to tell me that." After taking a moment to summon the courage she needed, she looked him in the eye and lowered her voice in case little ears were nearby. "I know how to turn you on and just how to touch you to make you shout when you come. I know what makes you tremble and what makes you sigh with pleasure, but I didn't know about the most important person in your life until someone else told me about her. I don't know what you hope for, what you dream about, what you *want* for yourself. All I'm asking for is the chance to know *you*, Shannon, not just what turns you on."

He broke the intense eye contact and looked down at the ground. After a long moment, he finally returned his gaze to her, seeming devastated by what she'd said. "I'm sorry to have disappointed you this way. I never intended for that to happen. Jesus, I never intended for any of this to happen." He caressed her face, his touch electrifying her as it always did. Then he kissed her forehead. "Give me an hour, and I'll be out of the house. I'm so sorry, love."

Riveted by the sight of him walking away from her, Victoria stood there until long after he'd disappeared around a bend in the path. Tears rolled unchecked down her face as she tried to process what'd just happened. He'd ended it with her rather than share himself, his past, his pain or his love with her.

Her chest tightened, the ache centered in her heart, which had been shattered in the scope of a few minutes. Blinded by tears, she bent at the waist, trying to force air into lungs that felt compressed by the magnitude of the pain. Nothing had ever hurt like this did.

Victoria had no idea how long she was there before she heard Seamus say her name.

"Come with me," he said, helping her to stand upright and guiding her toward his home with his arm around her shoulders.

Victoria pressed her face against his chest and let him lead the way for her. She was incapable of even the simplest things at the moment. He settled her on the sofa in their sitting room. Even though it was summer and hot outside, she shivered uncontrollably. Seamus pulled a blanket over her and then sat on the edge of the sofa.

"There now," he said in that hauntingly beautiful accent. "It's going to be okay."

Victoria shook her head. She had a hard time believing anything was ever going to be okay again.

"There's an old saying... I can't remember who said it, but it went something like this. If you love someone, set them free. If they come back to you, they're yours. If they don't, they never were."

A sob hiccupped through her, and tears fell in a steady stream. She already knew that Shannon wouldn't come back. He'd never been hers. She just hadn't understood that before now. "I... I should go. You don't need this here. The boys—"

"Are fine, and you're welcome here for as long as you'd like to stay." He pulled the blanket up farther. "Close your eyes and try to rest for a bit. You're in no condition to drive."

Victoria knew she ought to get up and go home to her own house to mourn in private, but she couldn't seem to make her body heed the call to move. So she stayed put on Seamus and Carolina's sofa and cried herself to sleep.

CHAPTER 7

Shannon guided the motorcycle out of Seamus's driveway and drove much faster than he should have on the island's winding roads, the careless disregard for his own safety an unwelcome reminder of the years that followed Fiona's death when he hadn't given a flying fuck about anything, least of all himself.

A jumble of mixed emotions assailed him—anger, grief, sadness, frustration and love. Yes, he loved Victoria. How could he not? She was amazing, sweet, sexy, smart and funny. They'd had an incredible year together, or so he'd thought. Apparently, it hadn't been as great for her, which was a huge surprise to him. He'd had no idea she was in any way unhappy until Seamus told him she'd been asking about his past.

No, he did *not* want to talk about Fiona. It had taken him years to be able to take a deep breath around the searing, agonizing pain in his chest after she died. It had taken years to be able to do anything other than relentlessly grieve. The last fecking thing in the goddamned world he wanted to do was talk about Fiona or what it'd been like to lose her. That would be like pouring battery acid on a festering wound that had never truly healed—and never truly would.

Crushed shells crunched under his tires as he pulled into the driveway at the home he'd shared with Victoria. It had been a good year, the best one he'd had since losing Fi. He'd never deny that or even try to. Vic said she wanted more. He didn't have more to give. It was that simple.

He parked the bike and went inside, where the familiar scent of home greeted him. Vic fancied her candles and smelly things. The memory of teasing her about a candle that smelled like laundry detergent stopped him in his tracks, the same way a punch to the gut would. Closing his eyes, he took a deep breath and let it out slowly, but that couldn't keep the old familiar despair from creeping up on him. He'd woken up this morning thinking everything was fine and now… Now it was a fecking mess again.

Life with Victoria had been peaceful and sweet and… *Fuck*, he was going to miss her. He sat down hard on the bed they'd shared for so many blissful nights and dropped his head into his hands. This, right here, was why he'd once vowed to never get involved with a woman again. Who needed this kind of pain when it ended? And it always ended.

Running his fingers through his hair, he thought about arriving on Gansett Island, meeting Victoria that first night and being instantly wowed by her. The first thing he'd noticed was her smile and the way it lit up her entire face. Her pervasive joyfulness had soothed him from the beginning. It hadn't taken long for him to become addicted to her joy and the way he felt when he was around her.

He hadn't come to Gansett looking for anything more than a couple of weeks away from the memories and the ghosts that had haunted him for the long years since Fiona was taken from him. To say that his relationship with Victoria had been a huge surprise was putting it mildly. Out of sheer necessity, he'd been with other women since he lost Fi, but Victoria had been the first relationship he'd had, and now that too was gone, leaving yet another gaping wound for him to contend with.

How many such wounds could one heart withstand in a lifetime and still beat the way it was supposed to?

Reaching under the bed, he pulled out the duffel bag he'd stashed there when he moved in and tossed it on the bed. Without thinking too much about what he was doing, he emptied the two drawers Vic had made available to him in her dresser and retrieved his shaving bag from the bathroom. Then he went to the closet to retrieve the few items he had on hangers and came face-to-face with the sexy black dress Victoria had worn to Dan and Kara's wedding earlier in the month. God, she'd looked beautiful that day.

He recalled being eager to get her home the whole time they were at the wedding and thought about slow dancing with her to one song after another. Then he'd watched her crazy antics on the dance floor with the other women to the faster songs. At the time, he'd thought she was life personified—energy, intelligence, beauty and joy. He kept coming back to that word when he thought of Victoria. In recent years, he'd had so little to be joyful about that it had been the first of many things that'd attracted him to her.

"Ah, bollacks," he muttered to the empty house. "What does it matter now what attracted you to her? It's over. You've seen to that."

Ten minutes after he began, he was completely packed, which made him realize that for all the time he'd spent in this house, he'd done almost nothing to make it his home as much as it was hers. Probably because he'd known, in his heart of hearts, that he wouldn't be here forever.

In the kitchen, he put down his bag and peeled the key she'd given him when he moved in off his ring, placing it on the table. His entire body ached with regret as he stared down at that key and everything it stood for, remembering the hopeful, excited expression on her face when she'd given it to him after he decided to stay on at the end of his two-week vacation. At the time, he'd figured he'd be here a month, maybe two. Now here it was a year later, and he'd found a whole new life here with a job he enjoyed, new friends and...

Sighing, he picked up his bag. The best part of his new life on Gansett was over now, and he'd have to find a way to accept that and move on. He pulled the door closed behind him and made sure it was locked. As he was strapping the duffel onto the back of his bike, his phone rang. Seeing the call was from Seamus, he took it.

"Hey," he said.

"Did you move out of Vic's?"

"Yeah."

"The company has a room at the Beachcomber. I left word at the desk that it's okay for you to stay there."

"I... um... Why are you helping me out after what I did today?"

"Because you're still my cousin, and I still care about you even if I think you're being an absolute gobshite to walk away from the woman who loves you."

Shannon closed his eyes against the burn of tears that infuriated him. He refused to be sucked into the bottomless rabbit hole of grief once again. "I know it's not possible for you to understand, but this is what's best for me right now."

"Fair enough."

"Seamus... I'm really sorry again about today. You've been... really good to me through all of it, and you deserve better than what you got from me today."

"And I'm sorry if I overstepped by talking to Vic, but I like her for you. I've enjoyed seeing you happy again after a long dark winter filled with despair."

Shannon's throat closed around a lump. He closed his eyes tight and tried to contain the rush of emotion. Everything his cousin had said was true, but none of it changed the simple fact that Shannon was no longer capable of the level of intimacy that Victoria needed and deserved from the man in her life. For the first time since he lost Fiona, he wished he could be different or more or whatever Victoria needed to make her happy. But that wasn't possible.

"Call me if you need anything," Seamus said.

His cousin's generosity in light of the day's events only added to the weight pressing on Shannon's chest. "I will. Thanks."

He stashed the phone in his pocket and straddled the bike, taking a long last look at the little house where he'd lived with Victoria. Seamus was right—he had been happy with her. He'd never deny that, but one of the reasons he'd been so happy was that she'd never asked for more than he had to give.

Until now.

Kick-starting the bike, he turned it toward the road and left behind the house he'd called home for the last year, weary at the thought of starting over.

Again.

VICTORIA WOKE TO DARKNESS, LOW VOICES AND THE GIGGLES OF LITTLE boys trying to be quiet. For a moment, she couldn't recall why she'd been sleeping in Seamus and Carolina's sitting room, but then it all came flooding back in a wave of painful memories that took her breath away.

Shannon was gone. Their relationship was over.

As she remembered their heated exchange in the yard and the despair she'd seen in his eyes, it literally hurt to breathe.

She gave herself a few minutes to get it together before she sat up, ran her fingers through her hair and hoped her ravaged face wouldn't scare the boys. After folding the blanket Seamus had covered her with and putting it over the back of the sofa, she took a deep breath and braced herself to face her friends.

The four of them were seated around the table eating hamburgers and french fries. Jackson had ketchup on his cheek, and Kyle was talking with his mouth full while Carolina gently corrected his manners. They made for such a sweet little family, and Victoria admired Seamus and Caro tremendously for what they'd done for the boys.

"She's awake!" Kyle cried when he saw Victoria. "Can we be loud now?"

Seamus laughed at the question and the mouthful of food that nearly fell from Kyle's face as he spoke. "Close yer mouth and chew."

"I'm so sorry you had to be quiet for me," Victoria said to Kyle.

"Hope you had a good nap," Seamus said, studying her with concern on a face that was almost as handsome as his younger cousin's, even when bruised and swollen. She would always be partial to Shannon's handsome face, whether they were together or not.

"I did. Thank you so much for letting me stay. I'll get out of your hair now."

"You're not in our hair," Carolina said. "How about something to eat?"

Victoria placed a hand on her abdomen. "I don't think I could, but thank you anyway."

Carolina stood to hug her. "Hang in there, and if you need us, you have friends here."

"Thank you," Victoria said softly, afraid to say anything more than that due to her shaky composure.

"I'll walk you out," Seamus said.

Victoria waved to the boys and preceded Seamus out the door. When she reached her car, she turned to him. "Thank you for everything. You went above and beyond. I'm sorry that I put you in this position to start with. I never should've come to you yesterday."

"That's a load of shite. You didn't do anything wrong. You wanted insight. Who else should you have asked if you didn't feel comfortable asking him?"

"That's just it, though. If I didn't feel comfortable asking him, that should've been a sign to me that something was wrong."

"Maybe so, but your heart was in the right place trying to figure him out. And you suspected there were things he was keeping from you that would matter at some point."

Victoria ran her hand over the heart that ached from the loss of the man she loved. "How long will it hurt this bad?"

"For a while, I suspect. After Caro and I first got together, she decided our age difference was too much for her to take on. We went round and round for quite some time until I couldn't take it anymore. I actually gave Joe my notice, intending to go home to Ireland, because I couldn't be here if I couldn't have her."

"I had no idea you guys went through all that."

"Aye, it was a terrible situation for a long time. I know what it's like to have your heart feel like it's cracked down the middle and nothing can fix it except the one you love."

"What happened? How did you end up staying?"

"Joe told his mum that I'd given notice, and that night she came to find me, asking me not to go—and not because my departure would create a nightmare at work for her son, but because she wanted me to stay. What started out as one of the worst days of my life turned into one of the best." He drew Victoria into a hug. "I know it's awful right now, but don't give up hope. This break might be just what he needs to get his head out of his arse and see what's right in front of him."

Though she wanted to cling to Seamus's hopeful thought with everything she had, Victoria also had to be realistic. "I don't think that's going to happen, but I appreciate you trying to cheer me up."

He released her from his embrace. "You heard what Caro said. We're your friends. If you need us, you know where we are."

Victoria kissed the cheek that wasn't bruised. "Thank you." She got into the car and put down the window.

"Incidentally," Seamus said, "Shannon is staying in the ferry company's room at the Beachcomber. Just in case he left anything behind at your place."

"Good to know," she said, swallowing hard at the realization that he was already long gone from their home.

"I'll check on you tomorrow."

"Hey, Seamus? Carolina was smart to go after you."

"I know," he said with a shit-eating grin. "That's another thing I tell her every day."

Smiling, Victoria waved as she drove down the driveway toward the main road that looped around the island. At the point where she had to decide whether to go right to go home, she faced a quandary. The thought of going to her place to confront Shannon's glaring absence made her feel even sicker than she already did, so she took a left and headed for David's.

On the way, she called him to see if he and Daisy were home. He answered on the third ring, sounding out of breath.

"Hey, what's up?" he said.

"I was wondering if you're home, but it sounds like I might be interrupting something."

"Ha, very funny. I ran for the phone because I was over at Jared's and forgot to bring it with me. Daisy heard it ringing. So yes, I'm home."

"Do you mind if I come over and maybe borrow your sofa tonight?" As she asked the question, Victoria felt pathetic for being so needy, but she simply couldn't face her empty house. Not tonight anyway.

"Of course. Our sofa is your sofa."

"I'll be there in a few."

"Sounds good."

Victoria again had to remind herself to concentrate on her driving so she wouldn't end up in a ditch or worse, off the side of one of Gansett's many sheer cliffs. Somehow she managed to navigate the island's winding roads and arrive safely at the driveway to David's home.

Looking like the cute engaged couple they were, David and Daisy both waited for her, sitting on the steps to their apartment over the garage at Jared and Lizzie James's waterfront estate. Victoria cut the engine and tried to find the wherewithal to get out of the car, determined to keep it together until she could be alone again.

Her resolve lasted until David got up and came over to her, wrapping his arms around her.

Victoria broke down into heartbroken sobs.

To his credit, David said nothing. He only held her while she cried it out. Then he kept an arm around her while he walked her inside with Daisy leading the way.

"I'm sorry to barge in on you guys this way," Victoria said, wiping away her tears. "But Shannon moved out, and I didn't want to be there tonight."

"You didn't barge in on us," Daisy said, "and of course you should come to us. I don't blame you for not wanting to be at home tonight. I'm sorry to hear about you and Shannon."

"I guess your talk with him didn't go well," David said.

She filled them in on Shannon's fight with Seamus and the conversation that had led to their breakup.

"Dear God," Daisy said. "His girlfriend was *murdered*?"

Victoria nodded as she sank to the sofa, her legs feeling less than supportive. "Nine years ago."

"You've known all along there was something," David said, sitting next to her on the sofa while Daisy took one of the chairs. "I remember a few times when you've wondered whether he would ever want more with you."

"There was definitely a wall that I kept butting up against," Victoria said, swiping impatiently at tears that refused to quit. "And now that wall has a name, and I'm so heartbroken for her and for him."

Daisy got up and retrieved a box of tissues that she handed to Victoria. Then she sat on the other side of Victoria on the sofa.

Victoria sent her a grateful smile. Thank goodness for friends at a time like this. She wiped her face and blew her nose. "What does it say about me that this is the first time in my life that I have ever cried over a guy?"

"It says to me that you've been very, very lucky," Daisy said.

Victoria immediately felt like total shit for saying such a thing, knowing that Daisy had been beaten by the last man she'd been involved with before David. "I'm sorry, Daisy. That was insensitive."

"No need to apologize. I mean it when I say you're lucky if this is the first time you've cried over a guy. I've been crying over them for most of my adult life."

"Until recently," David said, smiling at her.

"Now they're all happy tears," Daisy said, returning her fiancé's smile.

"I want what you guys have," Victoria said. "Is that too much to wish for?"

"Not at all," Daisy said, hugging her with one arm.

"I never should've gone to Seamus," Victoria said, filled with regret over the thing that had led to their breakup. "If only I hadn't done that."

"If you hadn't," David said, "you never would've known what'd happened to Shannon, because he wasn't about to tell you, and you also never would've had what you really want with him. You've been chafing at the bit with him for a while now, Vic. Much to my dismay, you used to joke, *frequently*, about how you two were all about the hot sex. Lately, you haven't been making those jokes. You've been dissatisfied. We've both noticed that."

Daisy nodded in agreement.

"I thought I did a better job of hiding it from everyone."

"We know you too well," David said. "I saw it happening months ago."

"I kept hoping if maybe I stuck it out long enough, that he'd open up to me," she said softly. "I gave him so many chances, but he never did."

"And he wasn't going to," David said. "You were right to force the issue. It was either that or spend forever in this odd state of limbo."

"Well, I got what I was looking for. Some of it, anyway. Not that it matters now."

"It matters, Vic," Daisy said. "You love him, and I believe he loves you, too. I've seen the way he looks at you. If that's not a man in love, then I know nothing about love."

"And she knows love," David said in all seriousness. "Trust me on that."

Both women laughed.

"It helps to know you think he feels that way about me," Victoria said to Daisy.

"I'm not just saying what you need to hear. I believe it. Give him some time to see what life without you is like. He'll be back."

"I guess we'll see, won't we?"

David put his arm around her. "You're welcome to stay with us for as long as you want."

Victoria leaned her head on his shoulder. "The last thing you lovebirds need is me sitting between you."

"We don't mind," Daisy said.

"I can't stand to see you so sad," David said. "I like it much better when you're busting my balls or telling me inappropriate details about your sex life."

Victoria laughed even as she battled more tears. "You won't need to worry about inappropriate details for a while."

"I know it doesn't seem like it now, but you're going to get through this," David said. "I promise."

"Keep telling me that."

"Any time you need to hear it."

"How about something to eat?" Daisy asked.

"I'm not sure I could."

"Cereal?" David asked. "You never say no to that."

Victoria was about to decline when her stomach growled—loudly.

Laughing, David said, "I'll take that as a yes. Come on." He took her hand and pulled her up, towing her along to the kitchen. "Daisy got me Cap'n Crunch."

Suddenly, there was nothing she'd rather do than eat Cap'n Crunch with David. "She really does love you."

"She certainly does."

WHILE DAISY GOT VICTORIA SETTLED ON THE SOFA, DAVID TOOK A shower and thought about the terrible situation his friend had found herself in. He had no doubt whatsoever that Vic loved Shannon and had for quite some time. That said, however, he'd been increasingly concerned by Shannon's seeming inability to commit to anything more than what appeared, from the outside looking in, to be a somewhat casual domestic arrangement. Knowing Victoria wanted and needed more than that, David had worried about her getting hurt.

It was, he'd discovered, a tricky proposition to warn a friend about the man she loved. Daisy had advised him to tread lightly with his concerns out of fear of Victoria deciding to marry the guy knowing David had reservations. The last thing he'd wanted was to put any more doubts in her mind when she already had her own.

So he'd kept his mouth shut even as he watched her get more and more involved with Shannon as the last year unfolded. Now that she had, in fact, been hurt by the guy, he wondered if he should've done more to prepare her for that possibility.

He took those concerns to bed with him, where he waited for Daisy to join him.

She came in a few minutes later, closing the door behind her.

"How is she?"

"Not great. She's going to watch some TV and try to sleep." Daisy sat on the bed and kicked off her flip-flops. "I feel so bad for her. I can't imagine how hard it must've been to find out what'd happened to Shannon and then to lose him over it." She turned so she could see him. "You saw this coming."

"I didn't see this particular scenario, but you know I've been worried that he wasn't as invested as she is. I should've said something."

"No, I still believe you really shouldn't have. What if, down the road, she ends up married to him? Then you're the friend who doubted the man she loves. Take it from me. I've been the girl in a relationship where everyone in my life hated the guy. With good reason, as it turned out in all instances, but no one could've told me that when I was in it. Love makes people blind."

"Is that so?" He reached for her hand. "What are you blind to when it comes to me?"

"The fact that you're thirty years old and still eating Cap'n Crunch."

David laughed and feigned offense. "I love my Cap'n Crunch."

"I know." She leaned in to kiss him. "And I love you, which is why I buy it for you."

David drew her into bed with him. "What else are you blind to?"

"That sometimes you forget to put the seat down."

"I do not! I was raised with sisters. I know better."

"Once in a blue moon."

"I require proof of this character flaw."

Daisy giggled at his outrage. God, he loved her so damned much. Witnessing Victoria's heartbreak up close made him so thankful for Daisy and the life they had together.

"I'll take a picture next time."

"You do that. Is there anything else?"

"No," she said, smoothing her fingers through his hair.

"Would you tell me if there was?"

"If it was something important. Would you tell me?"

"You'll never be anything other than perfect to me."

She snorted with laughter. "That is such bull. How about last week when I saw a perfectly good chair by the side of the road that I wanted to bring home, and you said we don't need other people's junk?"

"What about it?"

"You don't think my attachment to other people's junk is a character flaw?"

"Not at all. I think it's a throwback to a time in your life when you couldn't afford better. Now you can buy your own junk brand new."

"But why would I waste money on something brand new when there's a perfectly good free version right in front of me that I can clean and paint and make new again?"

"So what you're telling me is you're always going to be a frugal Fannie?"

"Yep, and you're going to have to live with it."

"Most men would say that frugality in no way counts as a character flaw in a potential wife."

She raised a brow. "A *potential* wife?"

"I mean *future* wife. Nothing potential about it."

"That's much better."

David reached up to frame her sweet face with his hands. "I'm extra thankful for you tonight. I wish everyone we love could be as happy as we are."

"I wish that, too, but we worked long and hard to get where we are now. It wasn't always easy."

"Yes, it was."

"Are you remembering the same things I am?"

"I remember every minute of it, and it has always been easy to be with you. It was other things, outside stuff, that made it complicated."

"True."

David dropped one of his hands to her leg, teasing the hem of her sundress, raising it up until his hand cupped one of her ass cheeks.

"Stop," she said, wriggling. "We can't misbehave when our friend is heartbroken in the next room."

"Yes, we can. We just have to be really, really quiet."

"David..."

"Yes, Daisy?"

"We *can't*."

"We absolutely can." In one smooth move, he had the dress over her head and her on the bed under him. Then he reached over to shut off the bedside light. "Shhh." He brought his lips down on hers and knew he had her when her arms curled around his neck.

"We could go one night without, you know," Daisy whispered, her lips pressed against his. He could feel the curve of her smile.

"No, we can't."

"Yes, we can!"

"You're being quiet, remember?"

She poked his ribs, making him gasp and then laugh.

Looking to regain the upper hand, he sat back to remove her panties and bra and get rid of the pajama pants he'd worn to bed. Then he came down on top of her, taking a moment to gaze at her lovely face, visible to him in the nightlight coming from the bathroom.

She looked up at him with big eyes gone soft with love and desire.

"Even after all this time," he whispered, "you still take my breath away."

"Same here," she said in the same whisper. "I love you so much. More every day."

He made slow, sweet love to her, taking his time and reveling in her soft gasps and the quiet moans that he muffled by kissing her. Afterward, he held her in his arms, caressing her back and marveling at her soft skin. "That was so much hotter because we had to be quiet."

"I can't believe you talked me into that when we have a guest."

"I didn't exactly have to twist your arm."

"I'm far too easy where you're concerned."

"No, sweetheart, you're absolutely perfect where I'm concerned."

She kissed his chest and snuggled in closer to him. "She's going to be all right, isn't she?"

"In time." It had taken him a very long time to get over the explosive end to his engagement and to put his guilt over the pain he'd caused Janey in the past. And Daisy had suffered terribly in the violent aftermath of her relationship with Truck Henry. "We know how that works, right?"

"Mmm. All too well."

"We'll take good care of her and get her through it. Try not to worry." He said what Daisy needed to hear, but he too was worried about Victoria. He'd never seen her anything other than upbeat and happy. Her tears had really gotten to him, and he could only hope she'd bounce back from the heartbreak. She'd been such a good friend to him and Daisy that he'd do whatever he could to help her through this.

CHAPTER 8

Shannon unpacked his bag in the small room the company kept on the third floor of the Beachcomber. The room contained only a narrow bed, a dresser and a tiny bathroom, so it took him all of five minutes to empty his bag. At the bottom of the bag, he noticed the envelope he'd put there before he left Ireland, the envelope he hadn't once touched since landing on Gansett.

He withdrew it now and held it in both hands for a full minute before he could bring himself to open it. Inside were the photos of Fiona he had brought with him, for no other reason than he wanted to know he had them if he needed to see them. For an entire year, they had remained in his bag, under the bed he'd shared with Victoria.

In all that time, he'd never once felt the need to retrieve them or to look at them. Realizing how long it had been since he'd seen her face, he felt guilty and sick at heart. He carefully extracted the priceless photographs from the envelope and sucked in a sharp deep breath, as if that could somehow assuage the streak of pain that traveled through him at the sight of her achingly familiar face.

How could he have gone so long without needing to see her? That was proof he'd let this thing with Vic get way out of hand. Fiona, *his* Fiona, deserved so much better from him than a whole year without once looking at her photo. Not that he needed pictures to remember every detail. As he gazed down upon her face with the adorable sprinkling of freckles across her nose and the gorgeous green eyes that had always danced with such mischief, he was flooded with memories. For years after her death, he'd relied upon these images and many others to wipe away the ghastly memories of her violent death.

He'd been haunted by the horror he'd encountered in their cozy flat the night he returned home from work to find her dead. As he ran a finger over the golden curls that fell to below her shoulders, he was transported back in time to those awful first days. A shudder traveled through him, and he shook his head as if that could snap him out of the unwelcome trip down memory lane.

Shannon kissed one of the photos and returned them to the envelope. Then he put it back in his bag and zipped it closed, as if that could keep the memories contained in the past where they belonged.

"I need a drink," he said to the empty, lonely room. In the bathroom, he splashed water on his face and combed his hair. The face gazing back at him in the mirror reminded him far too much of the way he'd looked for a long time after Fiona died—haunted and hollowed, as if someone had cut the very heart of him out of his chest.

The one thing that had helped him then was the same thing that would help him now—Jameson Irish whiskey. He went down the two flights of stairs to the lobby and took a seat at the bar where Chelsea Rose, one of his many new friends on the island, held court most nights.

She came over to greet him with a smile, placing a cocktail napkin on the dark wood in front of him. "How're things?"

"Oh, um, good." Things were a fecking mess, but she didn't want to hear that. She was just doing her job, making conversation.

"What can I get you?"

"Jameson neat, please." He usually drank Guinness here, but tonight he needed something more.

If she was surprised by his drink choice, she didn't let on. "Coming right up." She placed the drink on the napkin. "Are you starting a tab?"

"Yeah. Thanks."

"No problem. Where's Vic tonight?" Chelsea punched information into the computer that acted as the register, so she missed the stricken look that crossed his face, but he caught it in the mirror behind the bar.

"She's...at home." He had no idea where she was, and he hated that.

"Heard she's had a busy couple of days in the baby business."

"Indeed. She's knackered." People would find out soon enough that they'd broken up, but no one would hear it from him.

"Define 'knackered.'"

"You would say wiped out."

"Ahh, I see. We're so lucky to have someone with her skills on the island."

Shannon nodded in agreement and then focused on his drink, hoping to send the message that he wasn't in a chatty mood.

Chelsea moved on to other customers and refilled his glass when he emptied it. She had something friendly to say to everyone who sat at her bar, keeping up a running banter as she served drinks and rang up sales and supported the waitresses and waiters who worked the dinner shift.

Shannon's stomach growled, letting him know he needed more than a liquid dinner or he was going to land on his arse before the night was through. On Chelsea's next pass, he ordered a bowl of New England clam chowder, which had become one of his favorite things to eat since he'd come to Gansett.

He ate the soup and was working on his third glass of Jameson when someone took the seat next to his. Glancing to the right, he saw Dr. Kevin McCarthy lean over the bar to kiss Chelsea. The two of them had been together for months now. He and Vic had hung out with them a couple of times, and Shannon had enjoyed the doctor's company as well as his wise insights on life.

"How's it going?" Kevin asked Shannon when Chelsea went to tend to customers at the other end of the bar.

"Good. You?"

"Never better." As he spoke, Kevin's gaze landed on Chelsea. They were madly in love, or so it seemed to Shannon.

"Glad to hear it."

"You here by yourself?"

"Yep." He didn't offer any explanation, and Kevin didn't ask for one. No time like the present to start getting used to flying solo again.

The two men made small talk as they sipped their drinks and took in the activity around the bar. A solo guitarist, another guy from Ireland named Niall Fitzgerald, added to the atmosphere on the deck that overlooked the ferry landing and South Harbor. Shannon took in the sight of the ferry that would make the first trip off the island tomorrow, a reminder that he wasn't allowed to go to work for the next three days. What the hell would he do with himself for that long without work or Victoria to be with or anything else to do?

He rubbed his chest, hoping the panicky feeling would subside.

"What's the matter with you tonight?" Kevin asked, shocking Shannon out of his ruminations.

"Nothing."

"You're wired and antsy and drinking like a man looking for oblivion."

"Don't shrink me, Doc." The comment came out more harshly than Shannon had intended.

"I'm not. Just commenting on what I'm seeing."

Shannon had no response to that.

"What happened to your hand?" Kevin asked, nodding toward Shannon's bruised and swollen knuckles.

"Got it caught in a door at work."

"Ouch." Kevin took a drink from the beer he'd been nursing for an hour now. "So, hey, I was talking to an old college friend of mine today. He just got back from a trip to Ireland. Said the highlight was Killarney. You ever been there?"

Relieved by the new topic that didn't focus on what was wrong with him, Shannon nodded. "It's down in County Kerry. Nice place."

"You from anywhere near there?"

He shook his head. "My family is from Wicklow on the Irish Sea side. Kerry is on the Atlantic side."

"Ahh, gotcha. I told him I had a friend named Shannon, and he said that's not a very common name for men in Ireland."

"Don't I know it," Shannon said with a grunt of laughter. "It was my mother's maiden name. She thought it would be unique. It's given me more grief than anything."

"Oh, I see. That makes sense."

"Glad it does to you."

"Visiting Ireland is on my bucket list."

"You'll like it."

"I have no doubt I'll love it. You ever get homesick?"

The question hit Shannon squarely in the chest. He hadn't been. "Not really. I like it here." Or he'd liked it here until today, when it all went to shite. *I love you, Shannon. I'm in love with you. I want a life with you. I want us to have so much more than a shared address, a shared bed and the best sex I've ever had. I want a family. I want kids and a husband and a commitment from a man who loves me and only me. I want the fairy tale.*

He couldn't stop seeing her tears or the imploring expression on her lovely face. His Vic didn't cry or beg. His Vic was a joyful, happy person, and he'd reduced her to tears.

"Where'd you go, man?" Kevin asked.

Shannon realized he'd checked out of the conversation. "Sorry, what were you saying?"

"I was just saying how much I like it here, too." As he spoke, Kevin's gaze landed on Chelsea. "Feels like home."

Shannon took a deep breath and exhaled it slowly. Gansett did feel like home, or it had while he was with Vic in their little house. Now, home was a tiny temporary room in a hotel. Goddamn, he'd made a fecking mess of things. He pointed to his glass, asking Chelsea for a refill. Was that his third or fourth? He'd lost count.

Niall took a break and came over to say hello, shaking Shannon's sore hand, which hurt like a bugger, and clapping him on the back. They'd met months ago right here at the Beachcomber, bonding over their shared heritage. Niall's dark brown hair was cut short, and he had big blue eyes that the ladies went nuts over.

"You know Kevin McCarthy?" Shannon asked.

"I do." Niall shook Kevin's hand. "Nice to see you again, Doc."

"Likewise," Kevin said. "Love your music."

"Thanks, mate." To Shannon, Niall said, "Where's Vic tonight?"

The ache in Shannon's chest intensified every time someone asked for her. He supposed he'd have to get used to that. "Taking the night off," Shannon replied as he took a deep slug of whiskey, relishing the burn of it landing in his gut.

Niall visited with them for a few minutes. "I've got something for you in the next set," he said to Shannon before he moved on to greet other friends.

"Nice guy," Kevin said.

"Yeah, he's great. He's a big deal back home. Came here to record with Evan at the studio," Shannon said of Kevin's nephew, Evan McCarthy, who owned Island Breeze Records. "Hoping to break out in the US."

"He's sure got the talent, and with Evan on his side, he'll get there."

A few minutes later, Niall returned to his post on the deck. "Sending this one out to my buddy Shannon and all my fellow Irishmen."

As Niall played the opening notes of "In the Rare Old Times," a song made famous at home by The Dubliners, the pain in Shannon's chest became so intense, he feared he might be having a heart attack. The song had been one of Fiona's favorites, and it brought back a tsunami of memories that, combined with his intake of whiskey, threatened to wreck him.

"Doc," he whispered to Kevin. "I… I need a friend. Get me out of here, will you?"

To his credit, Kevin didn't ask any questions. He signaled to Chelsea to let her know they were leaving.

"My tab…"

"I've got it. No worries."

Shannon didn't have the ability to argue. He'd square up with him later, when he could breathe again.

Kevin took him by the arm and escorted him out of the bar. Thankfully, Niall was engaged with his audience and didn't see them leave. They went out the back way and followed a crushed-shell pathway to a nearby set of stairs. "Go on up," Kevin said.

"What is this place?"

"My office."

Shannon trudged up the stairs and stepped aside to let Kevin unlock the door at the top. He ushered Shannon into the dark space and turned on a light.

"Have a seat."

Shannon landed in the first chair he encountered, dropping his head into his hands. How had it come to this? How had everything fallen apart again so suddenly, the same way it had once before?

"Drink this," Kevin said, handing him a bottle of water.

Shannon opened the bottle and took a drink, letting the cool liquid soothe his parched throat.

Kevin sat in the seat across from him and appeared to wait for him to say something.

Shannon appreciated that Kevin didn't push him, but let him know he was there if Shannon wanted to talk about it. He didn't. Not really, but the pain inside him was unbearable enough that it compelled him to speak.

"I've royally fecked it up with Vic."

"How so?"

"I kept something big from her the whole time we've been together."

"What did you keep from her?"

Shannon kept his gaze trained on the floor, visions of Fiona alive and dead spiraling through his mind like a kaleidoscope of soaring highs and the most crushing of lows.

"Nine years ago," he began haltingly, "my girlfriend, Fiona, was raped and murdered in our flat in Dublin. We'd been together since we were fifteen."

Kevin's deep sigh said it all. "Start at the beginning."

. . .

BLAINE WALKED BABY ADELINE FROM ONE END OF THE HOUSE TO THE other, patting her back and putting a gentle bounce in his step the way he'd seen Tiffany do earlier. As she'd practically been asleep on her feet, he'd sent her to bed, assuring her he could handle baby duty for a couple of hours on his own.

He'd never in his life been so intimidated by a seven-pound being who held his heart firmly in the grasp of her tiny hand. She looked up at him with big eyes that couldn't make out much of anything yet, or so Tiffany had told him. But she seemed to be studying him with wisdom well beyond her one day of life.

"I bet you're going to be a genius. One of those exceptional kids who skips grades and graduates early from college."

He laughed at his own silliness and continued to stare down at her, fascinated by every movement of her lips, every expression on her face. Hell, everything she did fascinated him. To think that he and Tiffany had created this new life together was among the most overwhelming things he'd encountered yet in his life.

Sitting on the sofa with his feet on the coffee table and the baby propped on his legs, he was thrilled by the squeeze of her hands around his index fingers.

"The first time I ever saw your mom, I knew she was going to change my life. She was the most beautiful girl I'd ever seen, until I met your sister, Ashleigh, and found out there were two beautiful girls to love. And now there're three of you. That makes me the luckiest guy who ever lived. You know that?"

Her lips made an adorable little bow, and then she blew out spit bubbles that made him laugh. "You'll go easy on your dear old dad, won't you? You should know from the beginning that I'm going to be kind of a pain about boys and all that nonsense. I know what they want, and they aren't getting it from my girls. I'll throw them in jail if they even look at you or your sister."

She did some more gurgling, perhaps in protest of his stance on boys.

"We might be getting a little ahead of ourselves talking about that now, but it's probably best if you know my position on these things from the beginning."

A soft tap on the back door had Blaine collecting the baby and rising to let in his brother-in-law, Mac McCarthy.

"Did you get my text?" Mac asked.

"Nope. Haven't been near my phone all day."

"Ashleigh forgot Boo Boo Blankie when she was here earlier, and there's a bit of a meltdown going on at my house. I told her I'd come get it."

"Oh damn, thank you. She won't sleep without Boo Boo. Let me get it for you." Blaine went up to Ashleigh's room and retrieved the beloved blanket. They'd had to buy a second one for when the original was in the wash. "Are you going to have a blankie, too?" he asked Addie, who stared up at him with those big eyes. He was convinced that she saw him clearly and knew exactly who he was. All the times he'd talked to her through Tiff's belly had paid off. She knew her daddy's voice.

Blaine took the blanket downstairs and handed it over to Mac. "Thanks for coming to get it."

"No need to thank me. We're all looking forward to actually sleeping tonight."

Knowing full well how Ashleigh was about that blanket, Blaine laughed. "At least someone will be sleeping tonight. Little Miss Addie is wide awake."

"How's she doing?" Mac asked, gazing down at her.

"She's great. We've been having a nice little talk about boys and how I'll throw them all in jail if they step out of line."

Mac laughed so hard, he startled the baby. "Sorry."

"Is it always like this?" Blaine asked his longtime friend who was now his brother-in-law, too.

"Like what?"

"So intense that you feel like your nerve endings are on fire or something." He couldn't describe the feelings that were all new to him.

"Nah. You get used to it after a while, and you settle into the new normal."

"That's good, because I don't know if I could handle this much emotion on a daily basis."

"When Maddie had Thomas, one of the ladies she worked with at the hotel gave her a pillow that said motherhood is like having your heart walking around outside your body. If you do it right, and you totally will, fatherhood is like that, too. It's not just about you anymore. It's about something so much bigger than you'll ever be."

"Yeah," Blaine said, gazing down at the tiny face that had become the center of his universe in one momentous day. "That's very true."

"You got this." Mac squeezed his shoulder. "And now I'm off to pacify your other little girl."

"You're the best uncle ever. Thanks for having Ash."

"We love having her. She keeps Thomas and Hailey thoroughly entertained."

"We'll talk to you guys in the morning."

"Try to sleep when she does," Mac said. "That'll be critical for the next couple of months."

"Will do." Blaine saw him out and locked the door behind him. "What should we do now?" he asked Addie. "Want to watch some *Sports Center*? Or maybe *Cops* is on and you can see how Daddy catches the bad guys. Not too many of them on Gansett Island, thankfully. It's more about the fools who don't know when to quit drinking around here."

"What're you telling her?" Tiffany asked as she came downstairs wearing a silk gown that showed off her incredible pregnancy curves. She'd told him they didn't get to keep the much bigger than usual breasts, so he'd enjoy them while he could.

"It's between my daughter and me. No mommies allowed. And why aren't you sleeping?"

Tiffany sat gingerly next to them on the sofa, grimacing from the pain. "Did I hear Mac down here?"

"You did. He came to get Boo Boo Blankie, which Ashleigh left here earlier."

"Oh jeez. How did we let her forget that?"

"A few other things on our minds today."

"How's she doing?" Tiffany asked, leaning in for a closer look at the baby.

"She's doing great. In fact, I think it's possible she might be intellectually advanced."

"And you can tell this how?" she asked dryly.

"She gurgles at all the right times, like she's trying to talk to me."

"I hate to tell you, but that probably means she has gas."

"Don't listen to Mommy. You don't have gas. Daddy knows best, and he says you're a genius." He couldn't stop staring at the baby. "Look at her. Have you ever seen anything more perfect than she is?"

"Only her sister at the same age. She looks just like Ashleigh did."

"I know. I've seen the pictures. I'm going to have two daughters who look just like their hot babe mother. What did I ever do to deserve such a burden?"

Tiffany laughed. "You fell in love with the wrong woman."

"No, baby," he said, stealing a kiss. "I fell in love with the best woman in the whole wide world, and she's made me so much happier than I ever knew I could be."

Tiffany rested her head on his shoulder. "You've made her just as happy."

CHAPTER 9

George Alexander Martinez II had one hell of a set of lungs on him, and he was giving them a full workout as his dad tried to settle him. But nothing Alex did would calm the little guy.

"Come on, buddy. Tell me what you need. Mommy fed you, your diaper is dry and you had a good long nap. What's the problem?"

Unfortunately, little George had no response to his father's query. For the hundredth time since George arrived, Alex lamented that babies didn't come with handbooks that told clueless dads what to do when their wives were off getting some much-needed sleep and they were left in charge of their precious bundle of joy.

"Let's go outside," Alex said. He had no clue whether that was a good idea, but nothing else he'd done had soothed the baby. He'd turned the AC way down, but it was still somewhat chilly in the house —maybe too chilly. Alex stepped out the front door into a warm summer night thick with humidity. Even over the sound of the baby's cries, Alex could hear the crickets and cicadas as well as the belches of frogs, the sounds of summer on Gansett. Overhead, the sky was full of stars, and Alex was reminded of the heat wave during which he'd met Jenny at the lighthouse.

"Did you know your mama threw tomatoes at me the first time we met? Hit me square in the back, too. She's got good aim, your mom. Don't mess with her. That's my advice."

Miraculously, the baby stopped crying. He blinked rapidly, as if trying to process his new environment.

Alex walked along the dirt laneway that led from his house to the house he'd grown up in, where his brother, Paul, now lived with his wife, Hope, and stepson, Ethan. Both their homes were located on the grounds of Martinez Lawn & Garden, the business George Martinez Senior had started more than forty years ago.

Since the baby's arrival, Alex had been missing his parents more acutely than he had since the day he married Jenny. His dad had died of cancer a decade ago, and his mother, who suffered from advanced dementia, was in a long-term-care facility on the mainland. He and Paul hoped to bring her back to the island when the new health care facility their friends Jared and Lizzie James had started opened in the fall. Alex wished he could show off his new son to his parents, that they could be part of his life. It made him unreasonably sad to know that couldn't be.

He hadn't intended to walk over to Paul's, but he ended up there anyway. Hoping he wasn't disturbing the newlyweds, Alex knocked on the front door. Yes, it was weird to knock on the door to the house he'd called home for most of his life, but the house wasn't his anymore, and he tried to respect his brother's privacy.

Paul came to the door wearing only a pair of shorts, his hair standing on end and his face in bad need of a shave. But what stood out more than anything else was the huge smile that never seemed to leave Paul's face now that Hope and Ethan were officially part of their family. "Hey, what's up?"

"Your new nephew wanted to come over for a visit."

"Come in," Paul said, holding the door for Alex.

"I hope we're not bothering you."

"Not at all. Hope is reading with Ethan, and I was watching the Red Sox."

They weren't inside two minutes when George started to cry again.

"He likes it better outside," Alex said. "Let's go out on the porch."

As the brothers settled into the rocking chairs on the porch, Alex was reminded of the night his mother had said awful things to Jenny and she'd come to find him right in this very spot, imploring him to believe that nothing his sick mother said to her could change how she felt about him. It'd taken him a couple of weeks to see the light. Thankfully, Jenny hadn't stopped loving him in that time. They'd also hired Hope to be their mother's nurse, right here in this spot, and now she was married to Paul.

"What're you thinking about over there?" Paul asked.

"All the things that have transpired on this porch."

"Some monumental things, for sure. I always picture Mom out here."

"It was her happy place."

"Remember how we used to tease her about liking it out here because she could keep an eye on her entire kingdom?"

"Yeah," Paul said with a chuckle. "It was true."

"I'm missing them both like crazy," Alex confessed.

Paul nodded in understanding. "Because of baby George's arrival. I felt the same way when Hope and I got married. We're young to have effectively lost both our parents."

"At least we have each other."

"Always. And now we have Jenny, Hope, Ethan and George, too. More to come, probably."

"You holding out on me, brother?" Alex asked.

"Nothing to report yet. Just a *lot* of effort."

Alex grunted with laughter. "Spare me the details."

"I owe you a *lifetime* of details after having to listen to the two of you for months on end."

"Touché." He and Jenny had lived with Paul while their house was being built.

"Mom and Dad would be so pleased by the baby's name. It's such a nice tribute to Dad."

"It was the only boy's name we considered. Helps that the British royal family made George a cool name again."

Paul chuckled. "True."

Ethan burst through the screen door with his mother hot on his heels.

"Don't scare the baby," Hope said.

"I'm not gonna scare him," Ethan said disdainfully. He'd recently turned nine and had been eagerly anticipating the arrival of his new cousin. "Can I hold him?"

"Sure, you can." Alex stood to give Ethan his seat and then carefully transferred George into his arms.

"Support his head because his neck isn't strong enough yet," Hope told her son as she took a couple of photos on her phone. "Tell Jenny I'll text her the pictures."

"I will."

"He's so little," Ethan said, sounding amazed.

"You wouldn't think he was so little if you could hear him cry," Alex said.

"How's Jenny feeling?" Hope asked.

"Sore and tired."

"She'll bounce back in a few days."

Alex's phone buzzed with a text. He retrieved the phone from his pocket to read the message from his wife.

Where have you gone with my son?

Over to Paul's. Be back soon.

My boobs are tingling.

Why does he get to have all the fun?

Six weeks, mister.

Alex groaned. "Does it really take *six weeks* before we can get back in the saddle?"

"You'll be lucky if that's *all* it takes," Hope said.

"She's mean, Paul. Do something about your wife."

Paul snorted with laughter. "You'll survive the famine."

"I'm not sure I will. I've got to take him home to his mom now, Ethan."

"Can I hold him again tomorrow?"

"You sure can."

"Let us know if you guys need anything," Paul said.

"Will do. Talk to you guys in the morning." With the baby on his shoulder, Alex traversed the dirt driveway that connected their two homes. He would be off for the next week, but then he had to get back to work since this was one of the busiest times of year for their landscaping business. When Jenny felt ready to go back to her routine, she planned to take the baby with her to manage the retail store. Somehow, they'd make it all work.

Arriving at the two-story house he'd built mostly himself, Alex went straight upstairs to the master bedroom, where Jenny was propped up in bed, reclining against a pile of pillows. As she held out her arms for the baby, she looked exhausted and overjoyed at the same time.

"Hey there," she said to the baby. "Did Daddy take you on a field trip?"

"Ethan got to hold him for the first time."

"That must've been sweet."

"It was. Hope said she'd text you the pictures. Ethan is thrilled to have another guy in the family."

"Hope and I are outnumbered. We need some more girls around here." She peppered the baby's face with kisses. "How's he been?"

"Fussy. Lots of crying, but funny enough, it stops when we go outside."

"He's a Martinez man. Of course he prefers to be outside. Future landscaper in the making."

"Ha," Alex said with a grunt of laughter. "I hadn't thought of that, but it's true. In the summer growing up, Paul and I would be outside until long after dark. Mom had to call us to come in."

Jenny reached for his hand. "I know you have to be missing them right now."

"Yeah, I am," he said, appreciating how well she knew him. "Having the baby has stirred up a lot of things."

"We'll take him to see your mom as soon as possible."

Even though his mom would be confused by them and the baby, he appreciated that Jenny would make the effort for his sake. "That'd be nice. Thanks. When are your folks coming?"

"This weekend. My dad can stay for a week, but my mom can stay for as long as we need an extra set of hands."

"So she'll be here for eighteen years, then?"

Jenny laughed as she bared her breast for the baby. "Nah. We've got this."

"Are you sure? He's awfully little. What if we screw him up somehow?"

"We're not going to screw him up."

"You promise?"

"I promise, and you know I never break a promise."

Alex watched in amazement as the baby latched on to her breast. "I could watch that all day and never get enough of it."

Wincing, she said, "I'm glad you are entertained."

"It hurts?"

"Kind of, but Vic said that's to be expected for the first week or two, like how your hands hurt every spring until you build up calluses again."

"Not sure how I feel about calluses on your nipples."

Jenny sputtered with laughter. "Stop! You know what I mean."

Alex curled up next to them, putting his arm around Jenny, snug against the baby. "Thank you for giving me a son."

"Thank *you* for giving *me* a son."

"I love you both so much."

"We love you, too. Throwing tomatoes at you was the best thing I ever did."

Smiling up at her, Alex forced himself to relax and enjoy the moment with his two favorite people.

AFTER BARING HIS SOUL TO KEVIN, SHANNON HADN'T EXPECTED TO sleep, but apparently, unburdening oneself was exhausting. He woke to the sound of Kevin's key in the office door, where Shannon had spent the night on the sofa.

Kevin came in holding a tray with two coffees. "Morning."

"Hey." Shannon cleared his throat and sat up, running his fingers through his hair. In the bright light of day, he experienced a pang of embarrassment over the emotional breakdown his friend had witnessed and helped him through. He'd even told Kevin the truth about how he'd hurt his hand.

Kevin handed him one of the coffees. "How're you feeling?"

"Not bad considering how much Jameson was consumed last night, among other things that transpired. Thank you for the coffee—and everything else."

"No problem at all."

"Sure it was," Shannon said with a small smile. "I kept you here until three o'clock in the morning."

"I'm glad I was able to help you."

"You did help. More than you know."

"So what's your plan for today?"

"I'm going to take a shower, get cleaned up and go find Victoria. At the very least, I owe her an explanation for the way I behaved yesterday and for why I haven't been able to fully commit to her."

"What're you hoping to accomplish? Have you decided if you want to get back together with her?"

Shannon drank from the cup of coffee and took a moment to consider his reply. "You've helped me to see that I'm completely in love with her, even if I didn't intend for that to happen when we first got together."

"Love happens when you least expect it. I can certainly attest to that." Kevin leaned forward, arms on knees. "You need to give yourself permission to be happy again, Shannon. What happened to Fiona wasn't your fault. You couldn't have done anything to prevent it. Her death was a senseless, awful tragedy."

"I know, and you're right. I have to stop blaming myself. Even if I had taken a dinner break that night, it might've been too late to stop what happened."

"That's right, or you could've ended up dead yourself."

Shannon stood and folded the blanket Kevin had given him,

leaving it on the sofa. He picked the coffee up off the table and extended his sore right hand to Kevin. "Thank you so much. I'll never have the words to adequately thank you."

Kevin carefully shook Shannon's injured hand. "I'm glad I was in the right place at the right time. I'll be hoping for good news about you and Victoria."

"Me, too. I'll call you for an appointment to start regular therapy." Kevin had made the suggestion in the wee hours of the morning, and Shannon had agreed to continue what they'd started.

"I'm here whenever you're ready."

"Thanks again." As he went down the stairs from Kevin's office and walked to the Beachcomber to shower and change, Shannon's stomach ached from more than just the whiskey he'd consumed last night. He was afraid he'd blown it so badly with Vic yesterday that she wouldn't be willing to talk to him today.

He had so much to say to her and could only hope she'd be willing to listen.

Shannon rushed through a shower and shave, and before he left the room, he retrieved the envelope containing Fiona's pictures to take with him. He set off for the clinic, hoping to catch Victoria between patients to ask if he could see her for a minute now or after work. He'd thought about texting her, but had decided this situation called for a personal appearance. Besides, he was suspended from work, so he certainly had the time to go all out to try to win her back.

He walked through the main doors at the clinic right after nine o'clock and encountered David Lawrence standing at the reception desk, speaking with Anna. David did a double take when he saw Shannon.

"David," Shannon said haltingly, "I wondered if I could have a word with Victoria."

"She's not in today."

His stomach fell at that news. "Oh. I guess I'll try her at home, then."

"She's not there either."

"Excuse me." Anna got up and went through the double doors to the treatment area.

Shannon took a deep breath and forced himself to look the other man in the eye, well aware that he was staring down one of Victoria's closest friends. "Do you know where she is?"

"I do."

Shannon understood that he was going to have to go through David to get to her. "Are you going to tell me where she is?"

"Depends on why you want to know."

"I want to make things right with her."

"She's very upset."

"I know. I... I'm sorry to have upset her. All I want is the chance to explain things to her."

"And then?"

"That'll be up to her, I suppose." He held David's steely stare without blinking. "I love her. I want the chance to tell her so."

David blew out a deep breath. "If I tell you what you want to know, you have to assure me that you won't hurt her again."

"It was never my intention to hurt her the first time. I... There are things, in my past, that I've never dealt with the way I should have. I'm taking steps to fix that now, and... I... I just want the chance to talk to her. That's all."

After a long charged moment, David said, "She's at my place. I'm going to warn her you're on your way. It'll be up to her as to whether she'll be there when you arrive."

"I understand. Thank you for being such a good friend to her."

"She is my good friend. I thought you were, too."

"I was. I *am*."

"Then don't make me sorry I helped you."

"I won't. I want to try to make her happy. If she'll let me."

"I would say that's a very big *if*."

Shannon already suspected as much, but hearing David confirm it didn't do much to reassure him. "Thanks again for your help." He turned to get the hell out of there before he lost the courage he'd built up with Kevin during the night. Kevin had helped him see that confronting his demons was the only chance he had to fix his relationship with Victoria and to live an authentic, happy life. Nothing could ever bring Fiona back, but to ruin his life too would only compound the tragedy.

The thought of losing Victoria forever made him panicky. He'd lost Fiona through no fault of his own, and somehow he'd managed to survive that loss. Just barely, but he had survived. If he lost Victoria, that would be completely his fault. He wasn't sure he'd survive that kind of loss a second time.

Straddling his bike, he fired it up and headed for David's apartment on the James estate, determined to do whatever he could to fix the damage he'd done to his relationship with Victoria.

CHAPTER 10

Victoria woke to total silence and a crick in her neck from sleeping on a strange pillow. Judging by the silence, David and Daisy were long gone to work.

Work. She needed to get to work. What the hell time was it anyway?

She looked at her phone and gasped when she saw that it was already after nine. Then she noticed the note David had left her on the table.

Take the day off. We'll cover for you. Hang here for as long as you'd like. I put a key on the counter if you want to go anywhere. Call me later. D

She sagged into the couch, thankful for the day to get herself together. Facing patients with her usual cheerful disposition would've been a huge challenge today. After a minute, she pulled herself off the sofa and went to use the bathroom and the new toothbrush Daisy had left for her.

Coffee. She needed coffee. David had told her to make herself at home, so she did just that, making a cup of coffee in the Keurig. She took it to the small deck outside to enjoy the warm sunshine.

Her phone buzzed with a text from David.

Shannon was just here. After making him work for it, I told him where you are, and he is headed over there. Up to you if you want to be there when he arrives, but he seemed different and said he wants the chance to make things right with you. Call if you need me.

Victoria's heart began to pound—and not from the sudden influx of caffeine. Shannon was on his way over. He wanted to talk. He seemed different.

Hope exploded inside her. Was it possible they weren't over and done with after all? Would he tell her what she needed to hear and commit fully to her, or was he coming to say goodbye?

The phone buzzed with another text from David. *Vic? You saw my message? Just making sure.*

Got it, she replied. *Thank you.*

Hope I did the right thing telling him where to find you.

You did.

Let me know…

I will.

Don't settle for less than you deserve.

I won't. That's what started this whole thing. Too late to turn back now.

He replied with a thumbs-up emoji.

When she took another sip from her coffee, she noticed her hands were shaking ever so slightly. Her entire body vibrated with excitement at knowing she was going to see him and fear over what he might have to tell her. She'd wanted to know more about his past, but was she prepared to fully experience the horror of it?

Probably not, but if that was the way forward toward a future she wanted with him so badly, then she would do whatever it took, even if that meant making his heartbreak her own.

Fifteen minutes later, she heard the bike in the distance and braced herself for his arrival.

Because he wasn't wearing a helmet, she could see his relief when he saw that her car was still in the driveway. He parked behind her car and shut off the bike, gazing up at her on the deck with a look of yearning on his face.

Her heart beat so hard and so fast that she worried she would hyperventilate, and he hadn't even gotten off the bike yet.

Then he was walking across the driveway to the stairs, coming up slowly, almost as if he was gauging his welcome. She noticed a manila envelope tucked under his arm.

"Hi," he said.

"Hi."

"May I?" he asked of the other chair on the small deck.

Victoria nodded.

"Thanks for seeing me." He bent to rest his elbows on his knees and ran his fingers through his hair, a sign that he was nervous about whatever he'd come to tell her. "I'm really sorry about everything that happened yesterday."

"How's your hand?" she asked.

He seemed surprised that she'd asked. Flexing it, he said, "It's killing me, but I suppose I deserve that."

She didn't disagree, so she said nothing about that. "I'm sorry that by talking to Seamus I made you mad and stirred up old crap you'd sooner forget. That wasn't my intention."

"I know, and you didn't do anything wrong. He's become your friend over the last year, and who else would you go to for insight about me if you weren't getting it from me?"

"I would've much rather have gotten it from you."

"I know." After a pause, he said, "What exactly did Seamus tell you about Fiona?"

Realizing his use of her name was a big deal—and a good sign—Victoria said, "Only that you'd been together for years when she was murdered."

Shannon nodded, and after a deep sigh, he began to talk. As always, Victoria was mesmerized by his accent as much as the words he was finally sharing with her. "We met in school when we were fifteen. Her family moved to Wicklow that summer, and she started school with us that year. I was immediately taken with her. We became the best of friends, and then, later, when we were older, much more. Looking back with hindsight, I think I was in love with her from the start."

"What did she look like?"

Shannon handed over the envelope he'd brought.

Victoria's hands trembled as she opened the envelope and carefully removed the priceless photographs of the stunningly beautiful woman he'd loved and lost. Fiona had curly strawberry-blonde hair, blue eyes, fair Irish skin and freckles across her nose and under her eyes. "She was beautiful," Victoria said.

"Aye, she was. Inside and out. You couldn't find a sweeter person anywhere. She never had a bad word to say about anyone and could find the good in even the most difficult people. She'd gotten into modeling and met some truly awful people at various jobs, but she didn't let them get to her. I admired her and tried to be more like her. I dealt with my fair share of idiots as a bartender, and she would tell me there was probably some reason they were that way, and to try to have empathy toward them rather than getting angry."

"She sounds like a saint."

"I wouldn't go that far," he said with a gruff laugh. "She swore like a sailor and could knock back the pints with the best of us. I think you would've liked her."

"I'm sure I would have." Victoria carefully returned the photos to the envelope and handed it back to him. "Thank you for sharing her with me."

"I should've done it a long time ago. Maybe if I had, we wouldn't be in the spot we are now."

"Will you tell me what happened to her?"

Before her eyes, his entire body went tense.

"If you can," she added. "I'd never ask you to talk about it if it's just too hard for you."

"It is hard," he said. "Even after all this time." He looked away from her and seemed to gather his thoughts. "We moved to Dublin when we were twenty-one so she could pursue modeling. I bartended at a local pub five nights a week, including Saturdays. It was walking distance to our flat, so I usually took a dinner break around nine and went home to eat and see Fiona for a little bit. That Saturday, my rugby team came in to celebrate a big win earlier in the day, so I never made it home until after we closed."

Victoria braced herself to hear the rest.

"When I got home, the door was open. Someone had kicked it in. I... I found her, on the floor. She'd been strangled. Later they told me she'd been raped, too."

Victoria wiped away tears and reached for his hand, needing to offer whatever comfort she could. "I'm so sorry."

"Thank you."

"Did they ever catch the person who did it?"

He shook his head. "It's still an open investigation, but the chances of catching him now are slim. We still hope they will, though. She deserves justice for what was done to her. When I think about her final moments..."

Victoria rose and went to him, sitting on his lap and putting her arms around him. "I'm so sorry if my questions to Seamus brought this all up again for you."

"You had no way to know what the answers to your questions would be, love."

"I knew there was something holding you back, and I thought if there was just some way to scale that wall you've put up around your heart that maybe we could make this work somehow."

"You have scaled the wall. You did it a long time ago."

"I... you..."

"I love you, Victoria. How could I not after everything we've had together this last year? Before I came here and found you, I was totally lost. Someone asked me last night if I was homesick for Ireland, and I hadn't been. Not until I thought I'd lost you. That's when I realized that Gansett has become home to me. *You* have become home to me."

Reeling from his words of love, she had to force herself to stay focused. "Yesterday, I told you I loved you, that I'm in love with you, and you walked away from me."

"I know, and I'm so sorry about that. After I left you yesterday, I moved into the Beachcomber and went to the bar to drown my sorrows in a bottle of Jameson. I ran into Kevin McCarthy and ended up in his office, talking until three in the morning about the many ways I've been fucked up since Fiona died, ways I haven't acknowledged until now."

"How do you mean?"

"For one thing, my plan was to never again become so involved with a woman that losing her would ruin me." He cupped her face in his big hand and ran his thumb over her cheek. "I was doing pretty well with that plan until I came here and met you."

"I want you to know that I believe you when you say you love me."

"I really do."

"But if this isn't what you want—"

He kissed her then, turning her face toward him to capture her lips in a deep, searching kiss full of love and the desire they'd felt for each other since the first night they met. "It's what I want," he whispered against her lips. "*You* are what I want, and I'm sorry I let you think otherwise for even one minute, let alone an entire night. I was completely overwhelmed to realize that in order to keep you I was going to have to tell you about Fiona. I never talk about her or what happened to her. Not ever."

"Maybe you should."

"Kevin has me convinced of it. He's got me starting regular therapy this week. I've never properly processed what happened, and he's made me see that until I do, I can't be what you need or deserve in a partner."

"You can't do that for me."

"I know, love. I'm doing it for me first, but I also hope it'll help to convince you to give me another chance. I want to make you happy. I want to continue to build a life here with you and make a family together. I want it all with you, Vic. If you'll still have me."

She wiped away tears that slid down her cheeks despite her fierce desire to keep her emotions in check. "I want all of that, and I want it with you. I want it so badly."

"But?"

"Just yesterday, you didn't want any of this, and now you do?"

"I wanted it then, too, but I was so wound up about everything from the past coming to the surface and having to confront something I've never dealt with properly. What happened yesterday wasn't about you as much as it was about that. I reacted poorly, and after a very intense evening with Kevin, things are much more clear to me."

Victoria wanted to take what he'd offered and run with it. She wanted that so badly, she fairly ached from wanting it. But the sting of his rejection was too fresh in her mind to leap without careful consideration.

"What're you thinking, love?"

"I need a little time to process all this."

"You can have all the time you need, but I want you to know one very important thing."

"What's that?"

"Any doubts I might've had were about *me*, not you. I've always known how amazing you are and how lucky I am to have met you."

"That's good to hear. It helps."

"I have a suggestion."

His lighthearted tone made her smile. "What's that?"

"I assume you're not working today?"

"You assume correctly. David gave me the day off."

"Since I'm not working either, what do you say we spend this beautiful day together? We could pick up some lunch and go to the beach. We can talk some more about any of this if you want to."

When Victoria had asked for some time, she'd wanted to spend that time alone. But his offer was too good to pass up. "Okay."

"Can you leave your car here and come with me? We'll pick it up later."

"Sure." Swept up in his effortless charm, Victoria was reminded of the night they met and the instant attraction she'd felt toward him. Nothing had changed since that memorable first impression. Even after what'd happened yesterday, he was still her favorite person to be with.

While he waited, she went inside to tidy up the sofa and to wash the mug she'd used. She left David and Daisy a note thanking them for their friendship and their sofa and let them know she'd be back later to get her car. Just in case the day with Shannon didn't go well, she took the key David had left for her and tucked it into her purse.

When she was ready, she locked the door and followed Shannon down the steps to the driveway. Shannon put a helmet on Victoria and fastened the strap. The brush of his fingers against her chin sent off a riot of sensation inside her. That was all it took to make her want him. The first few months they'd been together, she'd assumed their crazy attraction would wane over time, but it had only gotten stronger.

Smiling down at her, he kissed her and then got on the bike. "Hop on and hold on as tight as you can."

"You always say that."

"I always like the way you feel wrapped around me on my bike."

Victoria sighed because she loved him, even more so after hearing about the terrible ordeal he'd suffered through and somehow managed to survive. She had other questions and would get the answers she needed before she decided anything for certain, but she already knew she would give him a chance. How could she not after hearing what he'd been through and in light of the time they'd already spent together?

He'd come looking for her today, shared his pain with her, told her he loved her and that any hesitation he'd had about their relationship was about him and not her. He'd said and done all the right things so far.

For a day that had started off with such despair, things were definitely looking up.

CHAPTER 11

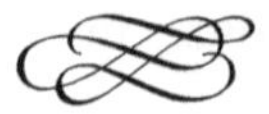

Shannon dropped Victoria at home and then went to the hotel to change and to the grocery store to pick up lunch. His spirits had risen exponentially after talking to her, and he was more hopeful now that they would find their way back to each other.

Determined to do everything he could to convince her to give him another chance, he bought her favorite salt-and-vinegar chips as well as the chocolate chip cookies from the bakery that he knew she loved. Anything to make her happy, to put the big smile back on her face and to dry the tears that had rattled him because he'd never seen her cry before yesterday.

He hated being the cause of her tears and was determined not to give her another reason to cry over him. Leaving the grocery store, he returned to the house to pick her up for the beach. She had a beach chair that she wore on her back like a backpack and a bag that he strapped to the bike for the short ride to the town beach.

The beach was busy for a weekday, so they walked along the shore a ways to a more deserted portion of sand, where Victoria spread the sheet she had brought. Then she removed the cover-up she'd worn, revealing a skimpy black bikini. Had she worn that one because she knew he loved it? He hoped so.

After they ate the lunch he'd gotten for them, Shannon stretched out on the sheet next to her.

"Will you do my back?" she asked, handing him the sunscreen. She lay facedown, her head propped on her folded arms, her gaze trained on him.

"Happy to." He took his time rubbing in the lotion on her soft skin. "You want me to do your legs, too?"

"Sure."

Shannon continued the sensual massage on the backs of her thighs and calves, noting the way she squirmed occasionally as he touched her. When he was finished, he lay down next to her. "Return the favor?"

"Of course." She gave him the same treatment he'd given her, and by the time she was done, he was hard as a rock.

Shannon ached so badly that he moaned.

Victoria giggled. "Everything all right over there?"

Delighted to hear her laughter, he said, "Are you teasing me?"

"Maybe a little."

He turned on his side, facing her, so she could see what she'd done to him, watching as her gaze traveled from his face to his chest and then his groin, focusing on the huge bulge in his board shorts.

"I did that?"

Shannon scowled playfully at her. "You know you did." He reached for her hand and linked their fingers. "I hated sleeping alone last night."

"I did, too. I've gotten very used to sleeping with you." Glancing up at his face, she said, "Could I ask you something else?"

"Anything you want." Kevin had helped him see that to make it work with Victoria, he had to open himself completely to her.

"Are there other things I should know about you? Things I don't know that I should?"

"No, you know all the big things about my life and my family."

"I didn't know you played rugby."

"Past tense. That's a young fool's game. I'm too old now to take that kind of beating on a regular basis."

"If I hadn't forced the issue, were you ever going to tell me about Fiona?"

"Probably not. Again, not because I didn't trust you with the information, but because it's just so damned hard for me to talk about it."

"I understand."

"I'm going to talk about it, though. I'm going to do the work with Kevin so I can be what you need and deserve in a partner. I want to be the guy who gives you your fairy tale, Vic, and I want to find a better way to deal with it for my own sanity, too."

"It means a lot to me that you'd put yourself through that, in part for me."

"In big part for you. The fear that I had lost you forever was a huge wakeup call for me. I hope you know that."

"Do you ever, when we're together, mistake me for her?"

He stared at her, seeming dumbfounded by the question. "*Never*. Not one time. *Ever*. When we're together, Victoria, there's no one else but you."

"Will you…"

"What, love? Anything…"

"Kiss me?"

"God, Vic, there's nothing I'd rather do." Mindless of where they were, he moved closer to her and put his arms around her, sliding his leg between hers. He gazed at her lovely face for a long moment full of the best kind of anticipation before he laid his lips gently on hers. Shannon watched her eyes close and felt the tremor that went through her when he deepened the kiss, stroking her tongue with his. After a while, he pulled back but only so he wouldn't get carried away, not because he wanted to stop kissing her. "Do you remember the first time we kissed?"

"Of course I do. We didn't stop until we'd done everything."

"Almost everything."

"More than I'd ever done with a guy I'd just met."

"We've been good together from the start." He kissed her again. "If you give me the chance to make you happy, I promise I'll give you everything I've got to give for as long as you want me around."

She released a deep breath. "I'm probably always going to want you around, if for no other reason than I'm addicted to the sound of your voice."

"Ah-ha, now the truth comes out. It's all about the bloody accent for you, isn't it?"

She dissolved into laughter. "Not *all*, but mostly."

He kissed from her lips to her neck, nibbling on her soft skin. "You've got me extremely hot and bothered here."

"You seem to be having the same effect on me."

"Let's take a swim and cool off." He got up and extended a hand to help her. "Don't look at it," he said of his obvious erection. "That only makes it worse."

Victoria laughed at the face he made at her.

In the water, they splashed and played and ended up wrapped up in each other again. As he kissed her, he cupped her breasts under the water and dragged his thumbs over her stiff nipples.

"*Shannon*," she said, sounding as desperate as he felt.

"Is tú grá mo chroí," he whispered in her ear.

"What does that mean?" He'd spoken to her in the words of his homeland before, but she'd never heard that particular phrase.

"'You are the love of my heart' in Irish, or you might call it Gaelic. We call it Irish at home."

"It's lovely. Say it again."

He said it over and over and over again, holding her close to him as he whispered words of love in the language of his home. "I want to be inside you so badly."

She clung to him with her arms around his neck and her legs wrapped around his hips. "I want that, too."

"Should we go home?" Pausing, he said, "No, wait. You said you wanted time, and I shouldn't pressure you—"

She kissed him. "Shannon?"

Dazzled by the way she looked at him, he said, "Yes, Victoria?"

"Take me home."

. . .

On the short ride, Victoria told herself she was doing the right thing taking him back and deciding to have faith in him. Their brief breakup seemed to have had a profound impact on him, and he'd come back to her with answers to her questions and the words she needed to hear, some of them said in a language and accent that set her blood to racing.

Shannon drove the bike into the driveway and cut the engine, the silence stark after the roar of the bike. He got off and then helped her, removing the helmet with fumbling fingers that she took as a sign of his eagerness. With his hand warm and firm on her lower back, he guided her inside, closing the door and locking it behind him.

When Victoria turned to him, he scooped her up and into his arms, walking toward the bedroom as he kissed her hungrily.

He put her down on the bed and removed his T-shirt as well as the cover-up she'd worn to the beach.

She had a brief moment of worry about getting sand in their bed, but then he kissed her again, and sand became the last thing on her mind.

"This bikini makes me crazy," he said gruffly as he ran his hands over her ribs and up to cup her breasts.

As she looked up at him, another question occurred to her, one that rocked her to the core and one she probably had no right to ask. But it could be the most important question of all.

Apparently, he sensed her withdrawal. "What is it? What's wrong?"

"I have another question, and I'm sort of afraid to ask this one because it's not a fair question but one I still want to ask."

"Whatever it is, you can ask me."

"I wondered if you might ever love me as much as you loved Fiona."

"Ah, Vic," he said on a sigh. "I already do, but it's a different sort of love I feel for you. It's more grown up and mature. Fi and I were so young and stupid and still figuring out life. You and me... We're past all that nonsense, for the most part."

"Are we?"

"Yeah, we are." He gazed down at her, using his fingers to brush the hair back from her face. Then he tipped his head and kissed her neck on his way to her chest. He untied the bikini top and removed it, leaving her breasts bare to his ravenous stare. "You're so damned beautiful. All I could think about last night is how I would bear to live without you, without your smile and your joyfulness. I need that so bad. I need *you*, Vic."

"You have me. I'm here, and I'm going to be here for as long as you need me."

"Forever?"

"That's an awfully long time."

"Won't be long enough." He kissed down the center of her, tugging at her bikini bottoms and helping her out of them.

"Hurry, Shannon," she said, sounding as breathless as she felt. "I want you."

His hair fell over his forehead and his cheeks were flushed the way they got when he was turned on. She loved knowing that about him, and other things, too, like how to arouse him to the point of madness.

Victoria held out her arms to him.

He removed his shorts and came down on top of her. "I wanted to take my time," he said.

She smiled up at him. "We have all day."

"Mmm, I like the sound of that. All day to love you and hold you and kiss you." He entered her in one deep thrust that had her arching into him, wanting to be as close to him as she could get. "Vic..."

Victoria held him tight against her as their bodies moved together in the perfect harmony they'd had since the beginning. "Tell me again, Shannon, in your words."

"Is tú grá mo chroí," he said. "The love of my heart."

She closed her eyes against the burn of tears. *"Is tú grá mo chroí,"* she said, tightening her hold on him. "Always."

Thanks so much for reading *Episode 1*! I hope you enjoyed it.

Turn the page to read *Episode 2, Kevin and Chelsea's story*!

enjoy Kevin +
Chelsea!
Marianne

CHAPTER 1

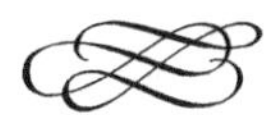

The meeting had been called by his brother Mac. As Kevin McCarthy made his way to the abandoned property at the far side of town, he had no idea what Mac was up to this time, but he'd know soon enough. Mac was known for his big ideas and even bigger personality, thus the nickname "Big Mac." They didn't call him that only because he had a son named Mac. Whatever he was up to now was sure to be interesting—and probably fun.

Kevin walked past the ferry landing, bustling with activity on a late August afternoon. Even after the peak summer season had passed, the ferry landing remained the epicenter of Gansett Island. Everything they used on the island, from gas to water to beer to cash to milk to mail, arrived via the ferries that also brought scores of tourists to the island. They came in cars, on bikes, pushing strollers, toting beach bags and coolers.

Though Kevin had visited his brother's family frequently through the years, he'd never given much thought to how island life functioned until he became a somewhat permanent resident and truly began to understand the essential role the ferries played.

He'd come to the island a year ago to attend his niece Laura's wedding to Owen Lawry. At the urging of Mac and their other brother Frank, who'd moved to the island after retiring as a Superior Court judge, Kevin had decided to stay for a while. He hadn't left the island once in the last year, and that had been just what he'd needed after the sudden demise of his thirty-one-year marriage. The three McCarthy brothers were back together for the first time since Frank left home, and no one was happier about that than Kevin.

He had a lot to be happy about these days, which was a stark improvement over the condition he'd been in a year ago, right after Deb left him for a younger man, sending him reeling.

The reek of dead fish hit him when he approached the pier where the fishing boats brought fresh catch to the island. Despite the stench, he enjoyed watching the skill with which the fishermen filleted and deboned the fish before selling them to island restaurants.

At first, he'd feared that island life would bore him. But with his sons, Riley and Finn, choosing to stay after the wedding and surrounded by his boisterous extended family, Kevin was never bored. His sons' decision to stay had surprised him, but with hindsight, he'd realized they'd initially stayed to support him after the demise of his marriage.

They continued to stay because their cousin Mac kept them so busy working for his construction company that neither of them had time to contemplate whether they'd rather be somewhere else. For now, they seemed content, and Kevin loved having them with him, so he didn't ask any questions about whether their move to the island was permanent.

As much as he loved having his sons living with him again and being close to his brothers and their families, the very best part of the last year had been his surprising relationship with Chelsea Rose. He hadn't been looking for love or sex or anything other than a cold beer when he ventured into the Beachcomber bar. But what he'd found with the sexy bartender could only be called true love.

In fact, as much as it pained him to admit it—even to himself—he was in love, truly in love, for the first time in his life. Yes, he'd loved Deb and the life they'd shared. But he'd never felt the kind of explosive passion for Deb that he did for Chelsea. Sometimes that realization made him feel a little sick—for himself and mostly for Deb, who'd deserved better than what she'd gotten from him—and vice versa. He'd tried his best. He'd been a faithful husband, a loving father to their boys and a hard-working psychiatrist who'd provided a nice life for his family.

It had taken a while for him to realize that Deb had done them both a favor by ending the marriage, leaving him free to pursue a relationship with Chelsea that made him happier than he'd ever been.

So, he had no immediate plans to leave the island that had become home to him. He'd even opened a small practice to stay busy, and most of his appointments were booked weeks in advance. People on an idyllic island like Gansett still had problems. People everywhere had problems, which kept him busy.

He liked helping people and feeling like he made a difference for others. Doing that on a smaller scale worked for him because it gave him more time to spend with Chelsea. They had fallen into a nice routine. He took appointments from two to seven most weekdays—except for Wednesday, when he spent the afternoon fishing with his brothers—and was done by eight, when he'd venture over to the Beachcomber for dinner and a beer or two with his favorite lady.

On many a night, he hung out until she closed the bar and then drove her home. They stayed up until all hours talking, laughing, making love, watching movies and enjoying each other. And in the mornings, they slept in. The guy he'd been a year ago, with the rigid nine-to-five schedule, barely recognized who he was today, but he liked this version of himself. This version fit in ways the previous version never could have, and much of that was due to Chelsea.

He walked up the sagging stairs to the old Wayfarer restaurant and hotel, which had been closed for several years. The owners had gone through a nasty divorce, and the property had been tied up in court ever since. It was a shame, since it occupied a prime spot in South Harbor due to its beachfront location and proximity to the ferry landing.

Back in the day, the Wayfarer had been the go-to destination for day-trippers right off the boat. He'd spent many a day on that beach in his younger years when he'd come to visit Mac and Linda after they were first married. The ladies and the liquor had been plentiful, and Wayfarer Beach had once been one of his favorite places.

Now the stairs weren't the only thing that sagged. The porch was nearly impassible as the ravages of salt air, wind and weather had left their mark. Shingles were missing, window panes broken, and the entire place was covered in a thick layer of seagull poop.

Kevin was almost afraid to touch the main door, even to push it open to step inside the cavernous room that had once been a shore dining hall and bar with a stage and dance floor to the right. Every surface was covered with grit. Ceiling tiles were missing, and the bar was littered with broken glass. Vandals had covered the walls in graffiti, including a sweeping mural someone had done of the beach and breakwater. Who ever said graffiti wasn't art?

Kevin followed the sound of voices coming from the other side of the building, which overlooked the beach, the one part of the property that had remained somewhat pristine despite the lack of care.

Passing through a door that had been propped open, he came upon Mac and Frank as well as Frank's kids, Shane and Laura. Mac's kids were there as well, Mallory, Mac, Grant, Adam, Evan and Janey, who was so pregnant, she looked like she could topple over if the passing breeze hit her just right. His gaze shifted to the beach, where his sons were standing together, sharing a laugh. They were both about six foot two, with wavy dark hair and the McCarthy blue eyes.

He marveled, as he always did, that he'd been part of creating two such handsome, funny, charismatic men. He loved them more than anything in the world and was so damned proud of them.

"Ah, there's Kevin!" Big Mac said, his volume set to High as always. "Everyone's here."

"What's this about, Dad?" Grant asked, checking his watch.

"It's about the Wayfarer," Big Mac said, spreading his arms to encompass the building and the beach.

"What about it?" Evan asked. He and his wife, Grace, were home for a week between dates on his tour with superstar Buddy Longstreet.

"I want to buy it," Big Mac said, drawing gasps of surprise and stunned looks from his children, brothers, niece and nephews.

"You wanna run that by us one more time?" his son Mac said.

"You heard me right the first time," Big Mac replied, grinning from ear to ear. "What you're looking at here, my friends, is what's commonly known as a gold mine."

"It looks like a dump to me," Janey said, rubbing her back as she spoke.

Kevin spotted an abandoned stool and grabbed it for Janey, testing it with his weight before he encouraged her to take a seat.

She sent him a grateful smile as she lowered herself onto the stool.

"The marina was a bigger dump than this when I bought it, and look at what that's become," Big Mac said. Turning to his oldest son, he said, "Do you think you and the boys could take this on over the winter, get her fixed up in time for next summer?"

Mac ran a hand through his hair as he took an assessing look at the building, seeing it now from the perspective of a contractor staring down a big job. He glanced at his cousin Shane, who worked with them at McCarthy Construction. "What do you think?"

"We'd need to bring in more people," Shane said bluntly, "especially if Riley and Finn are leaving at the end of the summer."

Wait, what? Kevin turned to his sons, both of whom wore noncommittal expressions. They were planning to leave? That was news to him.

"What does this have to do with the rest of us?" Frank asked.

"I was thinking it might be fun to do it together," Big Mac said.

"Define 'together,'" Adam said.

"We go in on it together as joint owners, and we'll call it McCarthy's Wayfarer," Big Mac said.

Grant and Evan exchanged glances while Frank stared at Big Mac.

"I just retired from one job," Frank said. "Not sure I'm looking for another."

"I'm not suggesting you go back to work or any of the rest of you abandon your existing careers—or your retirements," Big Mac said.

"I'm suggesting we put up the money together, hire people to run it for us, and hopefully, we'll all profit together, too."

"How much would you be looking for from each of us?" Mallory asked.

"Whatever you want to invest," Big Mac said. "It's going to take some coin to get this place back in shape, and it'll take a few years for investments to pay off, but I believe we're looking at a can't-lose operation here."

"For ten weeks a year," Laura said. "The rest of the time, it lies idle, needing constant upkeep."

She ought to know, Kevin thought, as the owner and proprietor of the Sand & Surf Hotel with her husband, Owen. "Laura makes a good point. With ten weeks a year to make or break, it could take a decade or more to recoup initial investments."

"It won't take that long," Kevin's nephew Mac said. "We went to high school with the former owners' kids. Their parents made bank here in the summer, enough to take the rest of the year off."

"How'd they let it get to this?" Janey asked, gesturing to the broken-down building.

"The parents went through a nasty divorce," Big Mac said. "They fought over it for years in court, and in the meantime, nothing was done to maintain it. They recently decided to cut their losses and sell. That's where we come in."

The usually boisterous group fell silent as they contemplated the idea.

"I have one concern," Mac said.

"What's that?" his father asked.

"I don't want any family strife. If we're all in business together, it needs to be hammered out ahead of time with no loopholes or other traps that'll lead to family crap. We don't have any now, and I think I speak for all of us when I say we don't want any in the future."

"That's where I come in," Dan Torrington said. Wearing a pink button-down shirt with madras plaid shorts and loafers, aviators covering his eyes, the hot-shot attorney grinned as he joined them. "Your dad and I have already started to put together an airtight partnership agreement that would prevent any issues down the road."

"The very last thing I'd ever want," Big Mac said to Mac before expanding his gaze to take in the rest of them, "is family strife. We'll make sure we're locked and loaded from a legal standpoint so there can never be any gray area in who owns what or who gets what or anything that could cause trouble." Pausing for a minute, he said, "I picture rentals on the beach—lounge chairs, beach chairs, umbrellas, boogey boards, as well as servers bringing drinks and food to beach-goers. We'll have tiki bars right there on the sand, and live entertainment every day all summer. Evan, I thought this would be a great place to showcase some of the talent coming here to record at your studio."

Evan glanced at the abandoned outdoor stage area. "I love that idea."

"We could do weddings on the beach, receptions in the restaurant and other events from May to October," Big Mac continued.

What he suggested went far beyond what the previous owners had offered, and Big Mac was right. It was a potential gold mine.

"No pressure," Big Mac said. "Go home. Talk to your significant others. Think about it, but think fast. It's officially going on the market next week. If we're going to do it, we need to act fast."

"I'm in," Frank said.

"Me, too," Kevin said. What the hell? Why not?

"Excellent," Big Mac said, beaming at his brothers. "It'll be just like old times when I was getting the marina off the ground, only you guys will be here to help this time around."

"It sounds like a fun challenge," Frank said.

"Everyone else can get back to me," Big Mac said. "Let me know if you want to invest, how much you'd like to invest, or if it's not a good time for you. Either way is fine with me."

"Thanks for the opportunity, Dad," Grant said. "I'll admit to being intrigued."

"Me, too," Adam said. "I need to talk to Abby about it, but I'm definitely interested."

"Same," Evan said. "Need to talk to Grace."

"And I need to figure out if we can make it happen from a construction standpoint," Mac said. "Shane and I will put our heads together to get you some numbers." To Riley and Finn, he said, "We'll also need to know if you guys are staying or going."

"We'll let you know," Riley said, his brother nodding in agreement.

Kevin wanted the answer to that question himself—and he wanted it soon. Island life wouldn't seem quite so great without his sons there with him.

CHAPTER 2

"You guys have time for lunch?" Kevin asked his sons after the meeting at the Wayfarer disbanded.

"Go ahead," Mac said to his cousins. "We're caught up for now."

"We'll check in after a while," Finn said.

"Sounds good," Mac said, taking a call on his cell.

Kevin and his sons walked to the South Harbor Diner, waving to Rebecca, the owner, as they took what had become "their" table. Kevin liked having routines and traditions with his boys. When they were little, he would take them for breakfast every Saturday morning so their mom could sleep in. Their Saturday morning breakfasts had been a tradition until Finn graduated from high school and left for college.

He'd missed that regular time with his sons after they grew up and flew the coop. It'd been great to have them back in his everyday life again over the last year, but he knew it couldn't possibly last forever. At twenty-six and twenty-eight, they should be pursuing lives of their own that they'd put on hold when his imploded. It was probably time to let them off the hook, as much as it pained him to think of them leaving.

After they ordered lunch—a BLT for him and burgers for them—Kevin decided there was no time like the present to address the elephant in the room.

"Pretty cool idea Uncle Mac has for the Wayfarer, huh?" Riley said before Kevin could bring up the elephant.

"All of Uncle Mac's ideas are cool," Finn said.

His brother had always been a favorite of his sons, from the time they were little boys and would come to visit Mac and his family on Gansett every summer. So it was no surprise to him that they were taken in by Mac's latest idea.

"What do you think, Dad?" Riley asked, sipping an iced tea that he filled with sugar, as per usual.

"It sounds like a great investment—and a lot of work."

"It'd be fun to be part of bringing that place back to life," Finn said. "Remember going there when we were kids?"

"I do," Riley said. "I love that beach. Some of the best body surfing on the island."

Kevin sat back to listen to them bounce ideas off each other for how the building renovation might unfold and where they'd start. Like their older cousin Mac, they were both civil engineers and had worked for a big construction company in Connecticut before taking leaves of absence from those jobs to spend some time on Gansett Island last year.

"Does this mean you guys are planning to stick around out here?" Kevin asked, trying to sound casual even as his heart beat a little faster while he waited to hear what they might say.

"That's my plan," Riley said. He glanced at his brother. "He's not quite sure yet."

"I heard from Missy," Finn said, his handsome face flushing with embarrassment at the mention of his longtime on-again-off-again girlfriend. "She misses me."

Riley rolled his eyes, and Kevin had to suppress the urge to groan—loudly. Finn and Missy—or *Melissa,* as she wished to be called these days—had been a disaster from the get-go, and they were the only ones who didn't seem to realize it.

"When do you have to tell work what you're doing?" Kevin asked.

"Next week," Riley said, "so it's put-up-or-shut-up time." That last part was directed at his brother.

"I know, I know," Finn said. He guzzled a cola and asked for another when the waitress delivered their food.

"You're not really going to make plans because Missy *misses* you, are you?" Riley asked.

Kevin wanted to thank his older son for posing the obvious question.

"Never said I was," Finn replied. "I merely said she misses me."

"It might be time to get off that merry-go-round," Kevin said, trying to keep it casual. "You've hardly ever dated anyone else. There're a lot of other fish in the sea."

"He's had his line out plenty in the last year," Riley said, smiling.

"Shut up, Riley," Finn said. "Dad doesn't want to hear that."

"Dad" wanted to hear everything they had to say, but Kevin knew by now what areas were firmly off-limits. If anything, he was glad to hear Finn had been mixing it up a little as the Missy relationship had gone toxic a while ago, at least as far as Kevin was concerned. That was another reason he'd been glad when Finn decided to stay on the island after Laura's wedding.

"Speaking from a purely selfish perspective," Kevin said, dipping a fry in ketchup, "I'd love to have you both make a permanent move to the island."

"Is the move permanent for you?" Riley asked.

"I think it might be."

"What about your practice at home?" Finn asked.

"I referred most of my patients to other therapists when I decided to stay, and I kept Sylvia on in the office, but she's ready to retire." He shrugged. "My practice here is growing every month, my brothers are here, you guys are here…"

"Chelsea is here," Riley said with a smirk.

"That, too."

"So it's more than a rebound fling with you guys?" Finn asked.

The question, though innocent enough, put Kevin's hackles up. "Much more."

"Hmm," Finn said. "Well, good for you."

"Something you want to say?" Kevin asked his younger son.

"Nope."

"That's not how it seems to me." Kevin wondered if he was making a mistake forcing the issue, but he wanted to hear whatever Finn had to say, or at least he thought he did.

"It's just that you went from being married for thirty-one years straight into another serious relationship," Finn said tentatively, so much so that Kevin could tell this had been on his son's mind for a while. "I wondered if maybe you might regret not playing the field a little more before you settle down again."

"I've never been a 'play the field' kinda guy."

"Because you've never done it," Riley said with a wink and a dirty grin. "Don't knock it till you try it."

"I'm happy with Chelsea," Kevin said.

"Which is great," Finn said. "She's really nice. And I don't mean anything personal against her. I'm just thinking about you going from one big relationship to another with barely a breath between them. What would you advise people in your practice who're coming out of a long marriage?"

"Not to do what I did," Kevin replied honestly, a pinprick of unease settling in his chest. "Look, I didn't plan on falling for Chelsea. It just happened, and she makes me happy."

"That's what matters," Finn said. "I didn't mean to stir the pot."

"You didn't." But he'd given Kevin something to think about. Had he been too hasty going all in with Chelsea when his divorce wasn't even final yet? Before right now, he would've said no way. Their relationship was the best thing he'd ever experienced with a woman. He was truly happy with her.

But...

Ugh, Finn was one hundred percent right about what he advised his patients who were coming off long marriages or the death of a spouse. No big decisions in the first year. No hasty new entanglements until they'd truly healed from the loss they'd suffered. Chelsea had expressed her own reservations about him not being divorced yet, and had insisted on making no further plans until he was. Even she had seen the issue more clearly than he had. Some psychiatrist he was.

The thing was, he didn't feel a sense of loss over his marriage. It pained him to admit that he actually felt nothing but relief now that he'd had some time and space from what had been a difficult situation for years. But Finn made a good point about the haste with which he'd gotten involved in a new relationship. What'd started as one night with Chelsea had turned into much more, and he'd encouraged it every step of the way.

He would have to talk this one out with his brothers. They were the ones he turned to when the therapist needed advice. Frank, in particular, would have good insight, having been widowed as a young man with two little kids to raise on his own. He'd only recently settled into his first real relationship since losing his wife, JoAnn, to cancer more than twenty years ago.

"I hope I wasn't out of line saying that," Finn said hesitantly after an unusually long silence.

"Not at all," Kevin said. "You make a good point."

"So, um, Mom has been making noise about coming out to visit," Riley said. "She says she misses us."

"I'm sure she does. When is she thinking about coming?"

"Next week."

Kevin hadn't seen her at all and had spoken to her only via text as they sold their house and their lawyers hammered out the divorce agreement that would be final in the next couple of weeks. He'd heard from the boys that the guy she'd left him for was history, which left him wondering if maybe she was looking for more than a visit with her sons by coming to Gansett.

God, he hoped not. He wasn't interested in revisiting history, and if she had regrets, well, that wasn't his problem. He would always be civil to her and respectful of her as the mother of his sons, but he had no desire for any kind of relationship with her other than a cordial one whenever their sons were involved.

Someday, they'd perhaps be parents of the groom at two weddings and would share grandchildren. For the sake of their boys, he wanted to be able to do that peacefully, without the acrimony that so often occurred after a divorce. He didn't have the stomach for that kind of drama and had gone out of his way to avoid it all his life. Now would be no different.

"Dad?" Finn said. "You okay?"

"Yeah, sure."

"Is it weird for you to think about seeing Mom again?"

"No, of course not. It'll be good to see her, and you guys need to see her more often."

"I'm still a little pissed off with her about the way things went down," Riley said. That was ten times more than either of them had said about the divorce in the year since it happened.

"You shouldn't be. I'm not."

"Really?" Finn asked, brows raised in amazement. "How is that possible?"

"Truth be told, things between us had been rocky for a long time."

"Even so," Riley said, "she should've told you she wanted a divorce. Not had an affair that humiliated you. You deserved better than that after thirty-one years."

"Maybe," Kevin conceded.

"*Definitely*," Finn said.

"Listen, you guys have every right to your opinions, and you're right that what she did wasn't the best way out of the marriage. But I'm over it, and you should move past it, too. She's still your mom, and she loves you both very much. You should never doubt that." This conversation was long overdue, and he was relieved to hear them finally expressing their thoughts on the matter. "You don't need to fight my battles for me. As far as I'm concerned, there's no battle to fight. She and I are done, but we'll always be your parents."

"Still," Riley said, "what she did was shitty, and she needs to own that."

"I'm sure she's gotten the message on how you feel over the last year," Kevin said. "I appreciate you guys being here with me for all this time. But if it's time to get back to your own lives, I'll certainly understand, as much as I'd miss having you around."

"I'm kinda digging it here," Riley said. "The work is challenging, and the cousins are always interesting."

"And entertaining," Finn added, making them laugh in agreement. "It's been fun to hang with them as adults rather than the bothersome little cousins we used to be."

"I'm leaning toward making it permanent, for now anyway," Riley said. "Mac and Shane are great to work for, and island life agrees with me. Way more than I thought it would."

"It does have a calming effect," Kevin said.

"And yet there're enough people coming here all the time that it doesn't feel like the small town that it is," Riley said. "Even the winter wasn't that bad."

"Did you hear that Jordan Stokes might be coming here to stay at her grandmother's place?" Finn asked.

"How do I know that name?" Kevin asked.

Riley rolled his eyes. "Really, Dad? She's only the biggest reality TV star in the world. Her ex-husband released a sex tape they made when they were together, and she's gone into hiding. Rumor has it, she's totally devastated and might be coming here to get out of the limelight."

"Okay, A, people, especially *famous* people, who allow themselves to be taped having sex shouldn't be surprised when something like this happens, and B, don't ever allow yourselves to be taped having sex."

"Easy, Doc," Riley said with a teasing grin. "You've already given us that lecture along with the safe-sex lecture. We're good."

"Don't forget the drugs, binge drinking, HPV and anything fun that's the slightest bit dangerous lecture series number nine hundred and twenty-six," Finn added.

"No, that was nine hundred twenty-seven," Riley said.

While the two of them cracked up and high-fived each other, Kevin sat back to enjoy the show. They were nothing if not as entertaining as their older cousins. "Have your fun, gentlemen, but you know I'm right."

"I feel kinda bad for her," Riley said. "From all accounts, she was madly in love with the husband, and he really screwed her over in more ways than one. Who knows if she even knew he was taping her?"

"That's a good point," Finn said. "How do we know if anything written or said about them is the truth?"

"Yeah, it could be manufactured drama," Riley said.

"I wonder if we'll see her around town," Finn said.

"If she's keeping a low profile, I doubt it," Kevin said.

"Tell us the truth," Finn said, zeroing in on his brother. "Have you watched the sex tape?"

"*No!* Shut up!"

Finn busted up laughing. "I think he sounds a little too *emphatic* in his denial."

Riley shoved his brother so hard, he nearly launched out of the booth.

"Children," Kevin said in his best stern-dad voice. "Behave in public."

"Doc's lecture series number eleven hundred and twenty-two," Riley said. "Behave in public even if you're hooligans at home."

Kevin shook his head at their antics. Some things never changed, no matter how old his "children" got. "On that note..." He signaled for the check and paid for lunch. The time with his sons had done him good—and it had given him a lot to think about.

CHAPTER 3

With plenty of time before his first appointment of the day, Kevin walked from the diner to Chelsea's place on the other side of town. They spent most of their time there, where they had privacy and space, two things they didn't have at the house he'd rented for himself and his sons when they decided to stay awhile last year.

Sooner or later, there would be decisions to be made about his living situation and his relationship, which was firmly in limbo until he was officially divorced. That should happen any day now. He was just waiting to get the official word from Dan Torrington, who was handling the divorce for him.

Chelsea had made it clear that she wasn't willing to talk about any kind of future together while he was still married. So they didn't talk about anything beyond what was for dinner or what movie they wanted to watch late at night when snuggled into her bed, usually after they'd had sex.

He'd had more sex with her in the last year than he'd had with his wife in the last ten years of his marriage. Chelsea made him feel young and vibrant and excited for the future in a way he hadn't been in a very long time. Perhaps he was nothing more than a fool to be so taken with a woman sixteen years his junior. But fool or not, he was taken by her. He thought about the night she'd first expressed an interest in him. They'd been at the bar of the Beachcomber, and a conversation about the demise of his marriage had turned flirtatious. She'd confessed to sleeping with his niece's husband years before Joe and Janey had gotten together.

Kevin had shrugged that off. "Sex happens."

"Does it?"

"That's been my experience."

"What do you think about it maybe happening tonight?"

For a moment, Kevin was rendered speechless. But then he recovered. "I'm fifty-two."

"Are you incapable?"

"No," he said with a laugh. "All the equipment works just fine, thank you, with no medication required. But I suspect I'm a hell of a lot older than you are."

"I'm thirty-six."

"That's sixteen years."

"A doctor who can also add." She fanned her face dramatically. "You don't find that every day."

She'd invited him to her place that night, and they'd been together ever since, settling into an easy, familiar groove that had worked for them for almost a year now. But was it a rebound fling or something more? A rebound didn't last a year, did it?

Kevin hated having those questions in his head, especially since he had no doubt that he was in love with her. Or was he in love with the sex?

"Fuck," he muttered under his breath. That wasn't it. No way. It was *her*. And suddenly, he was desperate to see her and confirm what he already knew. As enthralling as sex was with her, he was in love with *her*.

He picked up the pace, eager for some time alone with her before they both had to be at work. Rounding the last bend before her house, he found her in the garden she lovingly tended to in the front yard of the small cozy cottage she rented. She'd told him she liked being able to walk to work and anywhere else she needed to go.

As usual, her long blonde hair was contained in a braid that nearly reached her supple ass. She wore a beat-up straw hat and cutoff denim shorts that made him want to drool at the sight of her long, tanned legs. Then she bent over to pull some weeds, and he went hard at the memory of taking her from behind two nights ago.

"Hey, hon," he said, flipping the latch on the gate to the picket fence that surrounded her yard.

She turned to him, a welcoming smile lighting up her gorgeous face. "Hi there. I thought you had a meeting with your brother."

"I did," he said, closing the gate behind him. "And then I had lunch with my boys." He kissed her cheek and then her lips. "Missed you."

"You saw me three hours ago."

"Three hours is a long time." He gave her ass a squeeze because it was a great ass, and he couldn't resist.

"How was your meeting?"

"Interesting. Mac is looking to buy the Wayfarer and offered a stake to each of us."

"Each of who?"

"His brothers, children, niece and nephews. He wants to renovate it and have it opened for next season. Gonna call it McCarthy's Wayfarer."

"That's a great idea."

"All his ideas are great. Look at what he did with a ramshackle marina everyone told him not to buy."

"Are you interested? In investing in the new place?"

"Hell, yes. It's some of the best real estate on the island, and with the proximity to the ferry landing, an excellent lure for the day-trippers. My house in Connecticut is due to close in the next few weeks, so I'll have some money to invest."

"Sounds good," she said with a decided lack of enthusiasm.

"Does it?"

"Sure."

"What's wrong, Chels?"

"Nothing."

He took her hand and gave it a tug. "Come inside and talk to me."

"We can't talk right here?"

"I can't put my arms around you and hold you close while we're out here without causing a five-alarm Gansett Island scandal, as my brother Mac calls them." Tugging her hand, he convinced her to go inside with him.

In the small foyer that she'd turned into a mudroom, she took off her straw hat, hung it on a hook and kicked off the rubber clogs she wore for gardening. Then she went to the sink to wash her hands. Turning to him, holding a hand towel, she said, "What'd you want to talk about?"

So many things. "Whatever is on your mind. I mentioned making some plans, and you seemed troubled. I'd like to know why." Being with her had taught him to be more open about his thoughts than he'd ever been in any relationship prior to this one. He'd followed her lead. If she thought it, usually she said it, and he'd come to admire that quality in her.

"I've been doing a lot of thinking," she said tentatively.

Uh-oh. Please don't tell me you want out of this. Please... "About?" His heart pounded a mile a minute, and he seemed to have forgotten how to breathe.

"I just turned thirty-seven."

"I know." They'd celebrated with dinner at Stephanie's Bistro, and he'd surprised her with a diamond bracelet that she'd loved. At least she'd seemed like she'd loved it... "You don't look a day over twenty-five, if that's what you're thinking."

She offered him a small smile. "You're sweet to say so, but I'm not twenty-five anymore, and lately, I've begun to think about what's next for me."

Kevin felt like he was standing atop a trapdoor that was going to open any second and send him reeling. He couldn't seem to form any words, even to ask what was next for her and whether it included him. Then her eyes filled with tears, and he crossed the room to her, putting his arms around her. "Whatever it is that you want, Chelsea, I'll do whatever I can to make sure you get it."

She released a huff of laughter. "I doubt you'll still say that when you hear what it is, especially when I haven't wanted to talk about the future for us while you're still married."

He drew back from her, just enough so he could see her sweet face. Brushing away a tear that slid down her cheek, he said, "Tell me."

She took a deep breath, held it and released it. "I think I might want to have a baby."

For a moment, his mind went completely blank. Of all the things he'd thought she might say, that hadn't been in the top ten. Hell, it hadn't been in the top one hundred. Felled by shock, he tried to think of something to say. "I... um... a baby. Well..."

"I've totally shocked you."

"To say the least." Not once in the year they'd spent together had she ever mentioned wanting a child. He tucked a strand of her hair behind her ear and ran his fingertip over her cheek. "What brought this on?"

"Something my sister-in-law said when they called for my birthday."

"What'd she say?"

"She was only joking, but she said my eggs are getting old, and if I'm ever going to have kids, I'd better get busy."

As if that trapdoor had opened, Kevin felt like he was spinning through space, not sure where he was going to land. He had *not* seen this coming. "I... I don't know what to say."

"You don't have to say anything."

"Surely I need to say *something*."

She rested a hand on his chest, right above his fast-beating heart. "I don't expect anything from you, Kevin."

"You don't? Really? After a year together, you expect *nothing* from me?"

"I mean I don't expect you to father my child."

For some reason, her statement made him feel like he'd been gut-punched. "So what're you saying? You're going to find someone who will?"

"No! I'm not saying that at all."

"I'm afraid I don't understand what's happening here, Chels. I'm going to be fifty-three next month. My sons are twenty-six and twenty-eight. I'm hardly thinking about starting a new family at this stage in my life."

"I know."

"I feel kinda blindsided by this, hon. I had no idea this was something you wanted."

"Neither did I," she said, new tears filling her eyes, "until I was reminded that time is running out, and if I'm ever going to do it, I need to do it now."

Kevin turned away from her, running a trembling hand through his hair. "Where does this leave us?"

"I don't know. I don't want to lose you. That's the last thing I want, but I completely understand if what I want isn't what you want."

There were, after all, sixteen years between them. That'd never mattered before, but it certainly did now. "I… I need a little time to process this, honey. I hope you understand…"

"I do. Of course I do. And I'm sorry to do this to you, but we promised to always be honest with each other."

He turned back to her, took her into his arms and kissed her gently. "You know how much I appreciate your honesty, and you should have everything you want out of life. I'd never stand in the way of your happiness."

"I don't want to lose you, Kevin," she said, looking up at him with eyes full of unshed tears. "I've been trying to reconcile my desire to have a baby with our relationship and…"

"It doesn't add up, does it?"

"Not easily. No."

"Will you do something for me?"

She nodded.

"Give me some time to process this. Nothing has to be decided today or even tomorrow, right?"

"Right." Hesitating, she said, "I'm sorry to do this to you—and to us."

"You haven't done anything to me or to us. We'll figure it out. I don't want you to be upset."

"When I think about losing you, that makes me upset."

He hugged her close. "You haven't lost me. I'm right here." He'd come here wanting to talk to her about his divorce being final, their upcoming first anniversary as a couple, the investment he would be making with his brothers and their families. She'd thrown him for a loop by telling him she wanted a baby. He had no idea what to do with that information, but he was going to have to figure it out—and quickly.

"THERE'S NO FOOL LIKE AN OLD FOOL," HE SAID LATER THAT NIGHT OVER poker at Frank's house. Big Mac and his best friend, Ned Saunders, were also there.

"What the hell ya talkin' 'bout?" Ned asked in his typical blunt style as he signaled for two cards.

Kevin, who'd dealt that round, gave him the cards.

Mac chewed on a nasty-smelling cigar while Frank refilled their glasses with whiskey.

"What are you talking about, Kev?" Mac asked, eyeing his cards shrewdly.

"Chelsea wants to have a baby."

The cards fell from Mac's hand, and he barely managed to keep the cigar in his mouth.

From across the table, Frank stared at him.

Ned began to laugh, his deep guffaws echoing off the walls in Frank's small dining room.

Mac spoke first, after removing the stogie. "You, she... A baby. You're gonna be fifty-three!"

"Believe me, I know how old I am *and* how old she is."

After another long silence, Frank said, "Do you *want* another child?"

"Truthfully? No, not particularly. But I do want her. She's... Well, she's the best thing to ever happen to me other than my boys, and I love every second I get to spend with her."

"You'd be seventy-one when the kid wenta college," Ned said.

Kevin scowled at him, and Ned cracked up laughing again. "Glad you find this so funny."

"'Tis funny," Ned said. "You'd think so yerself if one a us said it."

Kevin couldn't deny that, so he didn't try.

"What're you going to do, Kev?" Mac asked.

"I have no idea, but it's all I can think about since she told me this earlier."

"She'd never mentioned wanting a baby before now?" Frank asked.

Kevin shook his head. "Not to me."

"That's kinda unfair of her to drop this on you outta the blue after a year together," Mac said.

Kevin felt the immediate need to defend Chelsea. "I think it's a recent realization on her part, that time is running out, and if she's ever going to do it, she needs to get going." He fiddled with a pile of chips on the table, the cards all but abandoned since he dropped his bomb on their game.

"What it comes down ta," Ned said, "is whether ya wanta spend the rest of yer life with her. If ya do, then yer gonna have to be okay with havin' more kids. She says she wants one, but once she has one, she's gonna want another so the first one don't grow up alone. Ya know how women are."

He did know, not just from his own life, but from his practice. Babies often came in pairs. "Fucking hell. I'll be seventy-five with kids in college."

"But you'd have her," Frank said gently.

"True." And that was no small thing to Kevin.

"Just thinka this," Ned added. "Ya could allocate yer life insurance to their college tuition."

Mac busted up laughing.

Frank, to his credit, tried to at least hide his smile.

"You're not helping," Kevin said to Ned, who was taking far too much delight in his dilemma.

"Oh, sorry," Ned said, a twinkle of mischief in his eyes. "Didn't know I was supposa be helpin'."

Kevin smiled and shook his head at his brother's friend who'd become his friend, too, over the last year. They referred to Ned as the fourth McCarthy brother. "What am I going to do, you guys?"

"To me, it comes down to the relationship with Chelsea," Frank said. "If you can't imagine your life without her anymore, then the decision becomes somewhat simple."

"T'ain't nothin' simple 'bout havin' a baby at fifty-three," Ned said.

"No," Frank said, nodding in agreement. "That part is more complicated, but it's a baby, not a bomb. Imagine the joy you'll experience bringing a new life into this world. Doesn't matter how old you are. All that matters is that you'd love that child the same way you love Riley and Finn."

Kevin contemplated what Frank had said. As always, his eldest brother was full of wisdom. "What if Betsy came to you and said she wants to have another child?"

Frank's mouth fell open and then closed.

Kevin laughed at his reaction.

"I'm a lot older than you are, and besides, Betsy can't have more kids."

"Still, what if she could, and she came to you saying she wanted one?" Kevin asked.

Frank pondered that for a minute. "I love her so much, I'd give her anything she wanted, even a baby."

"Whoa," Ned said. "At yer age?"

Frank shrugged. "Like I said, it's a baby, not a bomb."

"True," Kevin said, "but at our age, a baby would be like a bomb dropping in the middle of a life that seemed to be going in a certain direction. Until it wasn't..."

"I just think..." Mac shook his head. "Never mind."

"Don't do that," Kevin said. "Tell me what you think. I want to know or I wouldn't have told you guys."

"My concern," Mac said tentatively, "is you doing something you don't really want to so you can make someone else happy. This is a big deal, Kev, as you well know. You've already raised two kids. You know what it takes to do it right, and if you don't honestly feel that you can do it right at this age, then don't do it."

"Well stated, Mac," Frank said.

Kevin looked down at the table where the cards and chips were scattered about. "Sorry to ruin poker night."

"You didn't," Mac said. "Who else are you going to talk to about this besides us?"

"Um," Ned said, "how 'bout his boys?"

The thought of broaching this topic with Riley and Finn turned Kevin's stomach. They would not be pleased to hear their father was even considering such a thing. "They'll think I'm a fool."

"Doesn't matter what they think," Frank said. "They're grown men who don't want you meddling in their lives. They owe you the same courtesy."

"Still," Kevin said, "we all know their opinion will matter to me, even if it shouldn't."

Mac put a hand on Kevin's shoulder. "Whatever you decide, we'll support you one hundred percent. Don't ever doubt that."

Frank nodded. "What he said."

Kevin smiled at his brothers. Their support meant the world to him, but he still had no idea what to do.

CHAPTER 4

Chelsea wiped down the bar for the third time in an hour. The Beachcomber was slow tonight, which was the exact opposite of what she needed to keep her mind busy. She couldn't stop thinking about Kevin's expression when she'd told him she wanted a baby. After their awkward conversation, she sort of wished she hadn't said anything.

He was going to be fifty-three in a few weeks. What the hell would he want with another child when his were in their late twenties?

Every time someone walked into the bar, her heart skipped a beat until she realized it wasn't him. Every time, the disappointment took her breath away.

God, how in the hell had she let this happen? How had she, who'd remained stubbornly and happily single all these years, allowed herself to fall for a guy who was at a totally different place in his life than she was in hers? How had she allowed him to become so indispensable to her?

After giving her a kiss and telling her to have a good night at the bar, he'd gone off to see a few patients before poker with his brothers. He never said he'd see her later or if she'd see him at all. It wouldn't surprise her if she never saw him again. Almost every night that she worked, he came by at one point to have a beer or a bowl of chowder, sometimes both. His visits were the high point of her shift, and she'd begun to look forward to his arrival.

He probably wasn't coming tonight, and she couldn't blame him. But that didn't quell the disappointment that festered within her. She'd made a huge mistake dropping this on him the way she had. He was about to be officially divorced, free and clear for the first time in more than thirty years. His sons were through college and fully grown. What in the hell would he want with another child at this point in his life?

Her heart ached at the thought of losing him. What'd begun as a one-night stand had turned into something so much more than she'd ever had with anyone else. The sixteen years between them had never been an issue until now.

Ugh, she felt sick. Why hadn't she kept her mouth shut about the baby? Things with Kevin had been *so* good...

"Hey, Chelsea," Niall Fitzgerald said as he took a seat at the bar. He was one of the regular performers at the Beachcomber and had become a friend during the summer he'd spent on the island.

"Hi, Niall. Guinness?"

"You know I never say no to that."

"Coming right up."

Chelsea went through the motions of pouring the thick, dark beer without giving it a thought. She'd done it so many times, it was like second nature to her. She placed the glass on a Beachcomber cocktail napkin in front of Niall.

"Thank you." He took a sip of the beer. "Mmm, that's good, and well poured as always. You'd make the bartenders back home very proud."

Niall had short brown hair and big blue eyes that, along with his gorgeous Irish accent and beautiful singing voice, got him a lot of attention from the ladies who patronized the Beachcomber. "When're you gonna leave that doctor of yours for me, my love?"

And he was a flirt of the highest order. Normally, Chelsea laughed him off, but tonight his question hit like an arrow to the chest and had her blinking back tears.

"Whoa, Chelsea… I'm sorry. What did I say?"

"Nothing," she said, waving off his concern. "I'm just having a rough day."

"Everything okay with Doctor Kevin?"

"Yeah, it's all good."

He leaned in and lowered his voice. "I've been told I'm a good listener. If you need a friend, I'm right here."

Chelsea was tempted. The bar was dead and her emotions were a jumbled mess. What would it hurt to air it out with a guy who'd become a friend over the last few months? "If I tell you, it doesn't go any further, right?"

He pretended to turn a key over his lips. "I'm a vault. I promise whatever you tell me stays between us."

Chelsea hesitated, but only for a second. She needed to talk to someone. With her elbows on the bar, she leaned in close enough to Niall that they couldn't be overheard by the few patrons at the bar.

"I told Kevin today that I'd like to have a baby."

To his credit, Niall didn't express surprise or shock or horror—any of the emotions she'd seen in Kevin's reaction earlier. "What'd he say?"

"He was freaked out, not that he said that, but I could tell."

"He looks about forty, but I think he's probably older…"

She nodded. "He'll be fifty-three in September."

Niall blew out a low whistle.

"And his sons are twenty-six and twenty-eight."

"Hmm. So I'll bet he isn't exactly walking around pining for another wee one."

"Not exactly," Chelsea said, feeling dejected. "Now I'm thinking I probably shouldn't have said anything."

"Why would you think that? If you want a baby, you should have a baby."

"But I want him, too," she said softly.

Niall reached across the bar to rest his hand on top of hers. "That's a tough one. I don't deny it, but if he's not interested in having a baby, you'll have to ask yourself which you want more—the baby or him."

"I can't imagine having to choose."

"You may have to, love."

"I know," she said, blinking back tears. "That's what makes this so hard. I really do love him. I didn't expect to, but that's what happened. And now…"

Niall raised a brow. "Now what?"

"Now I don't know where we stand or if we're over or what. I hate that I've put all this uncertainty into a relationship that was going really well before today." Out of the corner of her eye, she saw Kevin come into the bar. He stopped short at the sight of her talking to Niall. Then he turned and walked out.

"Kevin!"

"Go on after him," Niall said. "I'll hold down the fort for you."

Chelsea didn't hesitate to take him up on the offer. She bolted from behind the bar and ran through the lobby toward the back door. Outside, she saw him heading for the parking lot. "Kevin! Wait!"

He stopped but didn't turn around. The hard set of his shoulders told her he was pissed off.

She took hold of his arm and turned him to face her. "Where're you going?"

"Home."

"Why?"

"I didn't like walking in there and seeing you holding hands with another guy, especially after the way we left things earlier."

"I wasn't holding hands with him! I was talking to him about *you*, and he was *comforting* me."

He laughed bitterly. "Sure he was."

"Kevin, look at me." She waited until his gaze met hers. "He's my friend. That's all he is. You…"

"What am I?" he asked, his voice gruff with emotion.

"Everything."

He sighed, his posture losing some of its rigidness. "I'm sorry. I overreacted. I know Niall is your friend. I've just been really…"

"What?"

"Spun up about what you told me earlier."

"Let's just forget I said that and go back to the way things were."

His fingers on her chin forced her to look up at him. "We can't go back, honey. You were honest about what you want, and I always want you to be honest with me. But I need a little time to wrap my head around this."

Her stomach ached with worry and regret for having rocked their boat. "How much time?"

"I don't know. I need to think about this, Chels."

She shook her head. "I never should've said anything."

"Don't say that."

"I don't want to mess this up."

"You haven't messed up anything."

Though he said what he thought she needed to hear, she could tell by the furrow of his brow and the tension she'd never seen before in his jaw that she'd messed up everything. She took a step back from him. "I have to go back to work."

"Okay."

"Will I see you later?"

"I'm gonna go home tonight and get some sleep. I'll talk to you tomorrow?"

They hadn't spent a night apart in more than six months. She nodded, determined to remain unemotional until he walked away. The second he was gone, though, tears rolled down her cheeks. He hadn't kissed her goodbye or told her he'd be back so she wouldn't have to leave the bar alone at closing.

Chelsea watched him go, feeling like she'd lost something precious.

KEVIN FELT LIKE CRAP FOR LEAVING HER LIKE THAT, WITH SO MANY unanswered questions lingering between them. But he didn't have any of the answers, and he needed some time and space to figure out how he really felt about her, them, the possibility of more children. His brain was like a whirling pit of thoughts that refused to add up to anything that made sense.

In the kitchen, Riley was making a sandwich of turkey, cheese and white bread, whereas his brother would've wanted multigrain bread and every condiment in the fridge. They teased Riley about still eating like a kindergartener.

"Hey," Kevin said, dropping his keys on the counter.

"What're you doing here?" Riley asked.

"Um, I thought I lived here?" Kevin took a beer from the fridge and used the opener that was always on the counter to open it. Deb would've put it away. He left it out because he could.

Riley laughed. "You keep your clothes here. That's about it." Riley took a big bite of his sandwich and helped himself to the beer Kevin had opened.

"Sure, have mine. I'll get another."

"Thank you."

Riley sat at the table and ate the sandwich in four big bites. "You're not hanging with Chelsea tonight?"

"No, not tonight."

Riley raised an eyebrow. "You guys have a fight?"

"Nah, nothing like that."

"Something's up."

Kevin opened another beer and took it with him to sit at the table with his son. "Chelsea wants to have a baby."

Riley choked on a mouthful of beer. He coughed so hard, his eyes watered. When he could speak again, he said, "*What the hell did you just say?*"

Kevin scowled at him. "You heard me."

"You're seriously thinking about having another kid at *your* age?"

"You say that like I'm eighty."

"Dad, come on… Is this really what *you* want, or would you be doing something huge for her that doesn't work at all for you?"

"I don't know. I told her I need to think about it."

Riley sat back in his chair, but his gaze never wavered as he took a good long look at Kevin. "I know you really like her."

"I love her, Riley. Despite what you and your brother might think, this is in no way a rebound for me."

"Okay… But a *baby*? Really?"

"Your uncle Frank said it's a baby, not a bomb."

"At your age, it would be like a bomb going off in your life. Are you prepared to go through that again?"

"Not even kinda, but I completely understand that it's an experience she wants to have."

"Fair enough, but does it have to be with you?"

"I don't know, son. I don't want to lose her, and I want her to be happy. I'm trying to figure out where we go from here."

Riley started to say something but appeared to think better of it.

"Whatever it is, just say it," Kevin said. "I value your opinion."

"It's just that sometimes I wish you and Mom were still together and nothing had changed. That makes me sound like a big baby, but that's how I feel."

"I understand. Change is difficult, especially when it's your parents who you always pictured a certain way. But there's no going back. We can only go forward."

"I know that, and I want you both to be happy. I really do."

"That means a lot."

"Are you leaning in one direction or the other on the baby?"

"Not really. I'm still stuck firmly in the shock zone. She's never given the slightest inkling that this is something she wants until today."

"What brought it on all of a sudden?"

"Her thirty-seventh birthday and a teasing comment from her sister-in-law about now or never."

"So maybe this is just a moment of panic on her part, and in a week or two, she might rethink it."

"I suppose that's possible."

"Nothing has to be decided immediately, Dad. Take a breath and see what happens."

"That's good advice. Thank you."

Riley smiled, and Kevin was again struck by what a handsome man his son had grown up to be. His hair was a little longer than it had ever been, he hadn't shaved in days, and he had tattoos on both arms. He bore no resemblance whatsoever to the little boy he'd once been, but Kevin loved him as fiercely as he ever had. "Least I can do for the shrink who's been giving me good advice all my life."

The boys often joked about being the sons of a psychiatrist who had all the answers. Their cross to bear, they would say.

"I gotta get to bed," Riley said, standing. "We're starting early tomorrow on a new house."

"Where's your brother gone off to?"

"Who knows? He's gotta work early, too, so I'm sure he'll be home soon." Riley tossed his beer bottle in the recycling. "Night."

"Night, bud."

Kevin went to bed and was still awake when Finn came home at one. He watched one become two and two become two thirty. He rarely had trouble sleeping, but he also rarely had so many thoughts keeping his mind awake when he should be sleeping. Reaching for his phone on the bedside table, he texted Chelsea.

Are you awake?

She wrote right back. *Yeah.*

Can I come over?

I wish you would.

Her response filled him with elation. *Be there in ten.*

Kevin put on a T-shirt and basketball shorts, grabbed his wallet, phone and keys and crept from the house as quietly as he could, feeling like a teenager sneaking out of his parents' home. He decided to walk the short distance to her house, through the silent, sleeping downtown where the foghorn was the only sound he heard. From a few blocks away, he saw her front light go on. He picked up the pace, eager to get to her, to talk to her, to *be* with her.

As he went up the front stairs, the inside door opened. She wore a white nightgown that fell to mid-thigh, and her long blonde hair was loose around her shoulders.

Gorgeous, he thought. *Stunningly beautiful and all mine. Mine, mine, mine.* The thought of her with any other guy drove him crazy. He was so happy to see her that she could ask him for anything, even a baby, and he'd happily give it to her.

He stepped inside, wrapped his arms around her and breathed in the alluring scent of her skin.

This was love. It wasn't a rebound or a midlife crisis or anything other than love, as pure and as simple as anything he'd ever felt. Lifting her into his embrace, he kicked the door closed and carried her into the bedroom where they'd spent so many nights together. She'd lit one of the candles she kept on the bedside table, filling the room with the scent of lavender.

Chelsea had introduced him to candles in the bedroom, and he'd become a fan of the romantic glow the flame cast over the cozy room.

With her arms looped around his neck, she kissed his face and lips. "I'm sorry to have dropped something so huge on you like that. It wasn't fair."

"I'm sorry I freaked out."

"I don't blame you for freaking out. Anyone would."

He dropped his keys on the floor and laid her on the bed, coming down on top of her. "How is it possible that you've made it so I can't sleep unless you're with me?"

She raised her hands to his face. "I seem to have the same problem. I missed you tonight."

"I missed you, too."

"Have I ruined everything for us?" she asked in a small voice that was so unlike her that it made his heart ache.

"No, honey. Not at all."

"If it's a choice between you and a baby, I pick you, Kevin. I never expected this to be so..."

He gazed down at her, heartened by her words and the emotion behind them. "Important?"

"Yes. It's become the most important thing in my life."

"Mine, too," he said, kissing her. "Right up there with my sons."

"I didn't like how it felt to think I'd driven you away."

"You didn't." Drowning in the sweet scent of her skin, he kissed her neck and jaw, rolled her earlobe between his teeth and buried his face in her silky hair. "We're going to figure this out."

"Are we?"

He nodded. "We don't need to decide anything right this minute. We're going to take our time, talk it out, look at it from all angles, and figure out a next step that works for both of us."

Her hands moved under his T-shirt, pushing it up as she explored his back.

Her touch electrified him like always. No other woman had ever made him feel the way she did, simply by touching him. He drew back from her to pull off the shirt and help her out of the nightgown. Seeing that she wore nothing under it ramped up the urgency beating through him. He took in her full breasts, the flat abdomen that she kept toned through daily yoga, the neatly trimmed hair that covered the juncture of long, tanned legs.

Over the past year, he'd had reason to wonder—on more than one occasion—what he'd ever done to get so lucky to have a goddess like her care for him the way she did. He cupped her breast and bent to draw her tight nipple into his mouth.

Her hips lifted off the bed, pressing her core tight against his cock as she grasped a handful of his hair to keep him focused on her breasts.

He'd often thought that if he died right there, with his face buried in the soft wonder of her spectacular breasts, he'd go a happy man. Kissing his way from her breasts to her belly and below, Kevin set out to worship her, to show her how much he cared and how badly he wanted her. He rested her legs on his shoulders and opened her to his tongue and fingers, setting out to bring her as much pleasure as she could stand.

"Let me hear you, sweetheart," he whispered against her thigh, which quivered under his lips.

Her obvious desire for him was the greatest turn-on he'd ever experienced. If he was close to her, she wanted to touch him, hold his hand, run her fingers through his hair. He hadn't realized how starved he'd been for that kind of affection until she showed him. And he loved how responsive she was to him, how he could make her come so easily. Often, he liked to drag out the pleasure, to take her up and leave her hanging before backing off and starting over. He liked when she begged to come.

Tonight, he only wanted to make her feel good, so he didn't tease or torment her. He knew exactly what it took to send her flying, and gave it to her, loving the sound of her gasps and cries when she came hard around his fingers, her clit throbbing under his tongue.

She was still coming when he pushed his cock into her. The tight fit of her flesh gripping his never failed to take him to the edge of madness. Grasping her hips to hold her still, he drove into her. He'd never felt anything quite like the wild emotions that overtook him when he made love to her. She made him feel like he could climb mountains and conquer armies single-handedly. It was foolish, he knew, to have such silly thoughts, but the feelings couldn't be contained.

"Chels..." He dropped his head to her shoulder. "Love you. I love you so much."

She grasped his ass, pulling him deeper into her in a move that nearly finished him off. "I love you, too. I don't want to lose you."

"You won't." He punctuated his assurances with a deep, soulful kiss. Her tongue rubbing up against his drove him crazier than he already was. A thought occurred to him, making him falter.

"What?" she asked, tuned in to him.

He looked down at her. "You... You're still on the pill, right?"

Her face went blank with shock in the instant before her eyes flashed with anger. She pushed at his shoulder, struggling to get free of him. "Get off of me."

CHAPTER 5

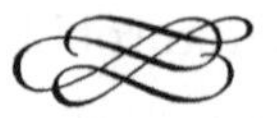

“helsea—”

“Get. *Off.*”

He withdrew from her, his cock throbbing with unfilled desire. Flopping onto his back, he tried to collect thoughts that were once again spinning through his mind like a cyclone.

She got up, put her nightgown back on and went into the adjoining bathroom, slamming the door behind her.

Fuck…

He sat up, ran his fingers through his hair and wished he could take back the last five minutes. Going to the bathroom door, he knocked. “Chelsea, honey, I’m sorry. I know better than to ask you that. It was heat of the moment. Forgive me? Please?” Receiving no reply, he knocked again. “Chelsea…”

The door opened, and she pushed past him. “You should go.”

“Baby, I said I was sorry.”

Sitting against the pillows, she wrapped her arms around her legs. “I can’t believe you would think for one second, heat of the moment or not, that I would *trap* you into giving me a baby.”

“I never thought you would do that.”

"Then why would you ask me if I'm still on the pill while we're making love?"

"Because I'm an idiot, and I wasn't thinking." He sat on the bed, putting a hand on either side of her hips. "I'm sorry."

Her chin quivered and her eyes filled. "You really think I'm capable of something like that?"

"No, I don't. I'm sorry." He rested his hand on her leg, waiting for her to kick him away, but she didn't.

Tears spilled down her cheeks, and he hated himself for making her cry.

"Come here, sweetheart." He held out his arms to her and was thankful when she allowed him to hold her. "I'm so, so sorry. I wasn't thinking."

"I would never do that you, Kevin. I swear to God."

"I know. I believe you." He'd come over here wanting to fix things between them, and instead, he'd made everything worse. Running his hand over her hair, he held her for a long time, while wondering if the damage they'd done to their relationship during the last twenty-four hours could ever be fixed.

CHELSEA COULDN'T SLEEP. SHE SHOULD'VE KICKED KEVIN OUT OF HER bed and her home after he'd had the audacity to ask her such a thing while they were making love! As if she'd ever have to trap a man or trick him into fathering her child! So insulting...

And yet, she couldn't exactly blame him for asking.

God, what a mess she'd made of things. Blurting out she wanted a baby to her boyfriend or lover or whatever he was hadn't been the brightest thing she'd ever done.

Of course, he freaked out. His sons were grown. The baby stage of his life was long behind him. What in the world would he want with another child at this point in his life? He wouldn't want that.

Her heart sank at the thought of losing him and the relationship that had come to be so important to her. She never would've expected that first night to turn into something so significant, but it had, and now she was deeply in love—for the first time in her life, if she were being honest—with a man who had already been there, done that with kids and had entered a new phase of freedom that he wouldn't want to give up, even for her.

She couldn't tell if he was asleep next to her. Usually she slept curled up to him, his arms around her, and she loved that and missed the warm comfort of his embrace.

"Are you asleep?" he whispered.

"No."

He turned to face her, putting his arm around her. "I'm so sorry I asked you that, Chels. I know you'd never try to trick me or trap me or anything like that."

"I wouldn't."

"I know that, and I shouldn't have asked."

"I don't blame you for asking after I dropped the baby thing on you out of nowhere."

"Still… It was shitty of me to ask you that, especially when I was inside you."

She placed her hand on top of his.

He turned his hand up and linked their fingers.

"It was shitty of me to drop something so huge on you out of the blue."

"You should be able to say anything you want to me. I want to know what you're thinking and what you want. How can I help you get it if I don't know?" After a long pause, he said, "I have to be honest with you… I was surprised to hear you want a baby because you've never said anything about that before."

"I know."

He waited, giving her space to collect her thoughts. "I told you about how my dad left us when I was in high school and ended up marrying my friend's mother, right?"

"Yes, you did."

"That really messed me up."

"Of course it did."

"I've been very determined, for my entire adult life, to stay single and unencumbered. I never wanted to be in a position to do to someone what my father did to my mother and our family." It was the most she had ever said to anyone about how her father's betrayal had affected her. "But then I met you, and my attempts to stay emotionally unattached failed miserably."

He laughed as he put his arms around her and drew her in close to him. "We said we'd reassess when my divorce is final, which it should be any day now."

"All this time, I've been sort of half waiting to hear that you're getting back together with her."

"I am *not* getting back together with her. Not now and not ever."

"Because of me?"

"In part, but also because of me. I didn't realize how truly unhappy I was with her until she left me and forced me to confront the truth. We were over long before we split, and I'm happier now than I've been in years—and that is definitely in large part because of you."

"Before I mentioned wanting a baby, what did you see happening for us after your divorce was final?"

"I was hoping you'd let me move in with you or, if you wanted, we could get a new place together."

"And what if..."

"What, sweetheart?" He ran his fingertip over her face and down to outline her mouth.

"What if you woke up a year from now and realized you never got a chance to be truly single before you took up with me? What if you had regrets about getting serious with someone else so soon after your marriage ended?"

"I'm not going to bullshit you and tell you that can't happen, because I've seen it happen in my practice."

Hearing that didn't do much to calm her fears.

"But what I can tell you for certain is you make me happy. Being with you makes me happy, the kind of happy I've never been before. Can I promise that what we have is going to last the rest of our lives? No, I can't. No one can make that kind of promise. All I can do is tell you I love you and assure you that when I tell you that, I *mean* it."

Chelsea gazed into his eyes, the waning light from the candle allowing her to see his face. "I know you do. I love you, too. I've never been in love like this before."

With his free hand, he cupped her cheek. "That's a damn good place to start."

She nodded. "Will you do something for me?"

"Anything."

"Will you tell me the truth if you really don't want to have a baby with me?"

"I'll tell you the truth as soon as I figure out what the truth is. I really do need some time to think about it."

"I understand. It's a big deal."

"Yes, it is. It's a lifetime commitment that we should both be sure we want before we dive into it. I'm not saying no, Chels. I'm saying we need to really talk about it and think it through and be completely certain we'd be bringing a child into this world for the right reasons. And I have to put this out there, but I don't want you to take it the wrong way..."

"Okay..."

"Realizing you're running out of time is not the right reason to have a child."

"I know. I've been thinking about that, too."

"When was the last time you spent time with a baby?"

"It's been a while. When my niece and nephew were small."

"What would you say if we offered to babysit for Laura and Owen some night soon? With three kids under the age of three, that'd give us both a good refresher course."

"I'd be up for that."

"I'll see how they feel about a night out on Sunday." That was one of her two nights off from the bar.

"Okay."

Kevin kissed her while continuing to caress her face. "We don't have to figure this out overnight, and we don't need to let it come between us."

"I don't want that any more than you do."

"Then let's take our time and make the best decision we can for both of us."

"Sometimes sleeping with a shrink has its advantages."

He smiled, and the turmoil that'd been swirling inside her settled.

"One thing I can promise you, sweetheart, is that I'll never, ever do to you what your father did to your mother or what Deb did to me. That's not something you need to worry about with me, okay?"

Chelsea nodded. "You don't have to worry about it, either."

"That's good to know."

"Were you really jealous when you saw me talking to Niall?"

"I was on fire with jealousy. I don't want other men touching you, even men you're friends with."

"That's fair enough, but he was just being nice to me."

"I didn't like it."

"You're very sexy when you're possessive."

"You're very sexy all the time."

"You got yourself in trouble before you could finish what you started," she said, rising to kiss his chest.

"So I did." He ran his fingers through her hair as she used her tongue to outline the lines and grooves of his abdominal muscles.

The time he spent in the gym was put to good use. If she didn't know how old he was, she would've guessed a decade younger. He had the stamina of a much younger man, and she'd had better sex with him than with men twenty years his junior. There was something to be said for maturity and experience.

After a year together, she knew just how to touch him and drive him crazy. Wrapping her hand around his hard cock, she stroked him as she continued to kiss his abdomen. His muscles tensed as he waited to see what she would do next. She didn't disappoint him, sucking the head of his cock into her mouth and adding her tongue to the mix.

He gasped and tightened his hold on her hair.

She took him as deep as she could while continuing to stroke him with her hand. The combination usually took him right to the edge of release. Knowing that, she backed off, slowed down and earned a deep groan from him that made her smile.

Chelsea released him and moved to straddle his hips, taking him into her slowly while his fingertips dug into her hips. Then she began to move, riding him until they were both gasping as they climaxed together.

After, she dropped down to his chest, and he wrapped his arms around her. "Feel better?" she asked.

"Much better. You?"

She nodded. They hadn't decided anything, but wrapped up in his arms, she could finally relax enough to get some sleep.

THE NEXT DAY DAWNED RAINY, GRAY AND COOL, THE PERFECT MATCH for Riley McCarthy's lousy mood. He'd been determined to throw himself into work so he wouldn't have time to think about what his father had told him last night, but that plan was failing miserably. All he could think about was his father having a baby with Chelsea. Riley couldn't get his head around the possibility of another sibling at this point in his life, nor could he imagine his dad with a newborn. Hell, he could be a grandfather before long, and he was thinking about starting another family?

It was ridiculous, but then again, much of what'd happened in the last year had been ridiculous, starting with his mother taking up with her personal trainer. What a cliché! The news of her affair had devastated his dad—and him and Finn. Being a grown adult didn't make you immune to despair when your parents suddenly and dramatically split.

If anything, he'd taken it harder than anyone knew, even the brother he was closest to. What did it say about him that his parents' divorce—and subsequent relationships with other people—had fucked him up? He should be past the point where anything they did could screw him up the way their divorce had.

With hindsight, he could see that the handwriting had been on the wall for them for quite a while by the time it finally happened, but it was *how* it'd happened that had stayed with him for all the months that'd followed. His mom had cheated on his father. That sentence still rankled more than a year later. How could she do that to him? His dad was the best man Riley had ever met, always willing to help someone in need, always there for the big and small moments in his sons' lives, a faithful husband and a hard worker.

What more could any woman ask of the man she married than what his mother had gotten from his father? He'd been so fucking angry with her after it first happened and had carried that anger with him for a year now. He hadn't seen her since he'd heard about what she'd done and had no desire to see her now, either.

But Finn wanted to see her, so he'd probably have to as well. But he didn't want to. The entire situation made him sad, and he was sick of being sad about something he had no control over.

"Hey, Riley," Mac shouted. "Go easy, will you? I can't build a house with splinters."

Riley snapped out of his musings to realize he'd been stacking lumber right off the ferry with no regard for how it was landing. "Sorry."

"Everything all right?" Shane asked when he came over to help.

"Yeah."

"You sure?"

"Yes." He liked Shane and appreciated his concern, but the last freaking thing he wanted was to talk about his parents' divorce and the many ways it continued to impact him. No one wanted to hear about that anyway. People had their own problems, and Riley was sick of thinking about it. He needed to go out tonight, get drunk and get laid.

That would make everything better.

"What the hell crawled up your ass and died today?" Finn asked when he joined him to finish unloading the pickup truck at the site of their next build. His brother hadn't shaved in weeks, and his eyes were rimmed with red from being out late on a work night.

"Nothing."

"Don't say it's nothing when anyone can see it's *something*."

Riley grasped another bundle of two-by-fours and hauled it from the truck, adding it to the pile next to the foundation that'd been poured last week. This time, he was careful to place the bundle rather than dropping it.

When he returned to the truck for another trip, Finn stopped him with a hand to his chest. "Tell me."

"You're going to be pissed."

"Tell me anyway."

"Dad and Chelsea are talking about having a baby."

Finn's hand fell from his chest, and his face took on an odd expression. "For real?"

"Would I have said anything if it wasn't for real?"

"This is just… It's…" Finn shook his head. "Whatever. We should've seen this coming. She's still young, and it's only natural she'd want kids."

"But with our old man?"

"Why not with him? They've been together a year, and he seems really happy."

"So you wouldn't care if he had another kid with her?"

"Why would I? He's not asking me to raise it."

Riley stared at his brother as if he had two heads. Could he really be so nonchalant about something so important?

"Riley!"

He turned toward Mac, who was on the phone and pacing. He waved Riley over.

"What's up?" he asked Mac, who held up a finger.

"Yes, I'm going to send my cousin Riley over to help you." Rolling his eyes, he said, "Yes, Riley knows what he's doing, Mrs. Hopper, or I wouldn't send him.

Mrs. Hopper was Jordan Stokes's grandmother. Suddenly, this day was looking up.

"He'll be there in ten minutes," Mac said, his voice dripping with exasperation. "Yes, ma'am. I know how important Eastward Look is to you and how much you love your granddaughters. We're on it."

It took another minute for him to extricate himself from the conversation and end the call. "For the love of God, that woman can talk!"

"What's up at the house?"

"The roof has sprung a leak, and the granddaughters don't know what to do. Can you go over there and see if you can shore it up until we can get there to make a more permanent fix?"

"Yeah, I'll take care of it."

"Thanks. Give me a call to let me know what we've got."

"Will do."

Riley jogged over to the company truck that was now empty. "Guess where I get to go?" he asked his brother.

"Where?"

"Jordan Stokes's grandmother's house."

"How come you get to do that?"

"Because I'm the one Mac asked." Riley flashed his brother a smug grin. "Try not to be too jealous."

"Finn!" Mac, who was on another call, pointed to the wood that needed to be sorted and distributed for the framing that was set to begin tomorrow.

"Not fair," Finn muttered as he stalked off to tend to the wood.

Riley laughed as he got into the truck and headed for the island's eastern shore.

CHAPTER 6

The ride gave Riley the opportunity to clear his head a little and to think about what Finn had said. It pained him to admit that his younger brother made a good point. It wouldn't be up to them to raise their father's new child, so really, why did it matter so much?

Probably because he was used to being part of a family of four that no longer existed, and now the makeup of his family might change yet again. Riley wasn't a big fan of change, as a rule. He liked things orderly, predictable, sensible, and hated drama of any kind. Finn was more of a roll-by-the-seat-of-his-pants kind of guy, who liked to shake things up and live on the edge.

That would never be Riley. Often, he wished he could be more like Finn, so he wouldn't get so stressed out about things he had no control over. His brother was always telling him to chill out and not worry so much, but Riley was a worrier. That was just how he was wired, and right now, he was worried about his dad.

On the way to the Hopper place, he drove past his uncle Mac and aunt Linda's home, the place the locals called the White House, as well as the entrance to their marina and hotel. As a kid, he'd spent a lot of time in all three of those places and had fond memories of those summer visits to Gansett.

Riley wondered what his uncle Mac thought of the possibility of Kevin having a baby with Chelsea. No doubt Big Mac had an opinion. He always did.

Another mile passed, the scenery spectacular as always. Stone walls, meadows full of colorful wildflowers, hidden ponds and pathways that led to the bluffs. The slower-paced island lifestyle had been good for him. He'd had the time to try to come to terms with his parents' divorce, to ponder whether he wanted to return to the hard-charging job he'd left in Connecticut and to give some thought to his long-term life plan.

He didn't have any answers to the last one, not yet anyway, but he was fairly certain he wanted to stay on the island and continue working for Mac. They were busy year-round, and they'd be doubly busy if Big Mac's plan to acquire the Wayfarer happened. Riley loved the idea of being part of bringing a place he had loved as a kid back to life.

Rain continued to fall, harder than earlier, and the windshield wipers beat a steady rhythm.

The one thing that concerned him about staying on the island was whether he had a chance of meeting someone he might potentially marry someday. Women flocked to the island in the summer, for the beaches, the bars and the boys, but most of them were transient. His cousins had found love on Gansett, but that didn't mean he would. Was he limiting his options by staying indefinitely? Probably, but he wanted to be here for now anyway. He'd probably give it another year and reassess.

Perhaps the reason he'd had such a strong reaction to his father's news last night was that he'd imagined himself as a young father. Was he jealous of his father? Nah, that'd be stupid. But still... He couldn't deny his dad's news had stirred up something in him—something that made him feel unsettled.

As the driveway to Eastward Look appeared on his right, Riley shook off the unsettled feelings to focus on the job that needed to be done. He pulled into the long gravel driveway that led to a large contemporary home perched on the coast.

The front door opened, and a young woman hovered in the doorway, as if she wasn't sure whether she should come out or stay in.

Riley zipped up the lightweight rain jacket he'd worn to work and got out of the truck, taking the stairs two at a time and landing on the porch in front of the door. "Hey, I'm Riley McCarthy for Mrs. Hopper."

"She's not here," the woman said, tucking a hank of dark hair behind her ear. Her huge brown eyes dominated a striking face.

"You... You're Jordan Stokes?" He felt like an idiot for stating the obvious.

She shook her head. "I'm her sister, Nikki."

"You look just like her."

"We're twins."

He'd never heard that Jordan had a twin. "That's cool. So, you want me to come in and check the leak?" Was she staring at him, or was that his imagination?

She blinked and seemed to recover her bearing. "Oh, um, sure."

"Lead the way." Riley followed her through the house, taking note of the big open rooms, the coastal decorating and the welcoming atmosphere that wasn't at all the stuffy, pretentious house he'd been expecting. No, this was a place where people could relax and put their feet up on the sofa. He liked it.

Checking out the house gave him something to do besides notice the way Nikki's shorts fit her excellent ass or how toned and sleek her legs were. He was here to do a job, not ogle Mrs. Hopper's granddaughter.

They went up to the attic via a staircase from the second floor. He could see whitecaps on the ocean through the dormer windows that looked out on the backyard, where there was an in-ground pool. "How did you discover the leak?"

"A wet spot appeared on the ceiling in my bedroom downstairs."

Riley made a mental note to make sure that got repaired, too.

"Is it going to be a big deal to fix it?" she asked.

"I'm not sure yet. Do you know when the roof was replaced last?"

Her brows furrowed with worry. "I don't, but I can ask my grandmother. She'd know."

"It would help to have that info. You might've lost a few shingles in the wind last night, which is an easy fix. But if the roof is old, it's going to keep happening."

She crossed her arms in a protective stance that tugged at him. He knew what it was like to fret over every little thing. It was exhausting.

"Try not to worry. I can shore you up for now until we can get up on the roof and see what we're dealing with."

"Can you do that today?"

"Probably not. We'll need ladders and other equipment I didn't bring with me. I need to get some stuff from my truck, and I'll get this contained for now. Tomorrow, we'll come back to do a more in-depth inspection of the roof and see what's up."

She bit her lip as she looked up at the wet spot in the plywood ceiling.

"It's going to be okay," he said, feeling the need to reassure her.

"I'm not sure how much more we can take," she said softly, so softly he almost didn't hear her.

"Excuse me?"

"Jordan... She's in bad shape. I brought her here because this place has always been home to us, but if the roof caves in..."

"It's not going to. You have my word on that."

"And are you a man of your word, Mr. McCarthy?"

As he met her intense gaze, the oddest sensation came over him, making him feel as if his answer to her question was the most important response he'd ever give to anyone. "It's Riley, and yes, I'd like to think so."

"That'd be a refreshing change of pace for us."

She'd been hurt by what happened to her sister. He could see it in the wary way she looked at him and in the protective way she carried herself, as if girding herself for battle.

"How about I talk to my cousin and we try to get those ladders over here today?"

The relief that washed over her features made him feel seven feet tall because he'd done that for her. He'd helped to relieve her burden somewhat. "That'd be amazing," she said. "Thank you so much."

"No problem." Mac would have his head for making a promise like that, but he was going to keep his word to her, no matter what Mac had to say about it.

ONE OF THE THINGS THAT KEVIN LOVED BEST ABOUT LIVING ON Gansett was the gatherings the family had for all occasions, big and small. This was a big one. His niece Janey and her husband, Joe, were leaving the island in the morning for Providence, where they would await the arrival of their second child, due in two weeks. They were hoping for a much less dramatic arrival this time around.

Janey had nearly died from a partial abruption of the placenta when her son was born, which would've been fatal had it not been for her ex-fiancé, Dr. David Lawrence. David had saved her life—and her baby son's life—by performing emergency surgery at a clinic ill-equipped to handle a crisis of that magnitude. David had since taken steps to equip the clinic in case another such emergency presented itself, but no one would rest easy until Janey had safely delivered.

Joe and Janey were taking no chances this time around, thus the two weeks they would spend at Frank's home in the city, close to the top hospital for women and children in the region. Tonight, the family was gathered at their home to send them off and to wish them well with the delivery.

Madhouse was the word that came to mind when he walked in and encountered the traveling circus known as the McCarthy family. Mac's son, Thomas, and his niece Ashleigh were the oldest of the kids, and they would start kindergarten after Labor Day. Thomas's sister, Hailey, and Laura's son Holden tried to keep up with the older kids. Every one of them was screaming, as were Laura's twins, Jon and Joey, and Janey's son, P.J.

Too bad Chelsea had had to work. It might've done her good to take in the mayhem unfolding all around him.

Was he out of his mind to be considering wandering back into that fray?

Watching Mac telling Thomas and Ashleigh to quit running in the house and to take the other kids outside to run in the yard, Kevin tried to picture himself chasing after a little one two years from now when he'd be fifty-five and way past the point when he'd thought he'd be wrangling babies.

Not that he didn't have the energy or stamina. He'd always had plenty of both. The big question was whether he *wanted* that for himself, and he honestly didn't know if he did. As he greeted his brothers, his sister-in-law, Linda, Frank's girlfriend, Betsy, and his nieces, nephews, grandnieces, grandnephews and a litany of friends who were like family, that question hung heavily over him.

Luke and Sydney Harris had brought their baby daughter, Lily, and watching Luke with his little girl had Kevin wondering what it might be like to have a daughter. The closest he'd come to a daughter was watching his nieces Janey and Laura grow up. He'd only met his third niece, Mallory, recently when she came to find her father, Big Mac, after her mother died, but she already felt like a surrogate daughter to him.

Big Mac came over to him with two beers, one of which he handed to Kevin.

"Thanks."

"How you doing?" Big Mac asked. "Thought about what you told us last night all day."

"You got any answers for me?"

"Nah," Big Mac said with a guffaw. "I ain't touching that one."

"Thanks a lot."

"I know you're the one everyone turns to for advice, but if you need someone to listen to you for a change, I'm here. I'll help if I can."

"I know, and I appreciate it."

"Hell of a thing," Big Mac said, watching the family dynamics unfold around them. As usual, the guys had overtaken the kitchen while the women were gathered around the babies in the living room.

"What is?"

"The spot you're in. Do you give the woman you love what she wants, potentially at the expense of your own happiness, or do you tell her it's not what *you* want and lose her in the process?"

"She says I won't lose her if I decide against having a baby."

"Hmm."

"What does that mean?"

"It's just that if she denies herself something she really wants because it's not what *you* want, will she resent you for that someday?"

Kevin sighed. "I don't know. Maybe. I'm so out of my element on this one, Mac. I don't know whether I'm coming or going."

"Can't say I blame you. It's a big deal. A lot to consider."

"I talked to Riley about it last night."

"And?"

"I think he was too shocked to share his true feelings."

"You know that in the grand scheme of things, it doesn't matter what he or Finn thinks, right?"

"And you and I both know that the thought of doing anything that hurts our kids, even if our kids are adults, is unfathomable to us. Besides, the divorce has hurt them enough. I don't want to pile on."

"You've been a great father to those boys, Kev. They've never wanted for anything on your watch. Whatever you do next should be for you. It may surprise or shock them at first, but they'll get over it. A baby brother or sister is one more person for them to love. It's not a disease you're bringing into the family."

"True." Kevin rubbed his chest. "I just wish I could separate what I feel for Chelsea from how I feel about becoming a father again at my age."

"You can't separate those two things. They're one and the same."

"What're you two boys so serious about over here?" Mac's wife, Linda, asked when she joined them.

Mac looked to him, raising his brow, letting Kevin know it was up to him whether he wanted to share his dilemma with Linda.

Kevin loved his sister-in-law and had always valued her opinion. He'd like to hear what she had to say about his situation. "Chelsea wants to have a baby."

"Oh," Linda said on a long exhale. "Wow."

"Yeah."

"Do *you* want to have a baby?"

"It wasn't exactly at the top of my to-do list before two days ago."

"I'm sure it wasn't."

"Tell me what you really think, Lin. I feel like an old fool to be even considering this."

"I love Chelsea. I think she's been very good for you."

"I agree."

"And I don't think having a baby at fifty-something makes you an old fool. Not if you would give that child everything you gave the boys."

"I would. Of course I would." But could he coach Little League and run the athletic boosters and help with scout campouts and supervise fundraisers at sixty-something? Why the hell not? He'd had to do all that while juggling a busy practice, too. If anything, he'd have more time to devote to his third child than he'd had to give to his sons.

"Then that's what matters. The older I get, the more I realize age is just a number. People assign expectations to certain ages, but no one says we have to live up to those expectations. Look at how happy Carolina is with Seamus," she said of Joe's mother, who'd married a man sixteen years her junior. "That girl is happier than I've ever seen her. Just think what she would've missed if she'd let society dictate what she should do."

"You make very valid points," Kevin said, intrigued by Linda's perspective.

"My wife is a very wise woman," Mac said, putting his arm around his petite, blonde wife.

She smiled up at him. "Said the man who knows that a happy wife is the secret to a happy life." To Kevin, she added, "Chelsea may not be your wife, but her happiness matters to you."

"Yes, it does."

"On another note," Linda said tentatively, "I heard from Deb today. She said she's coming over to see the boys and would like to get together. I have to admit, seeing her isn't at the top of *my* to-do list."

"It's okay," Kevin said. "I'm over it. You can see her if you want to."

"I'll never understand how she could cheat on you after thirty-one years of marriage," Linda said, her fierce loyalty making him smile. "If I see her, I'm apt to smack her."

"Easy, killer," Big Mac said.

"The way I've tried to look at it is that no matter what she did, she's still Riley and Finn's mom, and she always will be."

"That may be true, but that doesn't mean the rest of us have to welcome her back into the bosom of the family she turned her back on when she decided to have an affair."

"That's fair enough," Kevin said. "You can see her or not see her. Either is fine with me."

"I really don't want to."

"Then tell her you're busy."

"I think I will."

"Speak of your devils," Big Mac said, nodding to the door that Riley and then Finn came through, obviously fresh from after-work showers.

His heart never failed to swell with love and pride when he saw the handsome men who were his sons. "Hey, guys. Long day?"

"This one got us into a roof thing that mushroomed," Finn said, gesturing toward his brother with his thumb.

"Just keeping a promise to a woman in need," Riley said with a wink.

"Who happens to be a stone-cold fox," Finn said, smiling salaciously.

"Knock it off," Riley snapped. "Don't talk about her that way."

Interesting, Kevin thought. It wasn't like Riley to be so defensive about a woman.

"Is she or is she not a stone-cold fox?" Finn asked, clearly poking at his brother.

"I'm getting a beer," Riley said, storming off toward the kitchen.

"Leave your brother alone," Kevin said to Finn.

"I was testing a hypothesis," Finn said, his gaze shifting to Riley, now in the kitchen, surrounded by their cousins.

"What hypothesis is that?"

"He was weird about Mrs. Hopper's granddaughter Nikki. Insisted we get over there *today* to do a more thorough check on the roof, even though we had other work scheduled for today. I think he likes her, and he just kind of proved my point by flipping out."

"Aww, poor Riley," Linda said.

"Poor Riley is going to be spending a lot of time at the Hopper place," Finn said. "The whole roof needs to be done, and it needs to be done soon. It should've been done five years ago. More shingles are missing than not missing."

"Does that mean he's going to stay on the island for the off-season?" Kevin asked hopefully.

"Looks that way," Finn said. "He told Mac he'd take the lead on getting the roof done."

"How about you?"

"Haven't decided yet. I have until the Tuesday after Labor Day to go back to work in Connecticut, extend my leave of absence or offer my resignation. And now, I need a beer." He wandered off to join his brother and cousins in the kitchen.

"It sure would be nice to have them both here long term," Linda said.

"Yes, it would." The thought of Riley staying thrilled him, but Finn's indecision had him hoping his younger son would find a reason to stay, too.

CHAPTER 7

After dinner, Joe lit the fire pit and helped his hugely pregnant wife into a lounge chair.

"I can't believe I have to tote this cinderblock around for two more weeks," Janey moaned, her hands propped on her pregnant belly. She'd been on full bedrest all summer and was getting crankier about her restrictions with every passing week.

"You're almost there, sweetheart," Big Mac said, hovering over his daughter as he had throughout her pregnancy.

Kevin knew his big brother wouldn't truly relax until his daughter had safely delivered her new baby. Nearly losing Janey and P.J. had been a trauma the entire family wouldn't soon forget.

"Also on the agenda is the big snip-snip for Joseph," Janey announced, "so he can never, ever, *ever* get me pregnant again."

"Thank the Lord for that," Big Mac uttered to laughter while Joe just shook his head at his wife.

"The snip won't be *that* big," Mac said. "After all, we are talking about Joe here."

Joe gave his best friend the finger while the others howled and high-fived Mac.

"And speaking of good behavior," Mac said, "can we talk about my three-month streak of absolute perfection? Who bet on three months?" He held his hand up to his ear. "What's that? *No one* bet I'd last that long on my new grown-up streak? Bunch of chumps."

"He's right," Janey said, "as much as I hate to admit that. The longest bet was Maddie's at a month, so I guess she earns back some of the money she lost betting against him in the past."

"Excellent," Mac said. "Now that we've beaten you at your own game, I can get back to business as usual around here."

"Wait just a minute," Grant said. "Did you and Maddie collude against us?"

"Would we do that?" Mac asked.

"*Yes*," the others said in a chorus.

"Rigged," Adam said. "I call for an audit."

"Stuff your audit and pay up," Mac said. "Maddie is the rightful winner."

"Can anyone who has to live with you for the rest of their life actually be referred to as a *winner*?" Evan asked.

Maddie, who was a few weeks behind Janey in her pregnancy, held her belly as she laughed. "Quit making me laugh, or I'll pee my pants."

"She will," Mac said, his expression grave. "Happens once a day."

His wife glared at him. "Shut *up*, Mac!"

"How many times a day do you suppose she has to say that?" Riley asked.

"Hundreds," Maddie said.

Mac rubbed his hands together, his expression nothing short of diabolical. "I've had lots of time to think about our next move, gentlemen."

"There's not one man here who's gonna follow your lead after the skinny-dipping episode got us all cut off for weeks," Shane said.

"What he said," Blaine Taylor, Mac's brother-in-law, replied, using his thumb to point at Shane. "You've been replaced as the dictator of this banana republic."

"By who?" Mac asked. "Who'd want to take on this motley crew?"

"Anyone but you," Joe said.

"We'll see what you're saying when I come up with the perfect plan for retribution," Mac said.

"Why do you need retribution?" Grace asked. "We're the ones who were left naked on a beach without our clothes. The way I see it, you oughta be watching *your* asses."

"She makes me so hot when she talks dirty," Evan said, shivering dramatically.

Grace gave him a shove that nearly sent him flying off the deck.

While the others laughed at Evan, Stephanie said, "We need a strategic plan to get these men under control before we end up with a bunch of sons just like them."

"No kidding," Laura said. "I live in mortal fear of my boys growing up to be like cousin Mac."

"You'd be lucky if they were like me," Mac said.

Listening to their foolish banter, Kevin loved nights like this when the family came together for any reason or often no reason other than a desire to be together. Surveying the crowd, he noted Big Mac's daughter Mallory had arrived with her fiancé, Quinn James, and that Alex and Jenny Martinez had come by to see Janey along with Alex's brother, Paul, and his wife, Hope. They'd recently learned that Paul and Hope were also expecting a baby.

Slim Jackson and his fiancée, Erin Barton, were there, as were Victoria Stevens, the island's midwife, and her significant other, Shannon O'Grady. But the biggest surprise was the arrival of David Lawrence and his fiancée, Daisy Babson.

Janey held out her arms and hugged her ex-fiancé, who said something that made her laugh and then playfully punch his arm.

Joe shook hands with David and kissed Daisy's cheek before offering them drinks and food. After a man saved the life of your wife and son, Kevin supposed it didn't matter that he used to be engaged to your wife.

A consummate people watcher, Kevin enjoyed sitting back and taking in the family dynamics. Mac's sons, Frank's son, his sons... The cousins were close because the three brothers had always been tight. It was nice to see Shane laughing and bullshitting with the guys. For a while after his wife left him, they'd had reason to wonder if Shane would ever smile again. Since he'd gotten engaged to Owen's sister Katie, Shane smiled all the time, his gaze frequently landing on the woman he loved, who was on the other side of the deck with the women gathered around Janey.

Kevin took inventory—Maddie, Stephanie, Grace, Mallory, Tiffany, Jenny, Hope, Erin, Daisy. Where was Abby? He got up, grabbed another beer from the cooler and went inside. In the kitchen, Abby was at the sink washing dishes. He'd been seeing her regularly at his office since she'd been diagnosed with polycystic ovary syndrome and helping her come to terms with her fertility challenges. At least he hoped he'd helped her.

"Hey," he said when he joined her in the kitchen. "What're you doing in here when the party is out there?"

"Just cleaning up a little. Joe doesn't need to be left with a huge mess when they're leaving in the morning."

He leaned against the counter next to her. "Is that all it is?"

She glanced at him and then returned her focus to the dishes, but in that second of eye contact, he saw her torment.

"Abby..."

"Don't, Kevin. Please don't try to make me feel better when I'm a jealous cow. She's one of my *best* friends. I should be nothing but happy for her. For all of them." She applied vigorous effort to cleaning a pan.

He placed his hand on her arm. "Stop. You don't have to pretend with me."

"I don't want to be this person I've become. I hate this version of myself."

"Your feelings are totally understandable."

"Are they?" she asked, her eyes flashing with emotion. "Would my dearest friends and sisters-in-law really understand that I can't bear to be around them and their rounded bellies and their joyful families? Would they understand how fiercely I hate my body for turning on me this way? Haven't I had enough heartbreak in my life?"

Kevin ached for her, the way he did every time she opened her heart to him during their sessions. He did now what he couldn't do during therapy. He opened his arms to her.

She sighed, wiped her hands and stepped into his embrace.

All the fight seemed to go out of her when he hugged her. "I'm so sorry you're going through this."

"I'm sorry for venting. I hate that I have those thoughts. Saying them out loud only makes me feel worse. I love every one of those babies my friends and family have had. I really do."

"I know you do. Have you heard any more from the adoption agencies?"

"No, but they said it could be a year or two before we hear anything."

Keeping his hands on her shoulders, he looked down at her. "They approved your application. That's an important first step."

"I guess." She looked up at him, offering a wan smile. "Thanks for helping me through this. I'd probably be in a loony bin by now without Adam and you and everyone else who's supported me."

"Believe it or not, I think you're doing great, Abby. You're focusing on maintaining your health and your marriage and your business. You're doing everything you should be."

"I'm trying. I just wish I didn't feel so..."

"What?"

"Empty," she said, her despondence obvious. "I hate myself for that, too. I'm married to the most wonderful man who ever lived. I have a lovely life and a thriving business. Why can't that be enough?"

"Because there's something else you want, and that something else has proven hard to come by. Your feelings—all your feelings—are perfectly justified. Give yourself permission to be sad and mad and bitter, but don't spend too much time wallowing in the negative. That won't help long term."

"I know. I tell myself that every day."

Adam came in through the sliding door and came to a stop when he saw his uncle talking to his wife. "Everything okay in here?"

Kevin kissed Abby's forehead. "Call me if you need me."

"Thanks, Kev. For everything. I mean it."

"I know, honey. And for what it's worth, I think you're going to get everything you want. You just have to be patient."

Abby laughed, but there was a bitter edge to it. "Patience is not my best quality."

"You have a lot of great qualities. Don't ever forget that." As he turned to leave them alone, he squeezed his nephew's shoulder.

He felt for them and the difficult road they were on, but he admired the way they were fighting for their marriage. He'd had a few joint sessions with them that had reinforced his confidence in the state of their union. They were solid and facing the challenges of her condition head on. He admired them both tremendously and had his fingers crossed that they would get the baby they so desired—one way or the other.

"WHAT'S WRONG, HONEY?" ADAM ASKED WHEN THEY WERE ALONE.

"The usual thing," she said, forcing a smile for his benefit.

He ached for her as the months dragged on with no news from the various agencies they'd applied to and when her period arrived with maddening regularity. The doctors had told them to expect her period to be irregular, but that hadn't happened. No, it showed up every month, right on schedule, as if to mock them and remind them of how powerless they were.

Next month, they were due to begin aggressive fertility treatments that would put a further strain on Abby and her health, but they'd made the decision to try so they wouldn't have regrets later. He wasn't looking forward to that ordeal, but since there was absolutely nothing he wouldn't do for her, he'd be right by her side through it all.

He put his arms around her and tucked her head into the nook between his neck and shoulder. "You want to go?"

"Absolutely not. We're here to celebrate your sister and her new baby, and that's what we're going to do."

"You don't have to pretend with me, Abs. I know how hard this is for you."

"It is hard, but it's not Janey's fault, and it's not Joe's fault or

Maddie's or Jenny's or Syd's or Hope's or anyone else's. I absolutely refuse to let our sorrow be a drag on them. So get me a glass of wine, and let's put on our party faces."

"In case I forgot to tell you today, I love you, Mrs. McCarthy."

"I love you, too. There's no way I could deal with any of this without you by my side."

"There's nowhere in this world I'd rather be than right here with you."

"That makes me feel very lucky."

"We're both lucky to have each other, and I keep hoping that we'll be lucky in other ways, too, but even if we aren't, we still have more than most people get in a lifetime." He tightened his arms around her. "When it gets to be too much, hold on to me. I'll always be right here."

"That means everything to me."

"You mean everything to me. Don't ever forget that." He still worried from time to time that she would run away from him rather than subject him to the challenges her condition presented. That was why he held on to her as tightly as he could as often as he could, hoping she would never want to be anywhere but right here with him.

CHAPTER 8

The party broke up around ten with hugs and well-wishes for Janey and Joe. Kevin was one of the last to leave. He sat on the chaise and hugged his niece. "I'd say good luck, but you aren't going to need it. We McCarthys are a hardy stock."

"You make us sound like livestock," she said with a grin.

Kevin barked out a laugh. "You've got this, sweetheart. My money is on you."

"Thanks, Kev. Keep an eye on my dad, will you? He's worked himself up into a full panic over the delivery. I'm worried he'll have a heart attack or something before the baby arrives."

"I'll do what I can to keep him calm. Don't worry about anyone else but you and that little one. We can't wait to meet him or her."

"Neither can I."

"Love you."

"Love you, too."

"I'll keep in touch with your dad. Don't worry."

"Thanks, Kev."

Big Mac and Linda were accompanying Joe, Janey and P.J. to Providence tomorrow to help them get settled. They were due to return to the island in a couple of days. The island's chief pilot, Slim Jackson, was on standby to fly Mac and Linda to the mainland if Janey went into labor early. Otherwise, they were due to return to Providence two days before her due date so they could take care of P.J. while his mom and dad were at the hospital.

Kevin hugged Joe, wished him the best and walked out with Mac and Linda, who'd stayed to help finish cleaning up.

"I can't bear this," Mac said when they were outside. "Maybe we should go with them for the whole time they're gone."

"We offered, and they said that wasn't necessary," Linda reminded her husband.

"Still, we could stay out of their way and help Joe with P.J. I'd feel so much better being there rather than sitting around here waiting to hear it's go-time."

"What about the marina?" Linda asked.

"Fuck the marina. Luke can handle it."

Linda glanced at Kevin. "Can you help me out here?"

"You need to calm the hell down," Kevin said. "Janey is worried about you."

"*She's* worried about *me*?"

"She just told me she's afraid you're going to have a heart attack or something equally dreadful."

Mac's shoulders drooped. "I don't want her worrying about me."

"Then you need to chill. I know this is so hard for you both. I can't even imagine how terrifying it must be in light of what happened last time. But they're doing everything right, getting themselves to the mainland well ahead of her due date. They're going to be right where they need to be to ensure a smooth, safe delivery."

"Keep telling me that, will you?" Mac asked.

"Any time you need to hear it." To Linda, he added, "That goes for you, too."

She went up on tiptoes to hug and kiss him. "Thanks, Kev."

"Love you guys. Everything is going to be fine. I promise."

Mac hugged him. "Love you, too. Thank you."

"Any time."

He waved them off and got into the sleek BMW he'd had sent from home when he decided to stay on the island. Funny how "home" used to be somewhere else entirely and now it was a tiny island in the middle of nowhere, surrounded by his big, boisterous family. He loved it here. He loved listening to their problems and trying to help them the way he had his patients for so many years. If only he had ready answers to his own problems.

He left Janey's intending to head home, but found himself parked in the Beachcomber parking lot staring at the door and trying to decide whether he should go see her. That debate was new. Two days ago, it wouldn't have been a question. He'd visited her almost every night she worked since they got together.

It pained him to realize that things between them had changed since she told him she wanted a baby. He didn't want the changes to drive them apart, so he got out of the car and went into the bar, taking his usual seat and waiting for her to notice him.

She was talking to customers on the other side of the bar, and when she turned to find him there, her bright smile went a long way toward soothing the disquiet swirling inside him. When she looked at him like that, he had no problems or worries. And when she came over to lean across the bar to kiss him, he felt like the luckiest bastard who'd ever lived, especially when he saw other guys in the bar looking on in envy.

"How was the party at Janey's?" She opened a beer for him and then reached for his hand.

He linked their fingers. "The usual McCarthy mayhem."

"In other words, it was a blast."

"As always."

"How's Janey?"

"Eager to get the baby out. Apparently, Joe is having a vasectomy while they're on the mainland."

Chelsea winced. "Ouch." Then she gasped, and her eyes went wide.

"What?"

"We never actually talked about whether you'd had one."

"A vasectomy? Nope. Deb had her tubes tied after Finn. I offered, but she said she wanted to be sure. Friends of ours had gotten pregnant after he had a vasectomy. Deb had rough pregnancies. 'Two and done,' she said."

"Well, it's good that you still can," she said, giving him a shy smile. "If we decide to try."

"I still can." Even if the thought of another baby made him more anxious than anything had in a very long time. "I talked to Laura about babysitting for them, and she said any time we want, so I made a date for Sunday."

She gave his hand a squeeze. "Thank you for arranging that."

"No problem. How hard can it be to get three kids under the age of two ready for bed and settled for the night?"

"Umm, is that a rhetorical question?"

Kevin laughed and then released her hand so she could tend to other customers.

"You're a lucky guy," a man on the next barstool said.

"Excuse me?" Kevin said.

"She's a beautiful woman," the man said, nodding at Chelsea, a note of wistfulness in his tone that put Kevin on edge.

"Yes, she is." Kevin took a subtle glance at the man, noting he was probably in his early- to mid-thirties. And, he admitted grudgingly, the guy was good-looking. He was the sort of guy Chelsea ought to be with, a thought that made his chest ache.

Was he holding her back by holding on to her? *Ugh,* now there was a cheery thought. Christ, when had the simplest thing in his life become so bloody complicated?

I want to have a baby. That was when. He took a deep drink of the beer he hadn't planned to have. What the hell was he going to do? One minute, he had himself convinced there was nothing he wouldn't do for her, including father and raise their child. The next minute, he was balking at the thought of becoming a father again at his age. The internal debate was driving him *mad.*

Kevin nursed the beer over the next two hours while Chelsea tended to customers, cleaned the bar and cashed out. The young man who'd admired her had left a while ago, wishing Kevin a good night, but he'd left him with a whole new set of questions.

When Chelsea was finished, they walked out together.

"Are you coming over?"

"Yeah, if that's okay."

"It's okay," she said, smiling.

He waited until she'd pulled out of the parking lot and then followed her home, parking behind her in the driveway. Inside, Chelsea went directly to her bedroom, pulling her Beachcomber T-shirt over her head and dropping her khaki shorts on the floor. "I need a shower." In the doorway to the bathroom, she turned to him. "Join me?"

Kevin was momentarily struck dumb by her sweet, sexy smile and the plea he saw in her lovely eyes. She knew things were "off" between them, and she certainly knew why. But she was trying, and that meant the world to him.

He pulled the shirt over his head and kicked off his jeans.

Chelsea's smile got even bigger before she disappeared into the bathroom to start the shower.

He stepped into the shower, wrapped his arms around her from behind and kissed her shoulder. He'd never thought shoulders could be sexy until he met her.

"Hi there," she said, resting her hands on his arms.

"Hi yourself."

"You okay?"

"I'm great. You?"

"I'm... anxious."

He hated to hear that. "What about?"

"You know. I feel like I've made a big mess of things."

"You haven't. Not at all, sweetheart."

"Do me a favor, Kev. Don't lie to me to make me feel better."

He turned her to face him, drawing her in tight against his erection. "I love you, Chels. That's the one thing you can be sure of."

"I know you do, and I love you, too. But we've both lived long enough to know that sometimes love isn't enough."

Settling her head on his chest, he swallowed the panic that seized him at the thought of losing her. This was one of those moments when he'd give her anything she wanted if it meant he'd get to keep her in his life. "There was a guy in the bar tonight. The one sitting next to me. He said I was a lucky guy to be with you."

"That was nice of him."

"I completely agree. I am lucky to be with you this way."

"Why do I hear a 'but' coming?"

"I could tell he thought you were hot, which of course you are, and I thought for a second that he was the sort of guy you should be with —young and handsome with his best years ahead of him, not behind him."

"Does it matter at all that I'm in the shower with the guy *I* want to be with?"

"Of course it does. That means everything to me. You know that."

"Then stop trying to replace yourself and acting like you don't bring anything to our relationship besides this." She wrapped her hand around his cock and gave a gentle stroke that his head falling back as he groaned. "You are so much more to me than this, Kevin."

He rested a hand on the wall of the shower because it was either that or fall over. "You could have anyone..."

"I don't want anyone but you. I haven't wanted anyone else since the first night we spent together."

God, she was so sweet and sexy and perfect in every way. He dropped his hands to her ass and lifted her, pinning her against the wall.

She gasped when her back met the cool tile and released her grip on his cock. "Kevin..."

"What, honey?"

"Make love to me."

"There's nothing else I'd rather do." He kissed her and groaned when her tongue twisted with his. As he had many times since the first time with Chelsea, he thought about what he would've missed if he'd never met her. He'd never had the kind of all-consuming sex he had with her, and he'd become addicted to it—and to her—over the last year.

Sliding into her tight, wet heat was like finding paradise. He loved the way she tightened around his cock, how she pulled his hair and left scratches on his back.

"Why would I want anyone else when I have you?" she asked, looking at him with her heart in her eyes. "No one has ever taken care of me the way you do."

As he throbbed deep inside her, Kevin closed his eyes against the rush of emotion.

Her arms wound around his neck, her fingers delved into his hair, and her lips skimmed his face. She made him feel cherished and wanted in a way his wife never had. Their connection had been electric from the beginning, and after all this time, that initial attraction had never faded.

The guy at the bar was right. He was a lucky son of a bitch to have earned the love of such an extraordinary woman, and he'd be wise to hold on to her, no matter what.

CHELSEA LAY IN BED NEXT TO KEVIN, HER MIND RACING WITH thoughts and worries that couldn't be quieted no matter how hard she tried. She could tell he was wrestling with the challenge she had brought into their harmonious relationship. Part of her wanted to say never mind, let's forget about it. But the other part of her knew that wouldn't be wise.

For years, her mother had yielded to her father's wishes to the detriment of her own dreams and had been rewarded for her loyalty by a husband who'd left her for another woman. Her mom had never recovered from that blow. To Chelsea's knowledge, her mother hadn't been on a single date or so much as entertained the idea of being with anyone else in the twenty years since her marriage ended in dramatic fashion.

As much as she loved Kevin, Chelsea didn't want to end up like her mother by sacrificing her own goals for someone else. Not that Kevin would ever ask that of her. He wasn't that kind of guy. In fact, one of the things she loved best about him was the way he supported and indulged her many hobbies, including gardening, cooking and photography.

For her birthday, he'd bought her gifts tailored to each of those things and had obviously put considerable thought and preplanning into each of them. Living on the island required careful planning for occasions when shipping was involved. His thoughtful gifts had touched her because he'd put so much care into choosing things he knew she'd love, such as the shiny new garden tools and the cookbooks. Not to mention the diamond bracelet she had loved.

No one had ever treated her the way he did, as if she were the most precious thing in his life even if his sons were at the top of his list, as they should be. But he made her feel damned important to him.

She turned over, put an arm across his abdomen, and without waking, he pulled her in closer to him.

Chelsea sighed with contentment. She felt happy and safe when he was with her, no matter what they were doing. Even when he sat at her bar and shot the shit with other patrons during her shifts. Being in the same room with him comforted her.

"You're restless, sweetheart," he said in a sleepy-sounding voice. "What's wrong?"

"I can't turn off my brain."

"Come here." He settled her head on his chest and ran his fingers through her hair. "Better?"

"Mmm."

"What're you thinking about?"

"My mother, of all things." Kevin had yet to meet any of her family, which would change when her brother's family came for a visit Labor Day weekend.

"What about her?"

"She never got over my dad leaving her for someone else. In twenty years, she's never so much as thought about being with another man."

"That's too bad. What's got you thinking about that?"

"I never want to be like her, you know? I've gone out of my way to avoid situations that could turn me into a younger version of her."

"I don't know your mom, but I do know you. And you went through a difficult thing when your dad left, but it hasn't made you bitter or angry."

"In some ways it did. I've been all about the drive-by relationships, because if you don't get too involved, you can't get hurt. I moved out here to get away from the family drama fifteen summers ago and never left. I feel like I've backed into my life rather than making deliberate choices about what I want."

"Do you realize you just told me more about *you* in one minute than you have in the last year?"

"Did I?"

"Uh-huh. Why do you suppose that is?"

"Are you shrinking me right now, Doc?"

"Nah. I just want to understand why it's hard for you to talk about yourself."

Chelsea thought about that. "You want to know something I've never told anyone else?"

"Very much so."

He made it so damned easy for her to be vulnerable with him. That was one of the things she loved best about him. "She blames me for my dad leaving."

Kevin shifted them so he could see her face. "*What?* Why?"

"He left her for my best friend's mom. I brought the best friend—and her mom—into our lives. She was different toward me after everything that happened."

"Chelsea, honey… It was *not* your fault. You have to know that, right?"

She shrugged. "I guess…"

"I guarantee you he was unhappy in his marriage long before he met your friend's mom and decided to leave."

"How do you know that?"

"Because if he was happy, truly happy with your mom, he never would've noticed anyone else. I've seen a lot of this very thing in my practice. An affair is almost always the result of years of unhappiness. That doesn't make it right, but most decent people don't just wake up one day and decide they want someone else. It's a long, slow process of disillusion and often loneliness that leads someone to look outside their marriage for fulfillment."

"You're very smart about so many things. When you explain it, something that has never made sense to me makes all kinds of sense."

Kevin snorted with laughter. "If I'm so smart, maybe you can tell me why my own wife was so unhappy she went elsewhere without me even noticing until it'd been going on for months."

"Sometimes we can't see what's right in front of us."

"That's very true." He ran his hand up and down her arm in a soothing caress. "I want you to do something for me."

"What?"

"I want you to repeat after me. It wasn't my fault that my father left my mother for my best friend's mom. Come on. Say it."

Chelsea smiled. "It wasn't my fault that my father left my mother for my best friend's mom."

"Do you need to say it again to truly believe it?"

"Nah, I'm good."

"I'm sorry you went through such a difficult ordeal at such a young age. It had to be devastating."

"It was," she said softly. "Everyone knew. People looked at me everywhere I went. In school, at the grocery store, the local pizza place. It was mortifying."

"I can only imagine. What about your friend? She must've been in the same boat."

"She was, and it was worse for her. Her parents had already been divorced for years, so her mom was considered the homewrecker by people in town. She… That's when she started cutting herself. It went on for years until she finally found a good therapist who got her back on a positive track, but her life has been kind of a mess."

"And she's your stepsister now, right?"

"Yeah, but we aren't really close anymore. The drama kinda killed our friendship."

"I'm sorry you had to go through all that."

"So am I, but it taught me a lot about what I didn't want in my own life."

"Like what?"

"Drama. Relationships that are too much work. People who are disloyal, especially to the ones they love."

"That's a good list."

"It's worked for me and so has island life. The drama can't find me here."

"It does have that advantage."

"I want you to know..." Her courage failed her before she could get the words out.

"What do you want me to know?"

"I never had the slightest urge to have children until I had someone in my life who made me feel safe to want more."

"Chelsea..."

"It's okay if you don't want the same things I do, Kev. I just wanted you to know that your love gave me the courage to want things I thought were out of reach for me."

"I'm so honored that you feel that way about me. I keep thinking I should step aside and let you go find someone closer to your own age who hasn't already been a dad for almost thirty years."

"I'm not looking to go off and have kids with just anyone, and I swear to you, if you decide it's not in the cards for us, I'll understand."

He reached out to caress her face. "I heard everything you said, sweetheart, and I love you for being honest about how you're feeling. It means a lot to me that our relationship has made you feel comfortable and confident enough to ask for what you want."

"It has."

"You want to talk about what it's done for me?"

"I'd love to," she said with a grin that made him smile, too.

"It's made me believe in love again. It's made me believe in myself again."

"I can't believe you ever didn't believe in yourself. You're too confident for that."

"That might be how it seems, but when your wife of more than thirty years walks out the door for a younger man, it does lead to a crisis of confidence."

"I hate that she made you feel that way. You're the best man I've ever known. Well, except for your brother, of course."

Kevin poked her, and she cracked up. Her "crush" on Big Mac was something they joked about often. "You know he's going to want to hire you away from the Beachcomber to be the general manager of the new McCarthy's Wayfarer, don't you?"

"Seriously?"

"Of course. He loves you as much as you love him."

"You say that so matter-of-factly, as if it wouldn't be a BFD for me. Did he actually say he wants me for that job?"

"Not yet, but I have no doubt you're on his radar. He'll pour on that famous Big Mac charm to woo you away from the Beachcomber."

"He could do it. That charm is *formidable*."

Kevin moved quickly to pin her to the bed. Hovering above her, he scowled playfully. "All this talk about your *affection* for my brother is making me jealous."

"Is this the same head doc who likes to say that jealousy is a wasted emotion?"

"The very same one. See what you've done to him?"

"What've I done to him?" she asked, her expression wistful and serious.

He leaned in to kiss her. "You've made him crazy and jealous and happy. So damned *happy*."

She raised her arms to curl them around his neck. "You make me happy, too."

"We're going to figure this out, Chels. I promise you that."

"You know you have no need to be jealous of anyone, right?"

"Yeah, baby. I know." When he kissed her again, she opened her mouth to his tongue and lost herself to the desire that overwhelmed her any time he held her this way.

If this was all they ever had, it would be enough, or so she told herself.

CHAPTER 9

Riley arrived at the Hopper house at six thirty the next morning with ladders, shingles and other material needed to patch the leaking roof until they could take on the bigger job of replacing it. The sun was just coming up on the east side of the island when he put the biggest ladder the company owned against the side of the house and began the long climb to the roof.

He loved this time of day on the island, before most residents woke up to begin their day, when the Salt Pond was still so flat calm, it looked like a mirror, when the roads were free of traffic and the beaches free of tourists.

As he reached the lowest dormer and got another look at the roof, he groaned. More shingles were missing than not, and in some places, bare plywood was visible. No wonder the roof had leaked when it rained. The farther up he went, the worse the situation became, but the diagnosis was simple. The Hopper family needed a new roof on this house, and they needed it right now.

However, this being Gansett Island, it would take some time and coordination to get the materials needed shipped over on the ferry.

Tentatively, he stepped onto the roof and moved carefully to get a closer look at the area that had been the source of the leak. He could go only so far, because the wood was so wet, it had begun to sag. Unless he wanted to end up inside the house, he didn't dare take another step.

He withdrew his cell phone from his pocket and called Mac.

"Hey," his cousin said. "What've you got?"

"It's worse than we thought. We've got actual sag in a few places."

"Great," Mac said with a sigh. "As I recall, that house is huge."

"Your memory is correct. About six thousand square feet, give or take."

"Crap. This was not in the plans for this month."

"I know, but with her granddaughters holed up here, I'd categorize it as critical from a structural standpoint. Another decent blow could take the roof off the place, and we're getting into hurricane season."

"Yeah, I know. All right, I'll give Mrs. Hopper a call and break the news to her. If she gives us the go-ahead to replace it, I'll order the materials immediately so we can get the ball rolling while the weather is still on our side."

"Sounds good."

"Thanks for getting over there first thing."

"No problem. I'm going to do some patching here, and then I'll meet up with you guys at the new house."

"Great, thanks. Don't fall off the roof."

Riley laughed. "I'll try not to." He'd spent the hottest, most miserable summer of his life working for a roofing company while in college. Thanks to that worst job ever, he knew how to keep from falling off a roof and how to do a repair that would keep the occupants dry until a more permanent fix could be done.

He got busy with the patch, losing himself in the work the way he always did. As the sun got warmer, he pulled off his shirt and downed half the bottle of cold water he'd tucked into his work bag. Shingles were flying from the roof to the yard as he moved across the area of greatest immediate concern.

"Shit," he muttered when he uncovered soaked plywood that would have to be replaced. That development made the "quick fix" much more complicated. He pulled out his phone and sent Mac a text.

Got to replace the plywood in one area. Gonna take longer than I thought here.

Okay. Keep me posted.

Will do.

"Excuse me? Mr. McCarthy? Is that you up there?"

Riley smiled at being called Mr. McCarthy by someone roughly the same age as he was. Moving carefully, he made his way down the incline of the roof and onto the ladder. He descended to find Nikki waiting for him, arms crossed, brows knitted with anxiety. Today she wore a formfitting tank with another pair of denim shorts. Her silky hair was pulled back into a ponytail that put her gorgeous face on full display.

As he landed on the ground a few feet from her, she took a long look at his bare chest, her eyes widening and her mouth falling open for a second before she caught herself, slammed her mouth closed and did that cute thing with her eyebrows again. The girl was a tightly wound ball of stress. "You, um, you forgot your shirt."

"I left it on the roof."

"Oh."

"Did you need something?"

"I need the banging to stop. My sister is in a very fragile condition and requires a lot of rest right now. We can't have all that noise."

"Well, I'm sorry to be the bearer of bad news, but your roof is about to cave in, and when it's raining inside the house, your sister will be a lot more disturbed than she is now."

She hugged herself even tighter as stress rolled off her in waves. "How long will it take to replace it?"

"A couple of weeks at a minimum."

To his horror, her eyes filled with tears. "This can't be happening."

"I'm sorry, but it's in really bad shape. If even a minor nor'easter comes through here, the roof isn't going to hold."

She ran trembling hands up and down her arms. "I... I don't know what to do. She's so fragile. The noise... It's just too much for her."

"Is there any way you could relocate for a short time? We'll get it done as fast as possible."

She shook her head. "It was all I could do to get her here, let alone eat once or twice a day…"

"I'm really sorry. I wish I had better news for you."

"Me, too."

Riley had the oddest desire to wrap his arms around her and tell her everything would be okay when he couldn't possibly know if that was true.

They coexisted in awkward silence for an uncomfortably long moment. He had no idea what to say to her or even if he should say anything at all.

She cleared her throat. "I don't mean to dump my crap on you. It's not your fault. We'll figure out something."

"I'm sorry you guys are going through such a tough time. I can't imagine how anyone does what he did to someone they supposedly love."

She released a harsh laugh. "He didn't love her. He used her to make a name for himself. Rather successfully, I might add."

"Surely there must be something she can do, from a legal standpoint."

"I'm sure there's a lot that could be done, if I could get her out of bed long enough to take a call from her attorneys. In the meantime, the video gets ten million new views per day."

Riley recoiled. "Ten *million*?"

"Yep. So while my sister is bedridden, her sex tape is going viral." Her words were matter-of-fact, but her rigid posture indicated the toll the stress was taking on her.

"Jesus," Riley muttered.

"He doesn't seem inclined to help us. Believe me, I've requested his assistance repeatedly since we first found out about the tape."

"I wish there was something…" Riley faltered when a thought occurred to him. "My cousin Adam…"

"Excuse me?"

"He's a computer whiz. Maybe he can help contain the damage somehow."

She bit her thumbnail as she considered that.

"And we know Dan Torrington," Riley added, not sure why he felt the need to get involved.

Her eyes nearly bugged out of her head. "You *know* Dan Torrington?"

Riley nodded. "He's a friend and an island resident."

Nikki glanced at the house, and he could almost see her trying to decide what her sister would think of this.

A flash of panic hit him. What the hell was he doing getting involved with people he didn't know in a situation that was already so far out of control as to be deemed epically disastrous? He swallowed hard, as the words *never mind* hovered on the tip of his tongue. But watching her panic, which easily outmatched his on a scale of two to one, he couldn't bring himself to say the words that would put an end to his temporary insanity.

She looked up at him, her big expressive eyes swimming with unshed tears. "I would very much appreciate whatever help you're able to give me."

He swallowed his misgivings, hoping he wasn't going to regret offering his assistance. "Sure, whatever I can do."

As the nine o'clock ferry cleared the breakwater leaving Gansett, Joe Cantrell released a deep sigh of relief, the second biggest sigh of relief of his life. The first being the one that followed the birth of his son, P.J., when he'd been told that both his wife and child were going to survive after the chaotic delivery. He still gave thanks every day for the quick action of David Lawrence, who'd saved both their lives.

Joe didn't like to think about what his life might be like today if David had failed to save them. Standing at the rail with his son in his arms, looking out at the familiar landscape of the island they called home, Joe shuddered at the thought of life without Janey and P.J.

The breeze blew through the baby's light blond hair, making him laugh from the sensation of the wind in his face. His son laughed at everything. He was the most joyful child Joe had ever known, not that he'd known many kids. But his son was special. His easygoing personality, ready smile and big blue eyes brightened every day for Joe and Janey. He was, quite simply, the best thing to ever happen to them.

If it'd been up to him, they would've quit while they were ahead. The thought of another child terrified him after nearly losing Janey and P.J. the first time around. They'd taken steps to avoid getting pregnant again, but something had gone "wrong," and now their second child was due in two weeks. This one would be born on the mainland, in a hospital equipped for any possible emergency. They were leaving nothing to chance.

And they'd left right in the nick of time. Janey had been feeling "off" the last few days, with a weird backache that had been keeping her awake at night and heartburn that had set his nerves to frazzle. David and the island's midwife, Victoria Stevens, had been keeping a close eye on her and assured them everything was fine. But Joe had a sixth sense when it came to Janey, and he could tell she was trying hard to hide her discomfort from him, knowing how he worried about her.

He wasn't the only one who was worried, which was why her parents had insisted on coming with them today to help with P.J. as they got settled at Janey's uncle Frank's house in Providence. He and Janey and P.J. would stay there until two days before her delivery date, when she would be admitted as a precaution. Janey's parents were due to return the night before she was to be admitted so they could care for P.J. while he and Janey were in the hospital.

He had the whole thing planned down to the last contingency. So while he was relieved to finally be leaving the island to get closer to the medical care Janey and the baby would need, he wouldn't take a full deep breath again until the baby arrived safely and Janey was out of the woods. And then he'd be getting a vasectomy immediately to ensure he'd never have to worry about getting his wife pregnant again. They were *out* of the baby business. Forever.

He laughed to himself, thinking of the conversation he'd had with Janey when he first realized she was pregnant again—and yes, both times, *he'd* been the one to put the pieces together.

"Let me tell you this, mister," she'd said, "if we *are* pregnant, after this, you're getting that thing snipped."

"That *thing*? Did you just refer to the part of me you love best as a *thing*?" Despite the insult to his manhood, he was relieved that she'd stopped sobbing.

"That's not the part of you I love best."

"That's not what you said the other night when you were all like, '*More*, Joe, give me *more*.'"

Her face turned bright red. "I never said that."

"Do I need to start recording these encounters?"

"If you do, I'll kill you."

P.J. poked at the corners of his mouth, smiling as big as his daddy. "Your mommy is silly."

The baby replied with baby gibberish that had Joe laughing some more. Someday soon, that gibberish would become actual words, and he couldn't wait to hear what his son had to say about the world around him. He was looking forward to teaching him everything—from how to throw a football with a perfect spiral to how to captain a one-hundred-foot ferry.

Someday, his children would inherit the ferry business, and he would make sure they were ready. Hopefully, they wouldn't have as much responsibility on them as he'd had at a young age when his grandfather died and left the business to him when he was still in his early twenties. But he'd made a go of it and would teach his kids everything they needed to know to keep it running into the next generation—if that was what they wanted. It hadn't been forced on him, and it wouldn't be forced on them, either.

"What do you think, pal?" he asked P.J. "Can you see yourself at the helm of this ship someday?"

"Joe!"

Later, he would remember that his name had never sounded quite like that coming from Big Mac McCarthy. In the moment, he simply turned toward his father-in-law, still smiling at his son, who continued to "talk" to him. The expression on Big Mac's face made his entire body go cold with fear and panic and disbelief.

The word "no" echoed through his brain as he ran as fast as he dared with the baby in his arms through the door that Big Mac held for him to find Janey on the floor of the ferry's cabin, surrounded by people. He couldn't think or breathe or move, not even to ask what was wrong or what possibly could've happened in the ten minutes since he'd left Janey sitting at a table with her parents while he took P.J. outside to get some air.

He forced air into his lungs and shook off the shock to focus on what Janey needed. "What… What happened?"

"Sharp pains in her back that traveled to the front," Big Mac reported, his expression grim and his eyes full of the same panic Joe was experiencing. "And her water broke." Big Mac gestured to a puddle on the floor under the table.

Joe glanced outside, saw that they were well past the northern point of the island and wrestled with the decision to press on or turn back. The idea that Janey's life—and the baby's life—could hinge on a decision he made had him holding back the need to vomit.

Janey cried out in pain.

Her mother, seated behind her on the floor, held her up as she leaned back. Janey looked up, her gaze frantic as she sought him out.

Joe handed his son to Big Mac and went to his wife. "I'm here, babe," he said, kneeling next to her and taking her hand. "Tell me what's going on."

"The baby," she said, panting. "It's coming."

"Now?"

Her eyes were wild as she nodded. "Right now. Look."

Joe tore his gaze off her face and looked under the skirt of her dress. When he saw the top of the baby's head, he nearly passed out.

"Joe!" Janey's frantic cry centered him and snapped him into action mode.

Looking up at Big Mac, he said, "Go tell Seamus to pour on the coal. Get us to Point Judith as fast as safely possible. Tell him to call 9-1-1 and have an ambulance waiting. *Hurry.*"

Big Mac handed P.J. to a kindly older woman who held out her arms to him, and then he took off for the bridge.

"I'm going to take him for a little walk," the lady said.

"Thank you." Joe hoped he was doing the right thing entrusting his son to a stranger, but what choice did he have at the moment? The ferry was all but deserted, and he didn't know anyone else on the boat that morning. "Breathe, sweetheart," he said to Janey. "Just like they taught us in the class. Remember?"

She nodded and started to huff and puff her way through the next contraction.

"I don't understand," Linda said, looking to Joe for answers he didn't have. "How could this have come on so fast?"

"The back pain," Janey said between huffs. "Might've been contractions."

Jesus, Joe thought. *Back labor is a thing?* "Wouldn't that show up when Vic monitored you?"

"Didn't have it while I was there," she said, continuing to puff.

Someone gave Linda a wet cloth that she used to wipe the sweat from Janey's face and brow.

"Hurts," Janey said, taking his hand and squeezing *hard*.

"She's not bleeding," Linda said. "Right?"

"No blood." Joe felt like he was having a heart attack. This could *not* be happening.

"That's a good sign," Linda said, her face devoid of color and her eyes big with fear that further unnerved him because her composure was legendary.

He wasn't sure who she was trying to reassure—herself or him. Joe heard—and felt—the moment when Seamus followed his orders to pour on the coal. The boat began to pick up speed that matched Joe's heart rate. "How're you doing, honey?"

"Okay," Janey said, crying out when another contraction hit her. "I need to push."

"Can you try to wait until we get there?"

"I don't think I can."

Joe glanced at Linda. "What should we do?"

"How do you feel about delivering a baby?" she asked.

"*Me?*"

"Do you have someone else in mind?"

"What if… What if I do it wrong or…"

"Joseph." One sharp word from his mother-in-law had him blinking and trying to refocus. "She needs you." To one of the deck hands who'd come in to see what was going on, Linda said, "Go up to the concession stand and get me as many *clean* towels as you can. We'll take everything they've got. Hurry."

Janey needs me. Janey needs me. Can't let her down. "Are we going to do this, babe?" he asked.

She bit her lip and nodded, her eyes bright with tears. "I'm so sorry," she whispered.

"Not your fault that our baby isn't interested in waiting two more weeks to make his or her debut."

"Go wash your hands with hot water, Joe," Linda said, while continuing to blot the sweat from Janey's face. "Quickly."

Joe kissed Janey. "Be right back. We got this, you hear?" He waited until she looked directly at him. "Everything is going to be okay. I promise."

She seemed to take strength from his promises.

He had to tear himself away from her to run to the men's room, where he thoroughly washed his hands with soap and the hottest water he could get from the sink. What if she got an infection because he didn't wash his hands correctly? Or what if the cord was wrapped around the baby's neck? What if…

"Stop," he said to his reflection in the mirror. "Just stop and get your ass back out there." Other than the day P.J. arrived, Joe had never been more terrified in his life than he was right in that moment. "Please, God, if you're listening, please help me. Help Janey and the baby. Please don't let anything happen to either of them." He bolted from the men's room, moving faster when he heard Janey screaming.

Big Mac had returned from the bridge. "What the hell are we going to do?" he asked.

"We're going to have a baby," Joe replied.

"Here?"

"Right here." To the people who'd gathered around them, Joe said,

"Thanks so much for your concern, but if you wouldn't mind giving us some privacy, we'd appreciate it."

With mumbled words of good luck and Godspeed, the small group of passengers cleared out of the cabin area, leaving Joe and Janey and her parents.

"Mac," Linda said, "go get some air. Right now. We don't need another emergency when you pass out and smack your head. Go."

"Princess..." he said, his tone full of agony.

"I'm okay, Dad. Go get your grandson and keep breathing."

"Love you."

"Love you, too." She grabbed Joe's hand, and the fierce look of concentration on her face filled him with pride. They hadn't gotten the chance to do this last time, and her determination went a long way toward defusing his panic. "I want to push."

"Wait for the contraction," her mother said. "As soon as you feel it starting, push your way through it."

Joe knelt between her legs, his hands shaking so hard, he feared he would drop the baby. His crewmember had brought stacks of clean linen from the concession stand, as well as a first aid kit. Was there anything in there that could help them now? He doubted it.

Janey... She had found her center. Her eyes were closed, her cheeks rosy, her breathing steady and her lips puckered as if she were about to receive a kiss. She'd never looked more beautiful to him, as he continued to pray for the safety of her and their baby. He made bargains with God, vowing to never again ask for anything for himself in exchange for Janey's safety and that of the baby.

In the background, he heard P.J. crying, but Big Mac would take care of him.

"Here we go," Janey said.

One minute she was Zen Janey, the next she was screaming her head off and terrifying her husband.

Linda supported Janey from behind as she pushed as hard as she could.

More of the baby's head appeared and then disappeared just as quickly when Janey sagged against her mother.

"So close, babe. I could see the top of the baby's head."

"Hurts," Janey said, whimpering.

"You're so strong," Joe said. "I know you can do it."

Before his eyes, she gathered herself again, marshaling the strength and fortitude she needed to finish the job. He'd never been prouder of her.

The contractions came closer together. Janey pushed and screamed through each one, but the baby didn't come.

Joe's gaze met Linda's, and he could see her worry and fear, which fed his.

"Janey," he said, waiting for her eyes to open. "We gotta get that baby out. The next one, let's go all in. Everything you've got. Can you do that?"

"I have been doing that," she said, whimpering again. "It's not working."

"You're so close. One huge push is going to finish the job. You've got this, babe. I'm so proud of you, and I love you so much. I can't wait to meet our baby." He reached for her. "Hold my hands as tight as you can. Let's do it together."

"Only if you let go when the baby comes," she said, breathing hard.

"I will. Don't worry. I won't let anything happen to either of you." That was a promise he hoped he could keep.

She took his hands and held on so tight, his fingers quickly went numb from the lack of circulation, but he paid that no mind as he helped her through the next contraction.

Janey screamed in agony that broke his heart. She pushed so hard that her face turned bright red and she nearly broke the bones in his hand.

"Don't stop, sweetheart. Keep pushing! Here it comes!"

She released his hands in time for him to catch the baby as it emerged slimy and bloody and the most beautiful thing he'd ever seen. Big eyes popped open, and Joe fell flat on his face in love for the third time in his life.

"Too quiet," Janey said, gasping. "What's wrong?"

"Nothing," Joe said, wrapping the baby in the cloths and a beach towel someone had given them so she wouldn't get cold. "She's absolutely perfect."

"*She?*"

"She," he said, meeting her gaze through a flood of tears. "We have ourselves a daughter."

With Linda still propping her up from behind and the cord still attached to the baby, Joe gently deposited the baby on her mother's chest.

"Hi there," Janey said, taking a visual inventory of her daughter's face and then dragging her index finger over the baby's cheek. "I wasn't expecting to meet you for a while."

Overwhelmed by the emotional punch, Joe dropped his head as tears ran down his face.

"Well done, you two," Linda said, her eyes full of tears.

"That was *all* her," Joe said, wiping the dampness from his face.

"That was all *us*," Janey said, smiling at him, her eyes full of joy and satisfaction. "And you're getting that *thing* snipped, you hear me?"

"As soon as possible," Joe said, more thankful than he'd ever been in his life.

CHAPTER 10

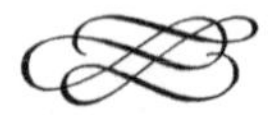

"So wait," Mac said to Maddie, who'd called him at work and asked him to come home for lunch because she had big news that couldn't wait for dinner. "Janey had the baby *on the ferry?*"

Smiling broadly, Maddie nodded. "That's right. Your mom tried to call you, and when she couldn't reach you, she called me. We have a new niece! Isn't it so exciting? I can't wait to meet her or to hear her name, which they haven't yet decided on."

As he listened to her, Mac tried to summon the expected enthusiasm for the arrival of a new family member, but he couldn't get past the fact that Janey had *given birth*—a *high-risk* birth, no less—on the fucking *ferry* of all places. His knees went weak under him, and he grasped the counter for support at the thought of something like that happening to Maddie, who was due soon with their fourth child. Their daughter, Hailey, had been born at home in the midst of a tropical storm of the same name. Their third child, Connor, had died in utero, something they were still recovering from more than a year later. Janey had nearly died having P.J. And now *this*...

Was it any wonder that Mac wanted to put a moratorium on babies among their family and friends?

"Mac?" Maddie watched him with concern furrowing her brow.

"What's wrong? I thought you'd be thrilled to hear that Janey had the baby and there were no complications."

He stared at her, agog. "*No* complications? She had a baby *on the ferry* after nearly *dying* the first time around. Everything about that is complicated!"

Wearing a small smile on her gorgeous face, the one that appeared whenever she was about to pacify or indulge him, Maddie closed the small distance between them and placed her hands on his chest.

He wondered if she could feel his heart galloping.

"You need to calm down."

Apparently, she could feel his heart going crazy. He glanced down at her hugely pregnant belly and rested his hands on their baby. "I want to go to Providence today. Right now."

"Mac—"

"I'm three thousand percent serious, Maddie. This baby is going to be born in a goddamned hospital. Not at home during a tropical storm, not in a poorly equipped clinic, not on the fucking ferry, but in a *goddamned hospital*!"

She continued to smile as she looked up at him. "You really need to calm down. It won't help me or the baby if you stroke out on me."

"If you want me to calm down, I want to hear you say we're going to pack our bags and go to the mainland today. We'll stay at Frank's." Mac pulled his cell from his pocket. "I'll call him now, but he won't care, especially if Joe and Janey don't need to stay there now."

Maddie took the phone from him. "Mac..."

"*What?*"

"We can't leave today."

"Why the hell not?"

"Because Thomas starts kindergarten next week, and we need to be here for that."

All the air left his body in one long exhale, because damn it, she was right. They couldn't miss the first day of kindergarten. "A few more days, and then we are leaving, do you hear me?"

"Yes, Mac, I think people on the mainland can hear you."

"I don't care if people on the mainland can hear me. As long as *you* can hear me, that's all that matters. And quit smiling at me. This isn't funny!"

"It is kind of funny when you lose your shit."

"I'm not losing my shit. I'm dead serious about getting you off this godforsaken island long before you have this baby."

"This godforsaken island is our home, and I don't like when you refer to it that way."

"You know what I mean. We should be raising our kids in a place with hospitals."

"Other than when babies are involved, when have we needed a hospital?"

"Just because we haven't needed one doesn't mean we won't. And look what happened when my dad fell off the dock." He shuddered with revulsion as he remembered the horror of that day.

"And he was totally fine thanks to you." She took his hands and gave a gentle tug. "Come with me."

"Where?"

"Just come with me." She towed him behind her as she headed for the stairs.

"I have to go back to work."

"You're on your lunch break, and you own the company."

Since he couldn't argue with either of those things and he was enjoying the view of her ass as she went up the stairs, he didn't protest.

"Where are my children?"

"Out to lunch with my mom and Ned."

Though still wound up and determined to get her to the mainland as soon as possible, he followed her docilely into their room, where she dropped his hands and turned to him.

"Take off your shirt."

"Why? I've got to go. We've got a big issue at the Hopper place, and Riley..."

She slipped her hands under his shirt and raised it, her palms flat against his stomach and chest. "Take. Off. Your. Shirt."

He reached behind him and pulled it over his head, tossing it aside. "It's off."

"Lie down on the bed, facedown."

"Maddie..."

She gave him a surprisingly forceful push that had him tumbling onto the bed, facedown the way she wanted him, causing her to burst out in a fit of giggles.

"I don't know what you think is so funny..." The words died on his lips when she straddled his back and began to massage his shoulders. Her touch, as always, was an instant turn-on. "Babe, that feels so good, but I don't have time—" He jolted when she pinched his ass—hard.

"Shut up and relax. Right now."

Something warm and slick slid over his skin, making him moan from the sensation of her hands on him. "What're you doing to me? I'm supposed to be working."

"I'm helping you relax so you don't have a heart attack or an embolism or some other sort of ism when your head explodes from stress. I am fine, the baby is fine, Janey is fine, our new baby niece is fine, Hailey and Thomas are fine, everyone you love is fine. You have to relax, Mac."

She was starting to turn him into a noodle with the gentle glide of her hands over his back. Then she added a light kneading of his muscles, and he might've started to drool. A little. "Won't relax until that baby is here and you're fine and the baby is fine."

"If we leave on the afternoon of the first day of school, will you be okay with that?"

"What about Thomas and school?"

"He can stay with Tiffany, and Hailey can stay with your parents or mine."

"What if it takes two weeks for the baby to come?"

"Then we spend two weeks away from our kids."

"That's a lot to ask of Tiff and Blaine when they have a new baby and Ashleigh, too."

"They won't mind. Thomas keeps Ashleigh entertained."

"I'll miss them if we're gone that long."

"We could ask Mom and Ned to bring them to see us on the weekends."

"True."

"Not to mention your business, which is busier than ever, what with the marina about to shut down for the season and the construction business booming, especially if your dad decides to go forward with the purchase of the Wayfarer. You'll be too busy to breathe."

He groaned at the thought of that massive project on top of everything else he had going on. No question he'd need to hire more guys if the purchase of the Wayfarer went through, and it was looking like it would. The thought of recruiting, hiring new employees and helping them find housing on the island made Mac tired just thinking about it. A couple of weeks off-island would put him deeply in the weeds, even with Shane keeping things moving while he was gone.

"*Or,*" she said, her hips moving in a suggestive rhythm, "we can stay here with our kids where we belong and have our baby at the clinic where the midwife I know and trust works and where the doctor who saved our daughter's life works."

"Are you manipulating me? Is that what this massage is about?"

"Absolutely not. I'm merely pointing out to you that taking off and going to the mainland to wait for a baby that might not arrive for weeks yet isn't as simple as you and me getting on a boat and leaving town."

He mumbled in reply.

"What's that you said?"

"I *know.*" The scented oil she was using must've had some sort of magic relaxing powers, because he suddenly felt like he could sleep for a year, except for the hard column of flesh beneath him that would keep him very much awake and far from relaxed until it was dealt with.

"Are you relaxing yet?" she asked.

"Most of me is. One part is still extremely agitated, and that's all your fault."

"All I did was rub your back."

"Right," he said on a low rumble of laughter. "That's *all* you did."

"I don't want to leave my kids for weeks, Mac."

"I don't want that, either."

"Then we agree we're going to stay here and have the baby at the clinic with the medical team that has monitored me throughout my pregnancy?"

He moaned, because that wasn't what he wanted, not at all. "The clinic is not a hospital."

"No, but after what happened with Janey, they're fully equipped for a C-section if it comes to that. I *trust* David and Vic with my life and the baby's life."

After several years of marriage, Mac was wise enough now to know when he'd been cornered and fully manipulated by the love of his life. "Fine," he muttered.

"Excuse me? I didn't quite hear you."

"*Fine*. Have it your way. But if anything happens to you, I will spank your ass until it's cherry red, Madeline."

"Oh yes, please. When can we do that?"

"Maddie! I'm serious."

"So am I. Nothing is going to happen, and I love when you 'punish' me for being an awful manipulative wife who knows just how to get what she wants from her adoring husband."

He grunted out a laugh. "You really are a shameless manipulator, Madeline McCarthy."

She kissed the back of his shoulder. "Stay there for a minute."

After the massage she'd given him, he couldn't have moved if the house had been on fire.

A towel appeared on the bed next to him. "Turn over and stay on the towel so the oil doesn't ruin my quilt."

"Yes, dear." After turning over, he opened his eyes and gasped at the sight of his gorgeous wife, standing naked before him, arms at her sides. Her pose touched him deeply as he knew how she felt about revealing her overly large breasts that were even more so when pregnant. To him, she was the most beautiful creature on earth. "Are you going to leave me in this stressed-out condition?" he asked, gesturing to his groin, all thoughts of work and the Hoppers' roof and hospitals obliterated by the sight of her, lovely and timid and all his.

Though his first impulse was to reach for her, he put his hands under his head to encourage her to take the lead.

She reached for the button to his shorts, unzipped him carefully over the huge bulge and tugged at the shorts to remove them and the boxer briefs.

Mac raised his hips, always willing to be helpful when his beautiful wife wanted him—and she'd wanted him a lot lately, not that he was complaining. He loved that pregnancy made her horny and was always happy to service her. The thought of saying that out loud had him choking back a laugh. She'd smack him if he said that, and he'd much rather she ride him than smack him.

He gasped in surprise when she leaned over him and took his hard cock into her mouth. Sinking his fingers into her silky hair, he closed his eyes and let the pleasure overtake him. To think, only a couple of years ago, he'd thought his single life in Miami was perfect. This… She… *They* were perfect. "Madeline…"

"Hmm?"

The vibration of her lips on his shaft nearly finished him off. Then she added some tongue action, and he moaned. "With you, babe. Come here." He reached for her and helped get her settled on top of him, the sight of her swollen lips and flushed cheeks making him even harder, if that was possible.

"Sexiest girl I've ever known," he said, gazing up at her.

She snorted with laughter. "*Right…* With my jumbo boobs and gigantic belly. Hot, hot, *hot*."

He took her face in his hands. "Sexiest. Girl. *I. Have. Ever. Known.*"

"You have to say that. You did this to me."

"I don't have to say anything, and I only say exactly what I mean, as you well know by now."

"You make me feel very lucky to have gotten knocked off my bike."

"Luckiest moment of my entire life," he said as she took him into her tight heat. "Although this one is shaping up to be rather lucky, too."

She smiled, her eyes dancing with joy. "Aren't you glad you came home for lunch?"

"I'm very, very glad." With his hands on her hips, he encouraged her to move. "God, that's so good. So, so good."

"Mmm, always is."

Needing to be closer to her, Mac sat up, wrapped his arms around her and kissed her sweet lips. "Is this comfortable for you?"

"Uh-huh, but our little friend is annoyed by the disruption." She took his hand and placed it over the skin that rippled with activity from within.

"Wow," Mac said, filled with wonder over what they'd created together. "Check that out." And he was unreasonably thankful every time he felt the baby move. After losing one, those little movements were so priceless to both of them. "I'm almost ashamed of what I'm doing to Mommy right now."

"You are not! Mac McCarthy doesn't know the word *shame*!"

He squeezed her ass cheeks, drawing a squeak of protest from her. "That is so not true. I am nothing if not humble."

Maddie lost it laughing.

Smiling, he massaged her back, which had given her so much grief during this pregnancy.

"That feels *so* good," she said, sighing. "I can't wait for the massages we're all getting at Daisy's bachelorette party."

Mac froze. "What massages?"

"I told you that."

"Um, no, you didn't. What massages?"

"I asked the team from the new spa to come give massages to all the girls. I know I told you this."

"You absolutely did not. Most of that 'team' are guys."

"So?" Her brows knitted with confusion.

"So I don't want some strange guy's hands on my wife."

"Oh, come on, Mac! They're professionals."

"Professionals or not, I don't want some happy-endings squad tending to my wife and her friends."

"You're out of your mind. *Happy endings?*"

"Everyone knows that's what massage is really about."

"Um, no, that's not true, and we're not talking about a massage parlor. We're talking about an upscale spa. For God's sake. Just when I think I've seen it all with you, you top yourself."

Mac was so disturbed by the thought of another man touching his wife, even in a professional sense, that he'd *almost* forgotten they were in the middle of having sex. "The other guys aren't going to be happy about this."

She swiveled her hips and tightened her inner muscles around his cock, drawing a sharp hiss from him.

"Don't try to change the subject, Madeline," he said through clenched teeth.

"Is that what I'm doing?" she asked, her expression innocent as she began to actively ride him.

His fingers dug into her hips, and he fought the sudden need to explode. He never let himself go until she had, not if he could help it anyway.

She picked up the pace, which made her breasts sway. And then she tossed her head back and stole the breath from his lungs when she cupped her breasts and toyed with her own nipples.

"*Fuck,*" he muttered, reaching down to where they were joined to coax her to an explosive finish. He was right behind her, coming so hard, he saw stars.

She sagged against him, her breathing ragged as she ran her fingers through his hair.

"You're not getting a massage with a guy, Madeline."

"Okay."

Her easy capitulation alarmed him. *His* Maddie was no pushover. He'd expected an argument, and her one-word answer made him only more determined to put a stop to her plans. No man was touching his wife. Mac didn't care how professional the guy was. Her body was a hands-off zone for all men, except for doctors and only when absolutely necessary. And that was his final word on the matter.

CHAPTER 11

Late on Friday afternoon, Kevin raced around the small house he shared with his sons, tending to dishes and dust and newspapers that'd piled up in the last few weeks. His housekeeping skills were better than they used to be, but there was still room for improvement. Chelsea's brother and his family were in town, and Kevin had invited them for a cookout tonight so she could enjoy her family without having to worry about cooking.

She'd taken the weekend off from the bar, and he looked forward to the time with her as well as the chance to get to know her family. He was also hoping to bridge some of the awkward distance that had persisted between them over the last few days, despite spending every night together.

By the end of the weekend, which would include their babysitting gig for Laura and Owen's kids on Sunday night, he hoped to have more clarity on the issue that had come between him and the woman he loved. The sad thing was, if you'd asked him a week ago if he could imagine anything coming between him and Chelsea, he would've said no, but that was before she told him she wanted a baby.

Speaking of babies, he'd spoken to his brother Mac earlier in the day and was happy to hear that Vivienne McCarthy Cantrell was doing splendidly and already had her grandpa wrapped firmly around her tiny finger. Thankfully, Janey was fine, too, and Joe was recovering from delivering his daughter on the ferry and having a vasectomy. They would have incredible stories to tell both their children about their births someday.

Kevin's cell phone rang, and he took the call without checking the caller ID.

"Kevin?"

The sound of his ex-wife's voice stopped him in his tracks. "Deb. What's up?" He'd never be rude to her, but he had no desire to stop what he was doing to chat with her, either.

"How are you?"

"Fine. You?"

"I'm okay."

"What can I do for you? I've got about two minutes before I need to be somewhere." That wasn't entirely true, but he hardly owed her any explanations.

"Did the boys tell you I'm coming over for a visit next week?"

"They mentioned something about that."

"I just wanted to check that it would be okay with you, too."

"Why would it matter to me if you're coming to see them?"

Her sigh sounded through the phone. "Because I'd like to see you, too."

"To say hello? Sure. I can make that happen."

"I was hoping we could talk, Kev."

Fuck. Fuck. Fuck. He had nothing to say to her. "About what?"

"Us," she said simply.

When had one little word packed a greater punch? He leaned against the counter and took a deep breath. "There is no *us* anymore, Deb. Our divorce will be final any day now."

"About that... I asked Len to put that on hold for the moment," she said, referring to her attorney.

Her statement shocked him. "*What?* Why?"

"Because I think we ought to be sure before we do something so permanent."

"Deb… I *am* sure. We're over. We were over long before you walked out the door and took up with someone else."

"I'm sorry about that, Kevin. I've told you that. It was a mistake that I genuinely regret."

"I'm sorry you have regrets, but ending the marriage shouldn't be one of them. That was the right thing for both of us." *Goddamn*, this was the *last* conversation he felt like having right now.

"Are you saying that because you have someone new?"

He'd wondered how much she knew about Chelsea. "I'm saying that because it's true. You and I stopped working years ago, and you know it as well as I do."

"It's because we stopped trying. Maybe if we put in some effort—"

"No, Deb," he said as gently as he possibly could. "I'm sorry if it hurts you to hear, but I don't want to go back. I'm happy with my life the way it is now."

"Because of your *girlfriend*?"

He gritted his teeth and held back the desire to snap at her. "In part, but also because I'm no longer in a relationship that made me unhappy for a long time. I take my share of the blame for that. Hell, I'll take more than my share because I should've done something about it years ago. But I can't go back. I can only go forward. And Chelsea isn't just my girlfriend. I'm in love with her."

"From what I hear, she's a lot younger than you are. Do you really think you can make a young girl happy long term?"

Her nasty question struck at the heart of his insecurities where Chelsea was concerned, but there was no way he'd ever let Deb know that. "Don't worry about her or us. Our relationship is none of your concern. I'm glad you're coming to see the boys, but I have nothing further to say to you about our marriage. The divorce is happening, so please stop trying to slow it down."

"Are you planning to marry her?"

"Again, not your concern. I hope we can maintain a cordial relationship for the sake of the boys, but I'd prefer that you not call me again. I have to go now."

"Kevin—"

"Bye, Deb." With shaking hands, he pressed the red button to end the call.

"Dad?"

He startled when Riley appeared in the doorway. "I didn't know you were home."

"I just came in a few minutes ago. I couldn't help but overhear that. Are you okay?"

"Of course," he said, forcing a smile for his son. "I'm fine."

"What did Mom want?"

"She… was hoping for a reconciliation, I think."

"I'm kind of surprised that she'd ask for that when the divorce is set to be final any time."

"Apparently, she's hit the Pause button on that, which doesn't please me." Kevin ran his hands through his hair, summoning calm and trying to put the uncomfortable conversation behind him so he could focus on Chelsea and their plans for the evening. "I feel bad that you had to overhear that."

Riley shrugged. "No biggie."

"She said she's coming to see you guys."

"Yeah, Tuesday into Wednesday."

"Does it bother you that I really don't want to see her?"

"I'd be surprised if you did after the way things went down a year ago."

"You'd tell me the truth, right?"

"It's fine, Dad. Don't sweat it."

"You're getting home late."

"I had some things come up at work today that I needed to deal with. Now I need a shower before I meet the boys for poker night. The ladies are having a bachelorette party for Daisy that has everyone up in arms."

"What now?"

"Apparently, Maddie hired male massage therapists for the party, and the guys are none too pleased."

Kevin huffed out a laugh. "They're ridiculous."

"I agree, but try telling them that. This ought to be an entertaining evening."

"I worry about you and Finn spending too much time with your cousins and deciding never to get married because of what you're learning from them."

Riley laughed. "Don't worry. I also see that they're stupidly happy most of the time."

"That they are."

"What're you up to tonight?"

"Chelsea is bringing her brother's family over for dinner."

"First time you're meeting her brother?"

"Yeah." Suddenly, Kevin was unreasonably nervous, which Riley picked up on.

"Don't sweat it, Dad. They'll like you. What's not to like?"

Kevin smiled at his son. "Thanks."

Riley went to shower while Kevin continued to clean up before getting to work on making a salad and slicing cheese to put with crackers. Then he got out the ground beef he'd bought, added his special blend of Worcestershire sauce and garlic powder to it and made the burgers using the "burger pounder" the boys had given him for Christmas after he said he wished he'd brought the one he'd had at home.

When they'd lived at home, Kevin had made burgers for dinner every Sunday night. That'd been the beginning and the end of his culinary prowess, which had expanded since his divorce to include Christmas turkey, omelets, spaghetti and barbecued chicken, to name a few things he'd attempted since being single. But the burgers were his specialty, and he hoped Chelsea's family enjoyed them as much as his did.

When the food was ready and the house as clean as it could be, Kevin went into his room to change into a button-down shirt and clean jeans. He sat on the bed and rolled up his sleeves, trying not to think about the things Deb had said, but they kept invading his thoughts. He reached for his cell phone and dashed off a text to his attorney, Dan Torrington.

Deb told Len to pause the divorce because she was hoping for a reconciliation that's not going to happen. Could you please get with him and make sure it's still moving? I want it final ASAP.

Dan wrote right back. *Absolutely. I'll reach out to him over the weekend and keep you posted.*

Thank you.

Try not to worry. You're close...

He was close, but not close enough. For months, as the divorce wound its way slowly through the various legal machinations, Kevin had been fearful that he'd lose his chance with Chelsea because it was taking too long. After what she'd been through with her parents, she'd never been entirely comfortable with his "separated and seeking divorce" status, so he'd been looking forward to the day he could tell her he was finally free and clear. Hearing Deb wanted to pause the proceedings made him feel panicked.

The doorbell rang, and he took a deep breath to change gears so he could focus on Chelsea and her family. There was nothing he could do tonight about Deb or the divorce, and a lot was riding on tonight for him and Chelsea. That was where his attention needed to be focused.

He went to answer the door and stepped back to allow Chelsea, her brother, sister-in-law, niece and nephew into the house just as Riley appeared, fresh from the shower.

Chelsea's brother extended a hand to Riley. "You must be Kevin. I'm Andrew Rose. It's so nice to finally meet you."

"Um, I'm Riley, Kevin's son." He pointed to his father. "That's Kevin."

Andrew's eyes widened in what could only be called shock, which he quickly tried to mask. "Oh. My bad." He reached out to shake hands with Kevin. "Nice to meet you."

"You, too." Kevin glanced at Chelsea and wondered why she'd failed to tell her brother he was older than she was.

Chelsea put her arm around Kevin, which went a long way toward reassuring him. "This is my sister-in-law, Lydia, and my niece, Josie, and my nephew, Travis. This is Kevin and his son, Riley."

"Nice to meet you all." Kevin shook hands with each of them. The kids were four and six and obviously adored their aunt Chelsea. "Come in and make yourselves at home. What can I get you to drink?" As he started to walk away, he caught the odd look Andrew directed at his sister, who ignored him and the awkwardness that had suddenly crept into the gathering.

"I'm headed out," Riley said. "You all have a nice evening."

"You, too, son."

"Nice to meet you," Andrew called after him. To Kevin, he said, "How old is your son?"

"He's twenty-eight, and his brother, Finn, is twenty-six."

"Huh," Andrew said as he accepted the beer Kevin had opened for him. Like Chelsea, he was tall with blond hair and gray-blue eyes, the resemblance between the siblings striking. His wife was petite compared to him and Chelsea, with dark hair and eyes. Both kids were blond with blue eyes and friendly smiles.

Kevin wanted to ask Andrew what "huh" meant, but he didn't. Rather, he served glasses of wine to the women and offered lemonade to the kids. "Let's go outside. It's nice out tonight." He showed them onto the back deck, which the boys had joked was bigger than the living room. They'd spent a lot of time out there during the summer, and Kevin would miss the extra space when the colder weather arrived.

Maybe by then, he would've convinced Chelsea that they should get a place of their own that was bigger than either of their two houses. Was he getting ahead of himself and their current dilemma by thinking about them living together? And why did he feel that everything was suddenly so uncertain, from the divorce to his relationship with Chelsea? He hated that and was determined to find a way past the uncertainty as soon as possible.

"I hope everyone likes burgers," Kevin said as he fired up the grill.

"Sounds great," Chelsea said, smiling at him. "What can I do to help?"

"Not a thing. Relax and enjoy." He went inside to retrieve the burgers from the fridge.

Andrew followed him. "How old are you?"

Startled by the blunt question, Kevin looked him directly in the eye. "Fifty-two. You?"

"Thirty-eight."

"What do you really want to ask me, Andrew?"

"What're you doing with my sister, who is, if my math is correct, *sixteen years* younger than you?"

Kevin stared at him, shocked by his audacity. But then he reminded himself that Andrew was looking out for his sister and kept his tone neutral when he replied. "I love her. I hope I'm making her happy."

Andrew's shoulders lost some of their rigidity, but he still seemed agitated. "She says you're still married."

"Not for much longer, and that was over before I met Chelsea."

"I don't mean to be a dick, but she's been through a lot..."

"I know."

Andrew looked up at him, and in one second of eye contact, Kevin could see the residual hurt he carried with him, too. "I don't want to see her hurt again."

"Neither do I. That's the last thing I want."

The screen door slid open and then closed as Chelsea came inside. "Everything all right in here?"

Kevin looked to Andrew to answer for both of them.

"Yeah, sure," Andrew said. "Kevin and I are getting to know each other better."

"You're not being a prosecutor right now, are you?" Chelsea asked her brother.

He smiled at her. "Me? I don't know what you're talking about."

"Sure, you don't." To Kevin, she added, "He's 'prosecuted' every guy I've ever dated."

Andrew put his arm around his sister. "Just making sure they're worthy of you."

Chelsea elbowed him. "I like this one. Don't run him off."

"I have a feeling this one won't easily be run off," Andrew said.

Kevin released a breath he hadn't realized he'd been holding, feeling as if he'd passed some sort of test with Chelsea's brother.

CHAPTER 12

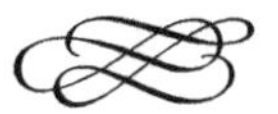

The rest of the evening passed without any further tension. Kevin enjoyed getting to know Andrew and his family. While the kids played in the yard, Lydia, who was obviously close to Chelsea, told a couple of funny stories about Chelsea that Kevin had never heard before,

"So, she really knocked someone into the cake at a wedding?" Kevin asked, incredulous.

Lydia couldn't stop laughing long enough to reply.

"Have you *seen* her on the dance floor?" Andrew asked. "Everyone is in danger!"

"That is so not true!" Chelsea protested. "I was *pushed*. That's my story, and I'm sticking to it."

"And the bride and groom," Lydia said between gasps of laughter, "they had to cut the cake from the *floor*."

Kevin laughed at the picture of chaos she painted.

"If you laugh at this story," Chelsea said with a menacing scowl, "I'm never having sex with you again."

Andrew put his hands over his ears. "Stop it right now. My baby sister does not have sex."

Kevin rolled his eyes. "You sound like my nephews. Their younger sister has two kids, and they still think she's as pure as the driven snow."

"Sisters don't have sex," Andrew said. "That's my final word on the matter."

"I wouldn't know," Kevin said. "I only have brothers."

"You're a lucky man. Sisters are a burden we brothers have to bear."

"Shut up, Andrew," Chelsea said, giving him a shove that had him laughing.

The kids wandered over to join them, and Josie curled up in Chelsea's lap while Travis stood next to her chair. She put one arm around the little girl and made her giggle with kisses to her neck while putting her other arm around her nephew to bring him closer to her. Watching her with the kids tonight had been a revelation to Kevin. She was so natural and comfortable with them, and he'd been given a glimpse of what kind of mother she would be.

"I hate to say it, but we need to get the kids back to the hotel," Lydia said. "This has been fun. Thank you for the hospitality, Kevin."

"It was my pleasure. I hope to see you again before you leave."

"Dinner tomorrow night?" Andrew asked. "On us?"

Kevin glanced at Chelsea, who said, "We'd love to."

"Excellent."

Andrew and Lydia helped them carry plates and condiments in from the deck and gathered their kids. "Thanks again for an enjoyable evening," Andrew said, extending his hand to Kevin.

"It was nice to finally meet you."

"Likewise."

Kevin stood in the doorway while Chelsea walked them out, giving her a minute to say her goodbyes. She rejoined him to wave as they drove off in her car. He put his arm around her. "That was fun."

"It really was, but I feel like I interrupted something between you and Andrew in the kitchen."

"Just two guys getting to know each other."

She raised a brow. "That's all it was?"

Kevin followed her to the kitchen, where they worked together to clean up. "He was a little concerned about our age difference."

"I almost died when he mistook Riley for you. I felt bad about that."

"I have to wonder why you never mentioned to him that I'm quite a bit older than you."

She shrugged. "Because it doesn't matter to me."

"That's nice to hear, but I think your brother would prefer to see you with a young guy like Riley rather than an old goat like me."

Chelsea slipped her arms around him from behind. "You're my old goat."

Kevin laughed and made a goat noise.

"Should I be concerned that you do that so well?"

He turned to her, put his arms around her and kissed her. "Hello."

"Hi there."

"I've been wanting to kiss you for hours."

"Me, too, but I'm mad at you for laughing at the cake story."

"I couldn't help it. That was hilarious."

"Not at the time, it wasn't."

"Maybe not for you, but for everyone else at the wedding, it was pretty damned funny."

"Luckily, the bride was drunk by the time she had to cut the cake and didn't realize her cake was on the floor."

Kevin smiled at her, enchanted as always when she was nearby. "I was thinking earlier…"

"About?"

"Our living situation."

"What about it?"

"This place is kinda crowded with three of us, and yours is too small for three of us." He shrugged. "I was thinking we ought to get a bigger place. Together."

"Wait," she said, shaking her head. "*Three* of us?"

"You, me and the baby we might have together." Kevin wasn't sure exactly when he'd come around to the idea of having a baby with her, but now that he had, the thought of their child excited rather than scared him.

"Kevin... What're you saying?"

"I'm saying I love you, I love us, and if we're lucky enough to have a child together, I'll love our baby, too."

"You mean it?"

"I'd never say it if I didn't."

She rested her forehead against his chest and took a deep shuddering breath.

"Are you okay?" he asked.

She nodded. "I thought I'd ruined everything."

"You haven't ruined anything. You told me what you wanted, and you should always do that."

Raising her head, she looked up at him, her eyes shiny with unshed tears. "And you're sure this is what you want?"

"I want you. And I want you to be happy."

"I want that for you, too. If you're only doing this for me—"

He placed a finger over her lips. "I'm doing this for *us*. Up until I met you, my boys were the best part of my life, and they still are. Don't get me wrong. But this, with you... I've never been as happy as I am with you, Chels. I just want you and this for the rest of my life. I might not have planned to fall madly in love with a woman who wants children, but that's what happened. So now I roll with it."

She wiped away a flood of tears. "Sorry to be so dramatic, but I've gone from thinking I'd ruined us to hearing you want to move in together and have a baby."

Smiling, he drew her into his embrace. "I don't mean to give you whiplash, babe."

She hugged him as tightly as he hugged her.

He kissed the top of her head. "Come on. Let's go to bed."

"We need to finish the dishes."

"They can wait until the morning."

. . .

RILEY'S HEAD WASN'T IN THE CARD GAME, WHICH WAS WHY HE'D ALREADY lost a hundred bucks to Mac, who was on fire. They were at Mac's house while the girls gathered at Janey's to celebrate her homecoming with baby Vivienne and Daisy's upcoming wedding.

"What's with you tonight?" Finn asked when they were on a beer break. "You're not usually so easily taken for a ride at the poker table."

"Tired. Long day at work."

"Where'd you disappear to all day? I thought you were just doing a patch at the Hoppers' and then coming back."

"The Hopper house is more complicated than we thought."

"Have you seen Jordan?"

Riley shook his head. "Just her sister, Nikki. Did you know Jordan's a twin?"

"Hadn't heard that," Finn said, studying him more intently now. "What's the sister like?"

"She's nice. Got a lot on her plate with what's going on with Jordan and a leaking roof."

"Huh," Finn said, taking a drink of his beer.

"What does that mean?"

"Nothing. Just wondering how you know so much about what the sister has on her plate. That's all."

Riley had walked right into Finn's trap. "Because she told me?"

Finn's eyes glittered with mischief. "I thought you were on the roof. Was she up there with you?"

Riley wanted to punch him, but before he could make a fist, a shout went out across the room that had him turning to see what was going on.

"*You've got to be fucking kidding me,*" Blaine Taylor roared, his face turning a scary shade of red. "Guys are *massaging* them?"

"That's what we heard," Adam said. "But we can't go over there."

"The hell we can't!" Blaine said. He still wore his uniform and had his weapon holstered at his hip. "No guy is massaging my wife except for *me*."

"If we go over there," Grant said, "they're going to mock us for the rest of our lives, and frankly, we'd deserve it."

"If you don't care about some strange guy having his hands all over your wife, then stay here," Blaine said, "but *I'm* going."

"I'm going with him," Mac said.

"Has it occurred to you that this is another setup?" Grant asked his brother.

"Why would she do the same thing she's already done to us?" Mac asked. "We'd see right through that."

"You're about to go running over there on the outside chance that guys are massaging them," Adam said.

Mac thought about that for a second. "Maddie told me she'd booked massages with the guys from the spa. I told her she'd better not have, but that doesn't mean she didn't do it anyway."

"If you girls are done sharing your feelings," Blaine said, teeth gritted, "I'm going to get my wife." He stormed out the door that led to Mac's deck and clomped down the stairs.

Mac chased after him. "Blaine! Wait for me."

Sighing, Adam said, "We'd better go with them to make sure they don't do anything stupid."

"It's probably already too late for that," Grant said as the two of them gave chase.

"I don't know about you," Riley said to Finn, "but I want to see this."

"Me, too," Luke said as Shane and Evan nodded in agreement.

"They never learn," Shane said.

"That's what makes them so entertaining," Luke said, shaking his head as he laughed.

They piled into Luke's truck for the short drive to Joe and Janey's and arrived right behind Blaine and Mac, who were in Blaine's truck. Blaine was in such a rush that he left the driver's side door open in his haste to get to Tiffany.

What might it be like, Riley wondered, to be so crazy about a woman that you did stupid things in the name of love, such as barging into a girls-only gathering like a battering ram on steroids? Riley wouldn't know because he'd never had those feelings for a woman.

Sure, he knew they existed, saw regular examples of it every day among his cousins and their friends, but he hadn't experienced it.

Sometimes he wondered if there was something wrong with him that had made him miss out on something even his own brother had experienced with Missy, not that he'd want that kind of relationship for himself. That was one chick who was *way* more trouble than she was worth, at least as far as he was concerned.

Following his cousins into Janey's house, he stood back to watch the show unfold, and what a show it turned out to be.

"What the hell is going on here?" Blaine bellowed, startling the women and waking the baby sleeping in Janey's arms.

Vivienne let out a lusty cry that had all the women scowling at Blaine.

Tiffany got up from her spot on the floor and went to her husband, placing a hand on his chest and pushing him backward out of the room where the women were gathered in a circle that also included Maddie, Stephanie, Daisy, Mallory, Victoria, Grace, Sydney Harris, Jenny Martinez, Hope Martinez, Erin Barton and Lizzie James.

From what Riley could see, there was no sign of men, except for Joe, who came downstairs and took the baby from Janey.

"What's the deal, boys?" Joe asked as he patted the baby's back and succeeded in soothing her.

Grant began to laugh, and he couldn't seem to stop. He bent at the waist and howled while Mac and Blaine scowled at him.

"What I think the deal is, Joe," Adam said, "is that our friends Mac and Blaine were led to believe there would be male massage therapists here tending to their wives, and apparently, that was a problem for our intrepid friends."

Joe laughed as he patted Vivienne's back, calming her instantly. "You guys never learn, do you?"

"Maddie told me there would be *men* giving massages," Mac said, scowling at his wife.

"I don't recall saying that," she said, giving her husband a sly smile.

"I said I'd asked them to give us massages. I never said they'd accepted. Turns out they were booked tonight. Such a bummer."

Blaine scowled at Mac. "*Seriously?*"

"She said it! I swear to God!"

"She was *pranking us*," Blaine said, fuming. "And you fell for it. *Again!*"

"So did you!"

Maddie began to laugh, taking the other women with her. "You are *so* easy," she said, gasping for air and wiping tears from her eyes. "So, *so* easy."

Mac glared at her. "Make no mistake about it, this is a declaration of *war*, my love."

Maddie dismissed his comment with a wave of her hand. "You don't scare me." The words were no sooner out of her mouth when she grimaced. Placing her hand over her pregnant belly, she took a deep breath.

"What?" Mac asked her.

"That felt like a contraction."

"Very funny," he said. "You've already had your way with me and won this round. Enjoy your success while it lasts."

She looked up at him, and the fear he saw in her eyes stopped his heart. "I'm not joking, Mac."

"No! Not yet. *You promised me no baby until after Thomas starts school and we can go to the mainland!*"

The words came out like one long chant that put Riley on edge as he watched the scene play out before him.

Maddie was about to reply when her face twisted once again in a grimace. "Ugh," she said, moaning. "*That* was definitely a contraction."

Victoria jumped into action. "Let's get you to the clinic so we can see what's going on. Daisy, will you please call David and have him meet us there?"

"Why do you need him?" Mac asked. "What do you think is wrong?"

"Nothing is wrong," Victoria assured him. "But if she's going to deliver this baby, I want him there."

"She is *not* going to deliver this baby," Mac said, "because it's not due for two more weeks!"

Adam stepped forward, took Mac by the arm and pulled him back. "You need to take a breath, man. If you have a heart attack, you won't be any good to Maddie when she needs you—and she needs you right now."

"This isn't supposed to happen yet," Mac muttered, his eyes fixed on Maddie, who was being helped up by Victoria and Stephanie.

"I know, but it *is* happening, and you need to get it together," Adam said, giving Mac a shake to snap him out of his stupor.

He crossed the room to Maddie, lifted her into his arms and carried her from the house with a new look of determination in his eyes.

"Holy shit," Finn whispered.

Riley couldn't have said it better himself. There was a lot to be said for being single—and staying that way.

CHAPTER 13

Mac told himself to calm the fuck down and focus on Maddie and keeping her safe. Although, calming down when your heart was about to explode was easier said than done.

"Mac," she said, gasping between contractions that seemed to be coming fast and furious—and how the *fuck* was that even possible? "Don't be mad at me. I was just teasing about the guys massaging us, and I honestly didn't know that the tightness I've been feeling was labor. I swear."

That she could think he was honestly mad at her made him feel like an asshole. "I'm not mad. I'm worried."

"Oh," she said, panting. "'Cause you look kinda mad."

"I'm not mad."

He kept his eyes on the road and both hands on the wheel, determined to get her to the clinic as quickly and as safely as possible.

A sniffling sound had him taking his eyes off the road to look at her. "Why're you crying? Does it hurt that bad?"

"It hurts, but it's nothing I can't handle."

"Then what?"

"I don't want you to be mad. I promised you there would be no drama this time, and now there's drama and—"

"Madeline."

She took a deep breath and hiccupped on a sob.

"I swear to God I'm not mad. "

"At least… it's not… *ugh*… being born… on the ferry," she said, releasing a long deep breath at the end of another contraction.

Mac grunted out a laugh. "There is that."

"See, so it could be worse."

He risked taking a hand off the wheel to grasp her hand and hold on tight. "It's going to be okay," he said, praying it was true.

"Kids… need… to call… parents," she said, panting her way through another contraction.

Had it even been two minutes since the last one? Was it possible to have a stroke from being afraid? "I'll call them. Don't worry about anything. I'll call your mom and ask her to keep the kids for us. My mom will help, too. Everything is fine. Don't worry about anything."

"Scared," she said, looking at him with big, frightened, caramel-colored eyes.

"Don't be. Victoria is the best, and David will be there, too. You've got this, babe."

With every word he said, Mac became more determined to put his own panic aside to focus on keeping her calm. When they arrived at the clinic, he pulled up to the main door, shut off the engine and bounded around to the passenger side to retrieve Maddie.

Victoria's car was already in the lot, and the lights were on inside. She directed Mac to one of the exam rooms down the hall from the waiting area, leaving a gown on the end of the bed. "Do you need my help to get changed?" Victoria asked.

"I'll help her," Mac said.

"I'll be back in a minute to get Maddie on a monitor and check where we are."

"Thanks, Vic," Maddie said. Her hands shook as she reached for the hem of the dress she'd worn to Daisy's party.

"I've got it, hon. You don't have to do anything."

"I ruined Daisy's bachelorette party," she said, tears sliding down her cheeks.

He raised the dress up and over her head and helped her out of her panties, leaving her bra on because he knew she preferred it. "You didn't ruin anything. Daisy will understand."

She slid her arms through the holes in the gown he held for her, and then gasped when another sharp pain gripped her. "God, I already feel the need to push," she said through gritted teeth.

"Not yet, babe," Mac said, helping her into bed. "Wait for Vic to give the okay."

"Here I am." Victoria breezed into the room wearing a big smile. Her dark hair had been contained in a ponytail, and she'd changed into scrubs. "Let's see what we've got." She positioned Maddie's feet in stirrups and raised the gown so she could examine her. "Oh, hello there!" Looking up at Maddie, she said, "You're about to deliver."

Tightening her grip on Mac's hand, Maddie said, "Please tell me I can push."

"On the next contraction," Vic said, "let's do it." She moved around the room, gathering the supplies she needed.

David came into the room. "Hey, guys. I hear your little one is upending your plans."

Mac looked at the man who would've been his brother-in-law and saw nothing but confidence and competence. Having Vic and David in the room went a long way toward soothing his nerves.

"She's set to deliver," Vic told him.

"Whoa, that was fast. What can I do?"

"Get her on a monitor for me."

Things got real after that, with Maddie pushing, Mac supporting her back, David keeping an eye on the fetal monitor and Victoria positioned between Maddie's legs. Fifteen minutes later, their son arrived, his little face red with rage as he let out a lusty howl.

"You did it, babe," Mac said, kissing her and wiping away her tears while she did the same for him. "He's beautiful."

"Just what this world needs," Maddie said with a tired smile. "Another McCarthy man."

Mac returned her smile and kissed her again. "Is he okay, David?"

"He's perfect. What's his name?"

Mac looked to Maddie, giving her the floor. After all, she'd done the hard work. She sighed. "Don't blame me for this, but meet Malcom John McCarthy the third. We've got *another* Mac McCarthy on our hands."

"Oh, dear God," Victoria said with a teasing grin for Mac. She was still tending to Maddie in the aftermath of the baby's arrival.

"Hey!" Mac said as he took the tiny bundle from David and gazed down at the gorgeous little face. "Don't worry, buddy. I'll show you how to be the best Mac McCarthy of the bunch of us."

"No, you won't," Maddie said, reaching for her son. "You'll be allowed contact with him once a week so you don't ruin him."

Mac laughed as he settled the baby in her arms. "Look at him," he said, amazed by the little eyes that moved around, checking things out. He'd learned when they had Hailey that babies couldn't see much of anything at first, but his son seemed to be looking right at him and liking what he saw.

It was hard to believe that Mac had once thought fatherhood wasn't in the cards for him. It made him sick now to think about what he might've missed if he hadn't crashed into a gorgeous woman on a bike.

"What're you thinking about?" Maddie asked him.

"The bike."

She smiled up at him. "Best thing to ever happen to me."

He kissed her again. "Me, too."

THE RINGING PHONE DRAGGED KEVIN OUT OF A SOUND SLEEP. HE AND Chelsea had crashed early, and he had no idea what time it was when he took the call from his brother Mac.

"What's up?"

"Sorry to wake you, but I had to tell you that Malcolm John McCarthy the third arrived two weeks early tonight! Two grandbabies in one week. Can you stand it?"

"Congrats," Kevin said, sitting up in bed. "How's Maddie?"

"Just fine, thank goodness. Mac's a mess. Can't stop crying, but everyone is fine, and this old man is relieved to have our new little ones safely here with hardly any drama this time around."

"I'm happy for all of you," Kevin said. "I know how concerned you were about both of them."

"You have no idea, my friend. Lost a lotta sleep worrying about something going wrong. Huge relief to have it over and done with."

"I can only imagine. Can't wait to meet them."

"Go back to sleep. I'll talk to you tomorrow."

"Tell Linda I said congrats."

"Will do. Night."

"Night, Mac." Kevin ended the call, put the phone on the bedside table and lay back down, wide awake after the big news.

"Everything okay?" Chelsea asked, snuggling up to him.

He drew her warm, naked body in closer to him and ran his hand over her silky skin. "Mac and Maddie had their baby, a boy named Malcom John the third. Another Mac McCarthy."

"Oh jeez. Just what we need!"

Kevin laughed. He had his own doubts about whether the world was ready for another Mac McCarthy. "My brother is weak with relief that both babies have safely arrived and their mothers are doing great."

"I'm sure. That's the downside to island life. No hospitals."

"We've got a damned good clinic here."

"Yes, we do, but still... It's not a hospital."

"One thing we haven't talked about in all these plans we've been making is whether you want to continue to live here. You want to have a baby, but there's no hospital here."

"I'd love to stay here, but only if that's what you want, too."

"I do. I love it here and feel totally at home after a year. If there's a baby, I guess we'll figure out the medical stuff the same way everyone else does."

"I still can't believe we're actually going to do this."

"I was thinking that we should probably get married at some point."

She gasped. "Really? I thought you never wanted to get married again."

"When did I say that?"

"In the bar one night, around the time we first met."

"Was I drunk?"

"It was the night I called Mac to come get you."

Kevin winced and ran his fingers through his hair, trying to find the words he needed, the words she deserved. "I was hurt and drunk and rejected and spouting off. I'm sorry you heard me say that and all this time you thought I meant it."

"I can understand why you felt that way. After what my dad did, I said I'd never get married, either."

"And now?" he asked, hanging breathlessly while waiting for her reply.

"Things change," she said softly. "The right guy comes along and suddenly it doesn't matter what my dad did, because he's nothing like my dad. He's loyal and honorable and family-oriented and the best friend I've ever had."

Kevin turned toward her, rested his hand on her face and kissed her. "You've changed everything for me, you know that, don't you? My life was in ruins, but then you came along and showed me a whole new beautiful way forward." He kissed her for a long time, pouring all the love he felt for her into the kiss.

"Are you *sure* you want to get married again?" she asked when they finally came up for air. "You're not even officially divorced yet. I'd understand if you need some time to—"

Kevin kissed her again. "I don't need time to know that I want to spend whatever is left of my life with you and my boys and the family we'll make together."

"If you're sure... I don't want you to feel pressured to do anything that doesn't work for you."

"I don't feel pressured. Although, it is kind of funny that my brothers are having grandchildren while I'm considering the possibility of another child."

"Our baby will keep you young at heart." After a pause, she said, "Did we just get engaged?"

"Not quite yet, but when we do, you won't have to ask."

THEY SPENT MOST OF THE NEXT DAY WITH ANDREW'S FAMILY AND WAVED them off on the four o'clock boat on Sunday afternoon.

"That was fun," Kevin said as they walked back to Chelsea's place to shower and change before heading to their babysitting gig with Laura and Owen's kids.

"It was nice to see them. And I'm glad you finally got to meet them. Andrew liked you."

"You think so?"

"I know he did. He told me so. He said he was skeptical of the fact that you're older than me at first, but after spending time with us, he can see how happy I am, and that's all that matters to him."

"I'm glad he approves."

When they were showered and dressed, they walked the short distance to the Sand & Surf Hotel, where Laura and Owen lived and worked. His grandparents had given them the hotel as a wedding gift last year, after the two of them had completely renovated the old hotel.

"I love this place," Chelsea said when they stepped into the lobby where Owen's mom, Sarah, was working at the front desk.

"Hi there," Sarah said. "Laura told me you were coming to babysit the hooligans. You can go on up to the third floor. Charlie and I will be around tonight if you need help."

"I'm sure we can handle it," Kevin said as a twinge of unease crept in. "How hard can it be?"

Sarah laughed. "You're about to find out."

"I'm scared," Chelsea said.

With his hand on her back, Kevin guided her toward the stairs. "Too late to turn back now."

On the third floor, they were greeted by the pervasive sound of crying babies.

Chelsea stopped walking. "Umm."

Kevin nudged her along. "We got this, babe. No worries."

"Easy for you to say. You're an experienced baby wrangler. I have limited experience."

"Just think—after this, you'll be an expert."

Her grimace made him laugh as he knocked on the door to Laura and Owen's apartment.

Owen came to the door, a wild look in his eyes and a massive stain in the middle of his pressed light blue dress shirt.

"Looks like you took a direct hit," Kevin said.

"You don't know the half of it." Owen stepped aside. "Enter at your own risk."

Kevin gave Chelsea another nudge to get her into the apartment, which looked like it'd been hit by a bomb made of toys and baby paraphernalia.

"Sorry about the mess," Owen said. "It's been a day and a half around here. Joey has been colicky, Holden has an ear infection, and Jon has diaper rash. Good times all around. Laura was going to call you to say this might not be the best night for you to watch them."

Disappointment radiated from Owen. This was a man who clearly needed some time alone with his wife, and Kevin was determined to make that happen. "No worries," Kevin said, rolling up his sleeves. "We can handle this, right, Chels?"

She gave him a deer-in-the-headlights look. "Umm..."

"The good news is Holden is down for the count, so we're back to a man-to-man defense," Owen said. "It's when they outnumber us that we get into trouble."

Laura emerged from the bedroom with a baby in each arm, both of them crying.

Owen took one of them from her and began patting the baby's back with practiced expertise.

"I meant to call you to reschedule," Laura said. Her blonde hair hung in shiny waves around her shoulders, and she wore a black dress that showed off a trim figure, despite having had three children in two years. She'd bounced right back from having the twins six months ago.

"If you guys still want to go, we don't mind watching them," Kevin said, wondering if he would regret his own generosity. But he felt for his niece and her husband, who'd obviously had a rough day.

Laura glanced at Owen. "What do you want to do?" She spoke loudly to be heard over the roar of crying babies.

"It's up to you. Will you be able to relax if we leave them in this state?"

"It's time for their bottles, so maybe that will settle them."

"We'll give them their bottles," Kevin said, taking one of the babies from Owen while Chelsea took the other from Laura. "You guys get out of here, and if we need you, we'll call."

"Let me change my shirt," Owen said, making for the bedroom, as if afraid Kevin might change his mind.

"You're sure about this, Uncle Kev?" Laura asked as she heated bottles in the apartment's galley kitchen while Kevin and Chelsea sat on the sofa with the babies, who were screaming even harder now that they'd been turned over to strangers.

"I'm sure, sweetheart. Take a break."

"Right at this moment, I love you more than anyone in this world."

Kevin laughed. "I remember what it's like to have little ones. It's intense."

"That's a good word to describe it." She handed him a bottle and gave the other to Chelsea. "They're both bathed, their diapers changed, and they're ready for bed. Miss Joanna almost always falls asleep having her bottle, so the goal is to transfer her into the crib if you can."

Chelsea nodded as she took the baby, knitted her brows in concentration and offered the bottle to Joanna while Kevin fed Jonathan.

The sudden silence made his ears ring after the loud crying.

Owen came out of the bedroom wearing a different shirt that hadn't been ironed, but he didn't seem to care. "Let's go while we can," he said, taking Laura's hand to tug her toward the door. "Call if you need us."

"Go have a nice time," Kevin said, transfixed by the sight of the little lips sucking on the nipple. "We'll be okay."

Owen tugged her through the door and closed it behind them.

"Holy crap," Chelsea whispered. "How do they do it?"

"Just think," Kevin said, in a teasing tone, "there's another one, too."

CHAPTER 14

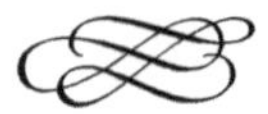

The babies put them through their paces—crying, diaper changes, more crying, waking each other up and eventually, waking Holden, too, which was when things really got interesting, because he wanted his mommy and daddy, *not* his uncle Kevin.

Hours later, the three of them had finally exhausted themselves—and their caregivers—and were blessedly asleep at the same time.

"Holy. *Shit.*" Chelsea dropped to the sofa, put her feet up on the coffee table and her head back, closing her eyes.

Kevin sat next to her, whimpering like a little girl. "I'd forgotten what that was like."

"I've never seen anything like that *in my life*!"

"Owen and Laura could run a class for teenagers that would reduce teen pregnancy to zero."

"That's for sure."

"Still want one of your own?"

"Absolutely not," she said, laughing as she glanced over at him.

"Aw, come on. You're not going to be that easily scared off, are you? It wouldn't be like this for us."

"And you know that how?"

"First of all, we'd be having one, not three, and second of all, you're hardly ever going to see colic, ear infections and diaper rash in the same kid on the same day. This was what's commonly known as a perfect storm."

"True." She looked at him, her expression uncertain. "You really think I could do this? That I'd be a good mother?"

He took her hand and brought it to his lips. "You'd be a wonderful mother." He brushed at something on her face.

"What?"

"Um, I think you have baby poop on your face."

She busted up laughing. "I do not!"

He took a whiff of his finger and groaned. "I'm afraid you do."

"Get it off me!"

Laughing, Kevin got up to wash his hands and get a paper towel for her and stubbed his toe on one of Holden's trucks. *"Fuck,"* he muttered.

"Language, Doctor McCarthy. If you're going to be a daddy again, you gotta clean it up."

"Christ, I just got to the point where I can swear again." He sat next to her and washed the smudge of baby poop off her face. "You look kind of cute with poop on your face."

"There is nothing cute about poop on my face."

Nodding, he leaned in to kiss her. "Everything about you is cute."

"So what time were we expecting Laura and Owen back? It's after midnight."

"Is it?" Kevin asked, surprised they were out so late. "Time flies when you're having fun."

"Maybe you should call them."

"I'll send a text." He pulled out his phone and sent a text to Laura asking if they were planning an all-nighter. The text was delivered but went unread. "Hmm." He waited a few minutes without a reply and then called her.

"Oh my God!" Laura shrieked as she answered the phone. "Owen! Wake up! The alarm didn't go off!"

Chuckling, Kevin held the phone so Chelsea could hear. "Where are you guys?"

"We checked into a room downstairs so we could sleep for a couple of hours."

"Seriously?"

"Dead seriously. Be up in a minute." She ended the call.

"They checked into their own hotel to get away from their kids?" Chelsea asked, incredulous as she laughed.

"Welcome to parenthood, sweetheart. Enjoy the ride."

ON TUESDAY EVENING, KEVIN AND CHELSEA ARRIVED AT HIS PLACE after an early dinner before her shift to find his ex-wife sitting at his kitchen table with their sons. Even though he'd known she was coming, seeing Deb in this place that had nothing to do with her still came as a shock to him, and apparently to Chelsea, too.

She dropped his hand and took a step back.

Kevin refused to allow her to feel out of place in his home, so he put his arm around her to keep her by his side, but her posture was rigid and her discomfort obvious.

Deb stood and came over to kiss Kevin's cheek.

He wished she hadn't done that.

"You're looking well, Kev."

"You, too." Deb had always been gorgeous, with shiny dark hair and brown eyes that looked at him now with longing. "Deb, this is Chelsea. Chelsea, Deb."

"Nice to meet you," Chelsea said, shaking her hand.

"You, too."

"Mom wanted to see our place," Riley said, a note of apology in his tone.

"Of course." Kevin felt nothing as he looked at his ex-wife—not anger or regret or sorrow. Just nothing other than gratitude for their sons. "Don't let us interrupt your visit," he said, glancing at the boys, who watched them warily.

"Kevin... I was wondering if we might be able to talk."

Fuming that she'd put him on the spot in front of their sons and Chelsea, he shook his head. "I'm sorry, Deb. I've said everything I've got to say to you. You take care." Ushering Chelsea out ahead of him, he left the room, hoping Riley and Finn would understand that he wasn't being rude to their mother, but he'd moved on from their relationship and wasn't interested in going backward.

"I'm really sorry about that," Kevin said to Chelsea after he'd closed the door to his bedroom. "I didn't know she'd be here, or I wouldn't have brought you here."

"It's okay. It was fine." As she spoke, she crossed her arms, rubbing them as if she were chilled.

Kevin went to her, put his arms around her and felt a tremble go through her. "She's no threat to you or us, babe. I hope you know that."

"I do."

"But?"

"You're still married to her. That part scares me."

"I'm not going to be married to her for much longer, and there is nothing she could say or do that would make me want to go back to her. I hope you believe me."

"I do..."

"You don't sound convinced."

"This has been a slippery slope for me from the beginning. You know that."

"I do, and I know why, and I respect that. I'm doing everything I can to move it forward as expeditiously as possible. I would've been divorced months ago if it were up to me."

She slid her arms around him, and they stood there, wrapped up in each other for a long time, until he felt her trembling subside. "She's very pretty."

"Who is?" he asked, being intentionally obtuse.

Chelsea poked his ribs, startling a laugh from him. "You know exactly who I mean, and I shouldn't be surprised that she's pretty in light of the two very handsome sons she gave birth to."

"They get their good looks from me."

Chelsea laughed, and Kevin felt himself relax a little. "Everything will be okay. I don't want you to worry about anything. I have no desire whatsoever to go back to where I was a year ago. Why would I want to do that when the present is so very, very sweet?"

She looked up at him. "I've put so much faith in you that sometimes it scares me when I think about the fact that you're still married to her."

"I'm not married to her in any way except legally, and that won't be for much longer. Your faith in me will be well placed. There is literally no other woman in the world who could have me considering having another child at this point in my life or thinking about getting married again. I love *you*, Chelsea Rose. *Only* you."

"I love you, too. So much. More than I thought I'd ever love anyone."

Keeping his gaze fixed on hers, he lowered his lips to hers and moaned when her mouth opened and her tongue brushed against his. He lost himself in her sweetness as he pressed his instant arousal against her heated center.

Chelsea broke the kiss, whimpering. "We don't have time. I have to go to work."

He kissed her neck. "Call in sick."

Laughing, she said, "I can't. It's too late to get someone to cover me."

"It's not fair for you to leave me in this condition."

"I'll take care of that after work."

Kevin sighed and released her. "After we're married, you won't have to work anymore. Unless you want to."

"I'll still want to. I love my job, and I like having my own money."

"Maybe you could work a little less."

She patted his face. "We'll see."

Mindful that Deb might still be there, Kevin walked her out and kissed her goodbye at the front door. "I'll come by later."

"I'll look forward to that."

"Have a good night at the office, dear."

Smiling, she kissed him and ducked out the door.

He waved her off, shut the door and turned to find Riley coming out of the kitchen. "Finn took Mom back to the hotel. I'm really sorry about that earlier. I wasn't sure we should bring her here, but she wanted to see where we were living..."

"It's fine, son. This is your home, too. You can bring anyone you want here. Did you have a nice time?"

"It was good to see her." After a pause, he said, "She had questions. About you and Chelsea."

"Is that right?" Kevin asked, annoyed that she'd pumped their sons for info about him. "What'd you tell her?"

"That you're serious about her, and it would be a good idea for her to finalize the divorce and move on the way you have."

"Did you? Wow, well, thanks for that."

Riley shrugged. "It's the truth, right?"

"Yeah, it is. In fact, can I let you in on a little secret?"

"Sure."

"Hang on a second." Kevin went into his room and retrieved the velvet jeweler's box he'd stashed in the dresser a few days ago. He opened it to show Riley the engagement ring he'd bought for Chelsea at the island's only jewelry store. The platinum band with the gleaming sapphire solitaire had seemed perfect for her.

"That's really nice, Dad. She'll love it."

"You think so?"

"I know so. When are you going to ask her?"

"The same day the divorce is final."

"Does this mean you've agreed to have a baby with her?"

"We've agreed to see what happens, up to and including adding to our family."

"I'm happy for you both."

"It means a lot to me that you and your brother approve."

"We do. Will you stay on the island?"

"That's the plan. I want to partner with Uncle Mac and Uncle Frank and you guys and your cousins on the new McCarthy's Wayfarer." With Dan Torrington's help, they'd set up a corporation in which Kevin and his brothers would own half of McCarthy's Wayfarer and their ten children would own the other half once the purchase was finalized. They had lots of plans and decisions to make, but Kevin looked forward to the challenge of the new endeavor. "Between that and my practice, I'll have plenty to keep me busy. I like it here. Feels like home to me. And you and your brother are here, at least for now."

"I've decided to stay for the time being, and Finn just added six months to his leave of absence with our company in Connecticut, so we're both here for now."

"That just makes it even better. A year ago, my life was in shambles and now..."

"People say Gansett Island has magical restorative powers," Riley said.

"It's certainly made a believer of me."

EPILOGUE

Kevin had put a lot of thought into how he would ask Chelsea to spend the rest of her life with him. He'd considered making a romantic dinner at her place and then popping the question over dessert. He'd thought about taking her away for the weekend, maybe to Boston or New York, and asking her while they were there.

All good ideas, but he kept coming back to one that refused to be ignored, and tonight he would ask her in the place where it had all begun for them—the bar at the Beachcomber—and he'd made a plan that he hoped she would love.

As of this morning, his divorce was officially final. Thank goodness. After her visit to the island, Deb had thankfully realized there was no point to dragging things out. And now that his past had finally been resolved, Kevin was ready to think about the future with the woman who'd profoundly changed his life over the last year.

She'd been patient and understanding while he went through the steps to end his marriage. That hadn't been easy for her after what'd happened to her parents' marriage years ago, but she'd done it for him, and he had no doubt that she loved him as much as he loved her.

In his relationship with Chelsea, he'd found everything that'd been missing in his marriage—enduring friendship, sizzling passion and a desire to be together every chance they got. Maybe some of that would wane as the years went by, but even if it did, she was everything he wanted. And if they ended up with a family of their own, he would be thankful for those blessings, too.

Earlier, he had shared his plans with his sons, both of whom had offered their congratulations and best wishes. Their support had meant the world to him, and he would always treasure the "bonus" year, as he called it, that they'd spent living together on Gansett. He'd been slowly moving his things into Chelsea's place, where they would live until they found a house to buy together.

As he approached the Beachcomber, a place he visited almost daily, he experienced an unexpected flutter of nerves. Maybe he shouldn't do this in the middle of her shift at the bar.

"Stop," he said as he crossed the street to the front steps of the iconic hotel. "She'll love it. Just chill the fuck out."

A woman passing him on the street gave him a funny look when she heard him talking to himself.

Kevin laughed as he imagined how he must appear to others. He took the stairs to the Beachcomber two at a time and walked through the lobby to the bar, which was quiet on that Tuesday night after Labor Day. Earlier, Kevin had received a flood of pictures of Thomas and Ashleigh's first day of kindergarten. Their parents and grandparents had all been there to send the excited kids off to school. If they had any idea how many years of school were ahead of them, they might not be so excited.

Chelsea lit up at the sight of him, and Kevin's mind cleared of all thoughts that didn't involve her and his plans for this evening. As she always did, she leaned across the bar to kiss him, drawing a catcall or two from the other guys seated at the bar. Her face flushed with embarrassment. "Don't mind the peanut gallery."

"They don't bother me. How're you doing?" He'd seen her three hours ago when they had dinner before her shift.

"Good, but it's quiet like always after Labor Day."

"Maybe you can close early."

"That'd be nice." She poured him a Sam Adams and put it on the bar in front of him. "Did you hear how the first day of kindergarten went for Thomas and Ashleigh?"

"Apparently, it was a big hit, and no spontaneous episodes of naked boy-naked girl, for which everyone is thankful."

Chelsea laughed. "They're never going to live that down."

"Ever," Kevin agreed. "That was an instant classic." *Do it,* he thought. *Right now while there's a lull in the action.* "So, the start of kindergarten isn't the only big news of the day."

"Oh no? What else happened?" She wiped down the bar as they talked.

"I got something important that we've been waiting for in the mail."

She looked up at him, eyes wide. "Really?"

"Uh-huh."

"So, it's final, then?"

"It is."

"And you didn't think to mention that to me earlier?"

"I was saving it as a surprise."

She crooked her finger to bring him in for another across-the-bar kiss. "I've never kissed you when you were completely single."

Grinning, he said, "Now you've done it twice. Want to go for three?"

Nodding, she kissed him again.

"Get a room," one of the guys at the bar said, teasing. "They've got lots of them upstairs."

"Shut up, Gary," Chelsea said without taking her eyes off Kevin. "We just got big news we've waited a long time for. Leave us alone."

Extending his right hand, Kevin reached for her left hand. "Thank you for staying with me through all this. You never wavered, even though I know how hard it was for you that I was still technically married."

"I didn't really have much choice after you made me fall in love with you."

"You had all the choices, and you chose to stay, and I love you for that and so many other things, which is why I want to marry you and have a life with you and maybe have a baby with you. If you'll have me, that is."

"*Kevin*," she said, gasping. "What're you saying?"

He opened his left hand to reveal the ring. "I'm asking you to marry me, Chelsea Rose. Right here in the place where we first started, I'm asking you to take this next step with me so we can spend the rest of our lives together. Will you marry me?"

She let out a little shriek that had all eyes on them. "Yes! *Oh my God, Kevin, yes, I'll marry you.*"

Cheers went up around them as the family and friends he'd invited to help them celebrate poured into the bar.

Kevin slid the ring on her finger and stood on the rungs of his barstool to lean across the bar to hug and kiss his fiancée. Then he sat back as she came around the bar and launched herself into his arms, laughing and crying at the same time. They accepted congratulations from Riley, Finn, Frank, Betsy, Mac, Linda, Shane, Katie, Grant, Stephanie, Mallory, Quinn, Mac, Maddie, Joe, Janey, Laura, Owen and Chelsea's many friends and coworkers from the bar. Kevin had arranged in advance for one of her coworkers to work the bar so she could celebrate her engagement.

"I thought about a bunch of other places to ask you, but this felt right," he said to her when the hubbub had finally died down.

"This is where it all began," she said, "so it was the perfect place."

"Do you like the ring?"

She held out her hand for another look. "I love it. It's gorgeous. I still can't believe you're finally divorced and now we're engaged, too. Best day *ever*."

"The first of many great days we'll have together." He kissed her again. "Are you happy, sweetheart?"

"I can honestly say I've never been happier in my life than I am right now."

Overwhelmed by emotion, Kevin gathered her into his embrace, thankful for all the days they'd already spent together and the lifetime of days they had ahead of them.

Thanks so much for reading *Gansett Island Episodes, Volume 1*! I hope you enjoyed it. Check out *A Gansett Island Christmas*, available now. Turn the page to read Chapter 1!

A GANSETT ISLAND CHRISTMAS NOVELLA

Janey Cantrell stood in the window and watched the snow come down in a total whiteout. She wanted to scream at the weather gods—not today! Not on Christmas! She looked forward to this day all year, and the snow was scuttling her plans. This would be the first Christmas of her life that she didn't spend with her parents and siblings. The thought of missing out on the McCarthy family madness made her want to cry.

Right away she felt silly for being sad. What did she have to be sad about? She had her wonderful husband, Joe, as well as their children, P.J. and Vivienne, who would celebrate her first Christmas. She had what she needed.

Except...

Evan and Grace were home, and Stephanie and Grant were back from a few weeks on the west coast...

Janey hadn't gotten the chance to see any of them yet. Plus, her brother Mac's baby son Malcolm the third—another Mac McCarthy, God help them all—would celebrate his first Christmas today, too. Janey wanted photos of him with Viv to commemorate the day.

She shook her fist at Mother Nature. As New Englanders, they hoped every year for a white Christmas, but no one asked for a *blizzard* on Christmas!

"What's the matter, babe?" Joe asked as he joined her at the window, taking a good look at the snow that had shut down the ferries for the day. "It sure is pretty."

"No, it isn't!"

"Um, yes, it is, and I thought you loved snow."

"I do love snow, but not when it ruins my Christmas."

"Aww, is my baby sad that she can't be with her mommy and daddy and her new sister and big mean brothers today?"

"Yes! I've never had a Christmas without them, and I don't want to start now."

"So what you're saying is that your wonderful husband and the two beautiful children he's blessed you with aren't enough for you?"

"Yes, that's exactly what I'm saying."

Joe laughed. "You could at least *try* to spare my feelings."

"Oh stop. You're as bummed as I am that we won't get to see the family today."

"You're right. I am, but we'll still have a nice day together." He put his arms around her. "The kids are down for naps. We can snuggle in front of the fire. It'll be great."

"No, it won't," she said, trying not to sound as whiney as she felt.

"Now, you're officially hurting my feelings. I'm very good at snuggling, as you well know."

"Yes, you are, but today I want my family. It's Christmas, Joseph. It's wrong that we're so close to them but can't see them."

"As much as I'd love for you to have everything you want for Christmas, there's no way I'm taking babies out in this. It's not safe to drive, Janey."

"I know!"

"Are you going to pout all day?"

"Not all day, but for a little while longer."

"I'll allow that." He tugged on her hand to lead her from the window. "But while you pout, I want my Christmas snuggle with my wife."

Janey followed him to the sofa and sat while he added wood to the fire. Outside the wind howled and the snow pinged against the windows. "It's only *two* miles."

"What if we get stuck? Then what?" He stood and came to sit next to her on the sofa. "You'll survive one Christmas without your family."

Evan and Grace, Adam and Abby and Grant and Steph would probably brave the roads because they didn't have babies to worry about. It would be so much fun! She wondered if Mac and Luke were as bummed as she was to be stuck at home with babies while everyone else got to go home for Christmas.

"Did you hear from your mom?" she asked Joe. "Did they make it to Ireland?"

"Safe and sound."

"Did the boys love the flight? They were so excited for their first plane ride."

"They did love it. Mom said they didn't want to sleep on the plane because they didn't want to miss anything."

"Caro and Seamus must be exhausted."

"She said they're hoping they can convince the boys to sleep for a while when they get to Seamus's mom's house."

"I hope so." Janey texted her brother Mac. *This weather sucks!*

I know, he replied.

Whose big idea was it to have babies?

Not mine, that's for sure.

Janey replied with laughing emojis. Her brother's aversion to babies being born on the island was well-known—and he had good reason with one chaotic delivery after another. She'd had Viv on the ferry, for crying out loud. Nothing ever went according to plan when it came to babies on Gansett Island.

What are you guys up to? Mac asked.

Joe wants to snuggle. Janey awaited his predictable reply.

Ewww. Gross.

Nothing gross about it...

Everything about that is gross.

What r u doing?

Walking the floor with Mac. He's cranky.

That's going around today.

Thomas is so excited to play in the snow. We told him he has to wait until it stops blizzarding.

That's not a word.

Did you get what I meant? If so, it's a word.

I'm going to snuggle now.

Barf.

"What's he barfing about?" Joe asked when he joined her on the sofa.

"Me snuggling with you."

"Nothing barfy about it."

"That's what I told him."

"Thank you for defending me, babe." He wrapped his arms around her. "Let's make out while we can."

"Don't you want your Christmas present?"

"Making out with you is all the present I need. Now kiss me."

"But I got you something cool."

Joe sighed. "Will it still be cool after you kiss me?"

Janey giggled at the pathetic face he made. "Yes, I suppose it will be."

"Then..."

"Oh, all right. If I must." Smiling, she laid her hand on his handsome face, which was even more so thanks to the stubble on his jaw, and kissed him.

"Mmm, more of that, please."

While her babies slept and the wind howled outside, Janey decided since she couldn't fight Mother Nature, she may as well enjoy the stolen interlude with her sexy husband. There were worst things that could happen on Christmas than having nothing better to do than make out with Joe Cantrell.

A Gansett Island Christmas Novella is available in print from *Amazon.com* and other online retailers, or you can purchase a signed copy from Marie's store at *shop.marieforce.com*.

OTHER BOOKS BY MARIE FORCE

Contemporary Romances Available from Marie Force

The Gansett Island Series

Book 1: Maid for Love *(Mac & Maddie)*

Book 2: Fool for Love *(Joe & Janey)*

Book 3: Ready for Love *(Luke & Sydney)*

Book 4: Falling for Love *(Grant & Stephanie)*

Book 5: Hoping for Love *(Evan & Grace)*

Book 6: Season for Love *(Owen & Laura)*

Book 7: Longing for Love *(Blaine & Tiffany)*

Book 8: Waiting for Love *(Adam & Abby)*

Book 9: Time for Love *(David & Daisy)*

Book 10: Meant for Love *(Jenny & Alex)*

Book 10.5: Chance for Love, *A Gansett Island Novella (Jared & Lizzie)*

Book 11: Gansett After Dark *(Owen & Laura)*

Book 12: Kisses After Dark *(Shane & Katie)*

Book 13: Love After Dark *(Paul & Hope)*

Book 14: Celebration After Dark *(Big Mac & Linda)*

Book 15: Desire After Dark *(Slim & Erin)*

Book 16: Light After Dark *(Mallory & Quinn)*

Book 17: Victoria & Shannon (Episode 1)

Book 18: Kevin & Chelsea (Episode 2)

A Gansett Island Christmas Novella

Book 19: Mine After Dark *(Riley & Nikki)*

Book 20: Yours After Dark *(Finn & Chloe)*

Book 21: Trouble After Dark *(Deacon & Julia)*

Book 22: Rescue After Dark *(Mason & Jordan)*

Book 23: Blackout After Dark

The Green Mountain Series

Book 1: All You Need Is Love *(Will & Cameron)*

Book 2: I Want to Hold Your Hand *(Nolan & Hannah)*

Book 3: I Saw Her Standing There *(Colton & Lucy)*

Book 4: And I Love Her *(Hunter & Megan)*

Novella: You'll Be Mine *(Will & Cam's Wedding)*

Book 5: It's Only Love *(Gavin & Ella)*

Book 6: Ain't She Sweet *(Tyler & Charlotte)*

The Butler, Vermont Series

(Continuation of Green Mountain)

Book 1: Every Little Thing *(Grayson & Emma)*

Book 2: Can't Buy Me Love *(Mary & Patrick)*

Book 3: Here Comes the Sun *(Wade & Mia)*

Book 4: Till There Was You *(Lucas & Dani)*

Book 5: All My Loving *(Landon & Amanda)*

Book 6: Let It Be *(Lincoln & Molly)*

Book 7: Come Together *(Noah & Brianna)*

The Treading Water Series

Book 1: Treading Water

Book 2: Marking Time

Book 3: Starting Over

Book 4: Coming Home

Book 5: Finding Forever

The Miami Nights Series

Book 1: How Much I Feel *(Carmen & Jason)*

Book 2: How Much I Care *(Maria & Austin)*

Book 3: How Much I Love *(Dee's story)*

Single Titles

Five Years Gone

One Year Home

Sex Machine

Sex God

Georgia on My Mind

True North

The Fall

The Wreck

Love at First Flight

Everyone Loves a Hero

Line of Scrimmage

The Quantum Series

Book 1: Virtuous *(Flynn & Natalie)*

Book 2: Valorous *(Flynn & Natalie)*

Book 3: Victorious *(Flynn & Natalie)*

Book 4: Rapturous *(Addie & Hayden)*

Book 5: Ravenous *(Jasper & Ellie)*

Book 6: Delirious *(Kristian & Aileen)*

Book 7: Outrageous *(Emmett & Leah)*

Book 8: Famous *(Marlowe & Sebastian)*

Romantic Suspense Novels Available from Marie Force

The Fatal Series

One Night With You, *A Fatal Series Prequel Novella*

Book 1: Fatal Affair

Book 2: Fatal Justice

Book 3: Fatal Consequences

Book 3.5: Fatal Destiny, *the Wedding Novella*

Book 4: Fatal Flaw

Book 5: Fatal Deception

Book 6: Fatal Mistake

Book 7: Fatal Jeopardy

Book 8: Fatal Scandal

Book 9: Fatal Frenzy

Book 10: Fatal Identity

Book 11: Fatal Threat

Book 12: Fatal Chaos

Book 13: Fatal Invasion

Book 14: Fatal Reckoning

Book 15: Fatal Accusation

Book 16: Fatal Fraud

Historical Romance Available from Marie Force

The Gilded Series

Book 1: Duchess by Deception

Book 2: Deceived by Desire

ABOUT THE AUTHOR

Marie Force is the *New York Times* bestselling author of contemporary romance, romantic suspense and erotic romance. Her series include Gansett Island, Fatal, Treading Water, Butler Vermont and Quantum.

Her books have sold nearly 10 million copies worldwide, have been translated into more than a dozen languages and have appeared on the *New York Times* bestseller more than 30 times. She is also a *USA Today* and *Wall Street Journal* bestseller, as well as a Speigel bestseller in Germany.

Her goals in life are simple—to finish raising two happy, healthy, productive young adults, to keep writing books for as long as she possibly can and to never be on a flight that makes the news.

Join Marie's mailing list on her website at marieforce.com for news about new books and upcoming appearances in your area. Follow her on Facebook at www.Facebook.com/MarieForceAuthor and on Instagram at www.instagram.com/marieforceauthor/. Contact Marie at marie@marieforce.com.

CPSIA information can be obtained
at www.ICGtesting.com
Printed in the USA
LVHW080953231122
733882LV00020B/380